THE PROMISE
OF PLAGUE WOLVES

For Olivia & Duncan

· STRANGE AND WONDERFUL ·

The Promise of Plague Wolves

First Printed in Latin, now Translated to English by

· COY HALL ·

A Discourse Relating a
TRUE AND MONSTROUS TALE OF CONJURATION
Lately Come to Pass in a Styrian Wood
This Present Year of 1686

A Case Fearful as Ever Seen or
Heard in the Memory of Man
Witnessed by Dorin Toth of Vienna,
A WORTHY GENTLEMAN
Brother of the Order of Saint Guinefort

NOSETOUCH PRESS
Anno 2023

The Promise of Plague Wolves

© 2023 by Coy Hall
All Rights Reserved.

ISBN-13: 978-1-944286-68-2
Paperback Edition

Published by Nosetouch Press
www.nosetouchpress.com

For more information, contact Nosetouch Press:
info@nosetouchpress.com

Cataloging-in-Publication Data

Names: Hall, Coy, author.
Title: The Promise of Plague Wolves
Description: Chicago, IL : Nosetouch Press [2023]
Identifiers: ISBN: 9781944286682 (paperback)
Subjects: LCSH: Horror—Fiction. | Paranormal—Fiction. |
GSAFD: Horror fiction. | BISAC: FICTION / Horror.

Cover & interior designed by Christine M. Scott.
www.clevercrow.com

Index Capitulis

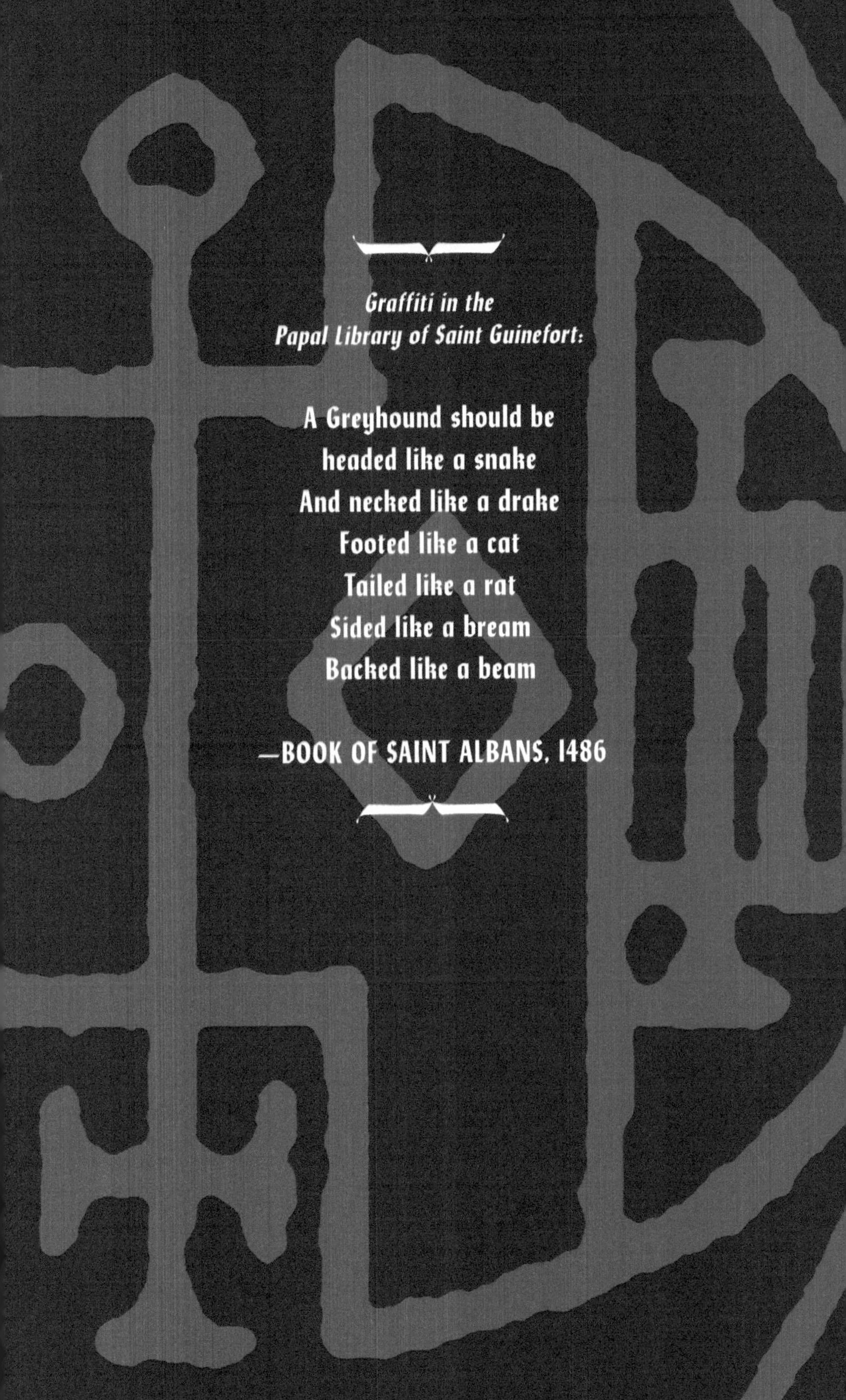

Graffiti in the
Papal Library of Saint Guinefort:

A Greyhound should be
headed like a snake
And necked like a drake
Footed like a cat
Tailed like a rat
Sided like a bream
Backed like a beam

—BOOK OF SAINT ALBANS, 1486

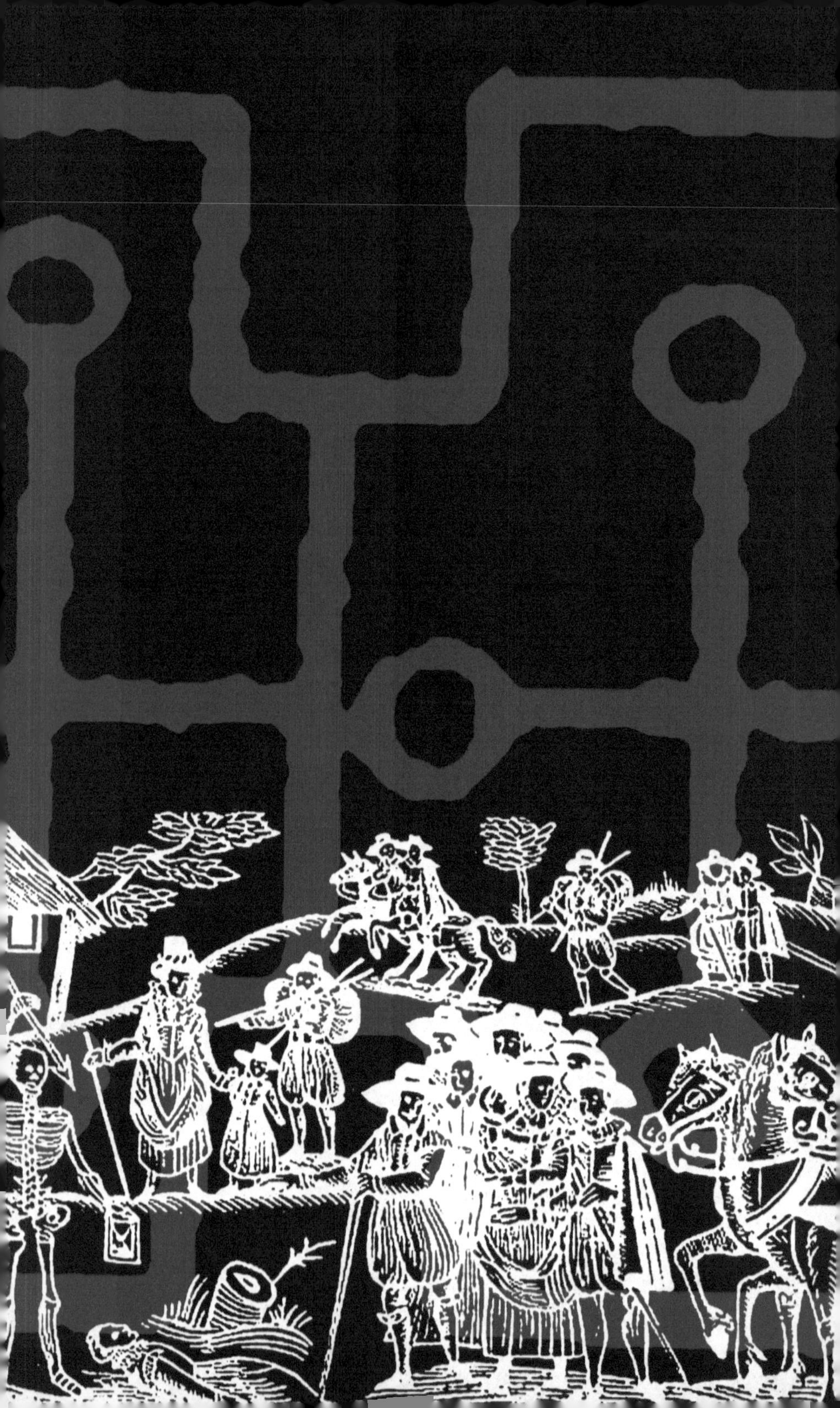

Ars
Pestis,
OR THE ART OF PLAGUE

I

CAPITULUM

A halo of light cut the fog, bringing the watchman to alert. With a lantern in his grasp, he stood to receive the travelers. The light pulsed up the incline until a cart emerged from the mist. Skeletal horses of ebony, with tendrils of steam roiling from their nostrils, pulled a freight of two passengers and three barrels. Jangling metal and creaking wood filled the guardhouse.

The bitter taste of dread glazed the watchman's throat, and his heart drummed.

Highwaymen do not abide by checkpoints, he thought with a beat of caution. *And good men do not travel at this hour.*

The watchman secured leather thongs on his breastplate. He considered the steel helmet on a peg by the door. This precaution he declined, for marching war-ready from the guardhouse suggested cowardice. He stepped into a muggy night rife with mosquitos. A torch hanging from the shack burned over his shoulder. A lone raven from the wood landed on the roof. The lantern burned in his hand.

Bravery, lad, thought the watchman. *Be firm.*

When the horses slowed, the cart rolled to a stop before the heraldry of Emperor Leopold Habsburg. A lattice of knotted ropes kept the sloshing cargo from tipping.

The driver, with hands covered in leather the color of human skin, relaxed his grip on the reins. From his perch, he frowned at the watchman. Only his face below the nose was visible. The lines of his mouth possessed shades of a rodent. With drama and impatience, the driver chewed a strip of leather. A breeze quivered the egret feather in his cap.

His proximity left a pit of disgust in the watchman. The fellow smelled like woodsmoke and decay.

The road ahead, an artery that ran from the mountains to Voitsberg, was empty save for fog. The dark treetops flanking the road swayed in the wind. There were no more checkpoints until the Voitsberg gates.

Be firm, thought the watchman.

He moved around the horses to the side of the cart. His face came level with the sharp knees of the driver. The stink of horseflesh and rot were intense. The stench brought a sexton's cart to mind. The wood was old and rotten, the metal rusted.

In archaic Bavarian, the driver asked, "Friend, is there no respect for the dead?" His words issued in a low rattle. He ripped the leather from his mouth and pointed at the barrels. His hands were unnaturally long. "Has that, too, been stolen from—"

"—Don't pontificate," interrupted the watchman. *Maintain control*, he thought. *Be firm.*

"Yes, be firm," said the driver. He spoke in a preternaturally calm tone. "Maintain control. Bravery, lad."

A finger of ice traveled the watchman's spine. He lifted his lantern, chasing shadow from the driver's face. Beneath the black cap was a cadaverous visage. The flesh was ashen. The rat mouth held a prominent overbite, with two incisors draping the bottom lip like a forked tongue. Sluggishly, the mouth curled into a grin.

"Are you a soldier of the parade sort?" the driver asked. "You smell of lavender, friend."

"That's enough of your insolence," the watchman said. "State your name."

"My name is Grau," said the driver. He gestured at his companion on the high back seat, a large man who was quite still. "His name is Toader. What's your name, little boy of pluck?"

"Make yourselves seen," the watchman ordered. He smoothed the tremble from his throat. He kept anger from his hands.

Grau lifted a lantern from the edge of the cart. He handed the flame to his companion. The man wore a monk's habit to hide his face.

The watchman adjusted his bandolier. The breastplate rattled. His mind went to weaponry. A harquebus hung on his back and a dagger was tucked at his waist. He mapped the route to both.

"By the look of your shack, you're alone on duty, friend," said Grau. "Even for a boy of pluck, that's an unfortunate burden. To guard the mouth of the forest is audacious for one so young, so unseasoned, so afraid."

The watchman's heart thudded. He touched the harquebus muzzle that peeked over his shoulder. The wick around his neck, however, was unlit, unprepared. There were too many steps between spasm and fire.

"You're a weak storm, child," said Grau. "Your confidence is misplaced. Go inside."

The watchman scrutinized Grau's busy hands. He narrowed his eyes.

"State your business," he demanded.

"War dead," Grau answered. "Our purpose is funereal. Three men to be transported home for burial. Three officers from the north."

Only officers from special families were escorted home. Common soldiers, the watchman knew, were buried in pits. Turk corpses were burned like flood debris.

The driver glanced at the barrels. "Those men are your superiors."

The watchman stepped to the rear of the cart and extended his lantern. The imperial insignia was burned into the staves. Leopold's prominent mark left him in doubt.

After a moment of consideration, he said, "The road to Voitsberg is closed to travelers. You know this. It's a matter of containing pox." He returned to the horses. "Unless you have a letter of entry, you'll turn this wagon around and head back. There's a village—"

"—There's nothing left of the village," Grau said. His tone grew severe. "Nothing, friend, but the pox and its dead."

"Then you'll not have trouble finding shelter," said the watchman. His chest tightened. "No one travels beyond the highlands until the pox is starved. That's an order from Vienna." He gestured at the heraldry, hanging in a puddle near the horses. "An order, friend, all the way up to Leopold."

"You'll grant no allowance for brothers in arms?" Grau asked.

"Not without a letter."

Grau handed the reins to Toader. He rose, a thin slash of black and pale.

The watchman reached for the blade in his belt.

"You're armed to the teeth, aren't you?" Grau said. "Hold, friend." He stepped into the bed of the cart, pressing Toader's massive shoulder for balance. "I'm sure I can find something with which to pay you. How many gulden will it take to make you sleep, soldier?"

"Sit down," the watchman ordered.

Grau accepted the lantern from Toader. Delicately, he navigated the ropes, moving between the drums.

Be firm.

"Yes, firm," Grau echoed.

The watchman drew his tarnished blade. He brandished the weapon like a Spanish officer, the way he'd been instructed.

"Friend, that blade's best for stabbing food," said Grau. "Why does a great Emperor not arm you more formidably?" He laughed. "They endow you with words but no ammunition.

Typical, isn't it, of the Lords of Vienna? Typical of all lords, eh?"

Grau kicked a barrel. The brine sloshed, and a heavy weight inside thudded against the wood.

"Be firm, now," Grau mocked. "Bravery, lad, bravery."

"I have no interest in a bribe, sir," said the watchman. He placed the lantern on the dirt. He straightened his back, lifted his chin, and wielded the blade. His heart was miserably fast.

"How about we bury them beneath your watch house? You could write your condolences to the widows of Bremen. Is that a preferable outcome, friend?" Grau shook his head. His grin remained, receding with the slowness of argil.

"Take the reins, turn your horses, and return to the village," the watchman ordered. "You are not to proceed." The quiver of terror filled his throat.

Grau swiveled his neck in recognition of the tremble. His dark eyes went through the watchman.

"Toader, help a weak friend," he said. "We'll dump the lieutenant here."

"You certainly will not," countered the watchman.

He began the laborious task of preparing the harquebus. He lifted the gun from his back. He uncoiled the wick. He bent to open the glass of his lantern to access fire.

When Toader stood, the cart creaked and the horses shuffled.

Seeing his shape from a kneeling position in the dirt, the man called Toader was truly a giant. He threw his leg over the seat and joined Grau. He was a head taller than the driver.

The gaunt horses were unbothered by the commotion. Their nostrils steamed, but their bellies did not move with breath.

The watchman unclasped a horn of powder and leveled the pan. His hands shook, his mind rushed, and his rage at being alone grew.

"This one will do," Grau said, pointing to a drum. "He's ready as he'll ever be."

Toader stepped through the ropes, jarring the cart with each footfall. With a bear hug, he wrapped the rearmost barrel. He lifted it, and then he threw the cask to the earth. The barrel smashed against the ground, crashing, splintering staves. The lid rolled into a ditch. A thick liquid gushed from the container, frothing in the dirt, imbuing the air with sweet-edged putrefaction.

The watchman stopped short of pressing his coil of wick to the lantern flame. He stood in disbelief.

"How could you do such a thing?" he asked. "In a time of suffering like this. No respect for the dead, you say, and then you do a barbarous thing like that. It's heathen, damn it. I'll see you both hang for it."

Grau shrugged. "You have a gun. Why not use it, lad? Why not be firm? You're losing your hold. I don't guess you've seen battle, have you?" He jumped into the mud, landing with a slap.

The horses held, still against violence, deaf to the world.

Toader stepped into the mud, splashing it over the wheels. His brown cowl fell back from his face. The sight shriveled the watchman's anger. The pink skin of a furless rodent caught the firelight. A few strands of hair erupted from open sores on his neck.

"If you can't use a gun, friend, perchance you can work a spade. Would you like to give this lieutenant a Christian burial?" asked Grau.

The watchman stared, uncertain. The ability and willingness to run converged too late.

Toader stepped nearer, pushing back the cowl until it bunched on his neck, rumpling in the manner his skin puckered at the back of his skull. His visage was enough to disarm a stout man, and it was more than enough to freeze a green one.

The watchman recoiled at the monstrosity.

Ulcerous sores pitted Toader's bald pate. His mouth was pinched. His ears were burned-off holes. Moss grew on his neck, chin, and hands. Without struggle, he snatched the harquebus from the guard. He tossed the weapon into the grass. He took the dagger and did the same.

"Bring him here," Grau said firmly. "Bring him close."

Toader grabbed the soldier. His fingers were thick and webbed. Mushroom-like fungus erupted from the palm. The watchman thrashed like a mouse snagged in a cat claw, but Toader forced him toward the broken drum. Through shattered staves, the watchman spied a wet corpse. The edge of Grau's lantern light was on the cadaver, and the moon silvered its ghastly flesh, pale as a fish gut.

"This lieutenant is ready," Grau said to Toader. "A bit underdone, but he'll finish. Hopefully you didn't bop his brains out."

With tremendous strength, Toader wrenched the watchman's neck, directing his gaze to the thing at his boots, whose claw-like hands lay against the dirt. The corpse rested in a fetal coil. There was no hair on the body. The face was slick, without features, without orifices. A hint of an ear marked the side of the skull.

"He'll grow quicker than a tadpole," Grau said.

"In God's name," said the watchman. He had no other recourse but to pray. Blood drained from his face. Courage seeped from his constitution until his eyes blurred with terror.

The corpse moved.

Grau furrowed his brow, observing the specimen on the ground. When the wet claw balled into a fist—a slow, deliberate, and painful gesture—he nodded satisfaction at Toader.

"Drown Master Pluck," Grau said. "We'll need his gear."

The grin was on his face, although his tone was hot with anger and hunger. Slowly, the hand of a sculptor undid the smile.

Toader throttled the watchman's neck until a bone popped. The agonizing snap was loud between his ears. Numbness ate away the sensation of pain. He shifted his arm to fight, but the limb was dead, locked at his side.

The giant lifted the watchman into the back of the cart. He raised a lid on an occupied cask, and then he shoved the soldier's face into brine, where his eyes met another pale form, this one unmoving and curled in the fluid of its womb.

"Don't ruin him," Grau commented from the ground. "He's a good morsel to sup on. I'll take him fresh."

These were the final words the watchman heard. The brine coated his face like a newborn's caul. His last vision was twitching awareness from the creature in the bottom of the barrel.

Presently, the carriage rumbled through a cobbled alleyway, scattering beggars.

"Get off the street and into a lazar house, you miserable shit worms," the driver shouted.

Something large, soft, and wet thudded against the rear door sash. Rot wafted into the passenger cabin.

Dorin Toth stroked the withers of the panting greyhound. Vinegar Tom dropped from the touch, going to his stomach on the floor, placing his chin on his paws. The dog's unease was infectious. He and Toth rode alone. At the station, three Austrians refused to ride through the streets of Old Graz with a "gypsy and mutt," as the men phrased it, so the driver forced Toth to pay extra for transportation to the Cathedral of St. Giles.

It was not an illuminating start to Toth's return to the city. From his time as a student, however, he knew Graz to be an insular town. Despite claims of worldliness, the city was distrustful, proud, irreconcilably Catholic, and venomous to the Slavs and Romani of Styria. Jews and Protestants were expelled from the region in 1496 and 1619, respectively, so diversity was in short supply.

The driver, an elderly man named Frantz, barked his call and gripped leather, and the carriage slowed to a stop. Frantz leaned back and smacked the door, his ring clanging against metal. The ring was the type worn by imperial veterans, Toth noted. Frantz was a boorish soul.

"St. Giles," he said. "Out, gypsy. Out with you and your stinkin', flea-fucked mutt."

"Easy, Tom," Toth said. He scratched the brindle coat, smoothing the dog's hackles. Vinegar Tom exorcised his rage with a wet-dog shake.

The pair exited the carriage to a bright street. The summer sun was hard, the sky cloudless. Pale buildings with burgundy roofs of tile lined each side of the thoroughfare. The commotion of carriages, wagons, and people surrounded Toth. Grazer Burg waited across the street from the Cathedral.

Frantz closed the door rudely, flicked the reins on his team of horses, and stuttered back onto the busy street without an exchange of niceties. He hurled colorful insults at pedestrians, parting the crowd like a tail fin through the sea. Tom performed another frenetic shake, clearing his mouth of nervous drool. A few passersby swapped looks of displeasure, but no words bridged the locals and the foreigner in their midst.

After three arduous weeks of journeying, Toth had finally arrived at his destination. Graz stood in marked contrast to Luxor, where his previous investigation wrapped. One city was medieval and one ancient, one was Catholic and one Muslim, yet both were scarred and angry from the recent wars between Emperor and Sultan. Both cities enjoyed proud, layered histories.

Toth and Vinegar Tom crossed a stone promenade, detaching from the traffic. The Cathedral of St. Giles reached high before them, its white façade brilliant in the sun, and its bronze-encased spire, weathered green and tipped with a golden orb, stretching into the sky. The remnants of a fresco showing three scourges of God broke up the austere stone. Three scourges, each a reminder of the Divine: The Black Death, swarming locusts in the fields, and a mad invasion of Turks creating rivers of blood.

"Fitting," Toth said to the dog. "*Ars pestis.*" *The art of plague.*

With the greyhound at his side, Toth passed beneath gothic windows of stained glass and entered a doorway ornate with carvings. One of the massive doors was parted, and cool air from the interior issued onto the street like the mouth of a cave. The air was welcome after the blistering carriage ride.

A subdeacon of St. Giles, a young man with tawny hair and a white dalmatic, waited within the entrance, prepared to greet Toth. He offered a somber smile, and then he looked at the greyhound with curiosity. There was admiration in his gaze. The feeling Toth received from the subdeacon was quite different than that of Frantz the coachman.

"Master Dorin Toth?" the subdeacon inquired, meeting Toth's eyes. He spoke in educated High German rather than Bavarian.

Toth adjusted the satchel on his shoulder and removed his traveling cap, a woolen bycoket. He gave a slight bow of assent. He folded the hat and tucked it away.

"We were told that you travel with an animal, Master Toth. May I have boys escort your hound to the stables to be fed and cleaned, sir?"

Toth straightened his mustache and smiled at Vinegar Tom. The dog's eyes wandered around the immense interior of the church. The whispers of busy craftsmen filled the air. The tangle of voices and smells had Tom ready to explore.

"As long as you pay him no mind when he grumbles," said Toth. "He'll suffer a cleaning if you feed him well."

"Very good," said the subdeacon. "Does the animal bite, sir?"

"Often," Toth admitted. "But only the right people. Or when he isn't treated like a dignitary. Or—Well, he's scarcely allowed in public."

The subdeacon did not find the situation humorous.

"Very well, sir," he said.

Two children, wearing white ruffs around the neck, came when called. With the excitement that boys have for dogs, they led Tom by his studded collar onto the sunny promenade. They scratched his ears and patted his ribs.

"Go on, Tom," Toth said. "You'll be happier for it in the end."

Reluctantly, the greyhound of Kent parted with his master. He wagged his tail when the children fawned.

The subdeacon tidied his stole, then he returned his attention to Toth.

"Why is it that you travel with a hound, sir?" he inquired. His voice, even in low register, echoed in the high chamber. The cathedral was an acoustic marvel. "I imagine it was no easy task to escort a hound in Egypt. It was the Arab prophet who said, 'The angels do not enter a house in which there is a dog.'"

"He did say that, didn't he? They're cat people. The Arabs didn't like it," Toth admitted, "but they do not like a lot of things. As to why I keep him: Tom's a spot of courage when needed, and he's a good friend. Moreover, I haven't found anyone else willing to suffer my traveling. It's constant these days."

"The world is worse in these times."

Toth grimaced at the millenarian strain of thought. He hadn't patience for it. He marked the subdeacon a child of Jesuit education.

"He goes with you everywhere, sir?"

"Indeed, he does. I'm never without him."

The subdeacon smiled with a trained air. He was from an elite family, and he'd rise through the ranks of the Church accordingly. Regardless, the young man fell into the trap of gossip. He broached the subject that he really wanted to know.

"Is it true that Vinegar Tom senses spirits when they're near?" he asked.

Toth raised an eyebrow. "I didn't think Bishop von Thun allowed occult thinking here, let alone talk of such things." The edge of his mouth curled.

"Truth be told, he doesn't, sir. It's more of a personal interest."

"Do people gossip about Tom?" Toth asked. "Is this what they're saying about him these days?"

"Word about you travels, Master Toth. Word travels quicker than you, in fact. There's been quite a laugh about your uncovering of the fraudulent mummies imported from Luxor to England."

Toth smiled. "Oh, yes. That. Lord May was snorting the cadavers as medicine, you know." He laughed.

"So, sir, was the Lord Bishop von Thun."

"No."

The subdeacon nodded.

"Well, don't make the same mistake, child. There's no medicine in the practice, and there's certainly no magic in it."

"Noted, sir. Does Tom sense spirits, sir?"

"I don't wish to disappoint an admirer of Vinegar Tom, but he senses things no better than you or me, I'm afraid. He's simply quick to anger, and he's quick to pounce."

The subdeacon hesitated. A shade of disappointment crossed his bright face. Then he smirked. "I scarce believe that, sir."

Toth gestured at the commotion in the nave. A checkered floor of marble stretched ahead, running beneath the pews, choir stalls, and gilded altar. The work of refurbishment was underway at the cathedral, a project of the Jesuits. Scaffolding surrounded the high pulpit, where a team of artisans argued and toiled. Scaffolding lined the opposite wall, as well, where a lone creative, high above, added color to a fresco.

"Are these men working to make the cathedral more ornate?" Toth asked.

As though there's a scarcity of gold, imperial eagles, and statues here, he thought. Toth was no admirer of Jesuits and their ways. He and The Order of Saint Guinefort experienced too many run-ins with their brand of pomp and zealotry. The University of Vienna was overrun with them.

"Indeed, sir, yes. Only the finest for St. Giles."

"I'm certain the good Saint appreciates gaudiness, but I can't decide if it's ethereal or tacky."

After a long, uncomfortable look at the nave, the subdeacon escorted Toth to the door.

"The Monsignor tends to side with you, sir. He's changed your place of meeting. He found the noise inside too bothersome."

"I see. It's no matter," Toth said. "Escort me, if you'd be so kind."

"Certainly, sir. It's no burden. Only if the day weren't so hot."

Toth and the clergyman exited St. Giles onto the promenade. The pair elbowed through heavy traffic to reach the grounds of Grazer Burg, a castle complex that filled an entire block and served as the city's seat of government. Grazer Burg was formidable and tall, rising five stories in certain sections. White chimney stacks and gabled windows towered above the busy street. Two guards with pikes minded the gate.

The subdeacon passed through without a word. One of the guards eyed Toth with curiosity, but he said nothing.

The *schloss* was a labyrinth of buildings, tunnels, and open spaces. The subdeacon led Toth across a stone courtyard and through an arched tunnel filled with shadow. Beyond the tunnel was a rosewood door that opened upon the Stairs of Reconciliation, one of the city's marvels. No traveler to Graz escaped without climbing the helix of stone. The double spiral staircase parted into twin paths at the base, reconnecting at each story as it twisted upward. Time on the stairs was dizzying to the eyes. A climb, whether it began left or right, ended at the same destination—such was the symbolism the stairwell conveyed.

Toth followed the young man, trailing in his wake rather than playing the game of "Hello—Goodbye—Hello" that many a soul enjoyed on the stairs. Before reaching the top, the pair halted on a landing with a closed door. Sunlight and the clamor of a horse came through the window opposite. Voices issued from behind the rosewood.

Toth listened. There was one voice he dreaded to hear— that of Kaspar Groza—but the voices were too low to distinguish.

"I'll introduce you, sir," whispered the subdeacon.

"Very well," said Toth. "Has Dr. Groza arrived?"

"He is within, sir."

Of course, he is, Toth thought. *Damn it. The screeching buffoon.* He cursed his fortune. He'd hoped his delay in reaching the city would leave he and the physician of Prague on separate itineraries. The horoscope Toth casted before entering Graz suggested this would be the case, but the stars were mistaken.

Toth gathered himself, adjusting the silk scarf that wrapped his neck. He straightened the blessed wax amulet from the tomb of Saint Guinefort that he wore as a necklace. Dorin Toth stood out in dress and style from men of influence in cosmopolitan cities. There was little modern about his manner. He wore no wig of curls. His color, his long dark hair and mustache, and the red scarf marked him as one of the Romani, a people Germans slurred as gypsies and pariahs. Not only was his look distinctive, but the same was true of his speech. Although Toth spoke Bavarian with ease, his native tongue was Hungarian, and an accent shaped his words.

The appearance and accent bred distrust. Neither of the attributes were shared in higher circles.

The subdeacon knocked politely, and then he opened the door.

Beyond was a tower library lined with books, lit with a rim of candles, and anchored by a table that matched the door in color. Three men, each with a goblet of wine and folio, ringed the table. An empty chair fronted with documents and goblet waited for Toth.

"Master Dorin Toth of the Order of Saint Guinefort is arrived, Monsignor," said the subdeacon. He gave a bow and backed from the room, careful not to turn his back on his superior. He left Toth alone. Delicately, the door closed. The room was stuffy and hot. The candles flickered. The noise of the courtyard ceased.

Toth offered a ceremonial bow of reverence.

Of the men at the table, Toth recognized Kaspar Groza, but the clergymen were unfamiliar. Judged by their garb, they were officers of the Church, one to represent Rome and His Holiness Pope Innocent XI and one to represent the Diocese of Graz-Seckau and its Bishop Prince, Johann Ernst von Thun.

The papal legate, the Monsignor, stood. His zucchetto was violet, and his vestments were a somber but expensive black. His face was a mix of grey edged with jaundice.

"Master Toth, welcome to Graz. Please have a seat."

He gestured at the open chair beside Groza.

Toth slid the leather satchel from his shoulder and stepped around the table. All eyes were on him. The other men didn't stand. Toth's chair scraped wood as he sat.

Kaspar Groza didn't return Toth's bow of recognition. Uncomfortably, the man stiffened and frowned.

"I am Monsignor Bellori," the legate continued in Neapolitan-accented German. "This is Father Melcher. This is Dr. Groza."

After gesturing at each with an open hand, Bellori sat.

The breathless subdeacon returned with a skin of wine. He filled Toth's goblet and exited the chamber once more.

Father Melcher watched Toth and Groza.

"We understood that the two of you worked together previously. Is that not so? Are you unacquainted?"

Groza nodded assent. When he finished, a touch of lavender powder from his wig stayed on his shoulder. He was a theatrically righteous and stormy man. Although Groza traveled in the imperial circle, he was common born, rural born.

"Kaspar and I worked on a case in Prague," Toth said. He placed his satchel on the floor, and then he tested the wine. It was sweet and warm.

"A case of witchcraft, as I understand it," said Bellori. He was more a diplomat than churchman, and it showed in his manner. The shrewd man steepled his fingers over the table.

"Possession and poison preceded by an attempt at witchcraft," Toth agreed.

Melcher narrowed his stare. "Yet neither of you are inclined to a warm welcome. Is there trouble between you that we should know?"

"Yes," the Monsignor agreed, "it's prudent to put any quarrels on the table now."

Groza's face trembled until he broke.

"There is no quarrel. It is simply that I am a man of education, of knowledge, and of science, and this gypsy Magyar is a heathen who dabbles in the magic of his nomadic forebears. Although I have no place for his views, I will not protest his presence. I will also not cower before the John the Revelator speech he is prepared to unleash."

"'John the Revelator'," Toth said. He stifled his laugh with wine. "It's wonderful to see you again, Kaspar. I wasn't dreading your presence, at all."

With every fiber of his being, Toth despised the pompous bastard of Prague, but it was unacceptable for Romani to directly insult a white man in front of superiors. The Monsignor did not tolerate such behavior, regardless of the respect he had for Toth's intellect and ability, regardless of papal weight behind the Order of Saint Guinefort.

Bellori betrayed no emotion, no pleasure or displeasure at the exchange.

"I'll admit," he said, "we were warned of the animosity that existed between you, but Bishop von Thun requested the pair specifically. By name." He eyed the physician, mustering authority. "I will remind you, Doctor, that the Order of Saint Guinefort is not heathen, regardless of the man's forebears. His Holiness Pope Innocent is inclined to favor it. You'll say no more on the matter in my presence. Is that understood?"

Curtly, Groza agreed.

The Monsignor faced Toth. "Speaking of challenging men, how is your superior, Brother Abelard, these days?"

"He's well in health," Toth said. "He is in Nubia presently."

"Brother Abelard, too, insisted on your attention to this case." He looked at Groza. "He didn't mention you."

Groza said nothing.

"Father Melcher," Bellori continued, "explain the task ahead to these men."

As though preparing for a sermon, Melcher stood. He wore a black cassock, which he smoothed downward, but otherwise he was unadorned by the vestments of his post. He walked around the contour of the windowless room, passing rows of books and dots of flame.

"Both of you have read what is known of the plagues that trouble Styria. One scourge, it is no mystery, is an outbreak of smallpox. Although pox has yet to enter Graz, it has worked its way through the Styrian highlands as far east as Voitsberg, and the death toll is immense. It is believed that either a corps of soldiers brought the ailment back from a campaign against the Turks or that Turks themselves delivered the ailment unto our people by vile means."

Dr. Groza gestured agreement with the latter.

"The Archduke will not allow Graz to be shuttered, so we have quarantined the infected area to slow its arrival."

"Keeping the city open is wise," the Monsignor added.

Melcher had his doubts, but he showed proper deference to his elder. He continued.

"Pox is *not* the concern of your investigation. Now, although the Voitsberg region on our flank is closed to travel, the two of you will be allowed entry and free movement therein. In the folio, you'll find documents of permission from Bishop von Thun and the Archduke to offer to soldiers at checkpoints. We are correct to assume that both of you are immune to pox by means of prior infection?"

"That's correct," said Groza.

"Yes, Father," said Toth. The pitted scars on his jawline proved a childhood bout.

"Good." Melcher grew grave. "The second plague *is* your concern. It is more mysterious than smallpox, and, as you gauged from the reports, we understand the ailment little, if at all. We can only report on its various symptoms, which, admittedly, are jarring. We know nothing of the cause.

"Some are saying it's a plague within a plague—another malady rising in collusion with smallpox, feeding on it. Dr.

Groza falls in with the twin plague line of thinking, from what I understand."

"You are correct, sir," said Groza.

"Others are saying this is a spiritual malady rather than physical. There are peculiar stories attached to it. Peculiar even for the Order of Saint Guinefort, Master Toth. Whatever it is, one village is under decimation. A second is in the embryonic stages. The two of you are tasked with finding the second plague's origins and formulating a plan to combat it. The Voitsberg region will remain under smallpox quarantine while you work."

"We are not expected to work in unison, however. Is that correct?" Groza asked.

"Cooperation will harm neither of you," the Monsignor said, "but that is correct."

"The lack of harm is highly debatable," Toth said.

Groza scoffed.

"Go on, Kaspar," Toth said, "cross your arms. Your tantrum isn't complete without flailing."

The Monsignor allowed the breach of decorum, but he eyed Toth.

"Notwithstanding, we hoped the region was large enough for the two of you to coexist. Bishop von Thun is interested in two sites in particular: one is a backwater village on the Lavant named Drunstall. It is under decimation. The other, Karnstein, is the site of a chateau under the charge of a family of the same name. Two leagues separate Drunstall and Karnstein."

Groza swiveled in his seat, facing Toth.

"I will not hamper your investigation, gypsy, which is inclined to be a circus and an embarrassment to our lords, and you will do nothing to interfere with mine. If that's agreeable, then I'm agreeable."

"I partially agree," Toth said.

"Which part?" asked Groza.

"How can you be so certain that nothing of the occult is involved?" Bellori asked the physician. Anger colored the Monsignor's cheek. It was the first hint that a human existed under the skin of the courtier.

Dr. Groza found himself on treacherous ground. Although his was a community of skeptics, the Church that employed him believed in the realm of Hell, regiments of demons, and cancerous witchcraft. What Groza believed to be illusionary, the Monsignor believed genuine and haunting. In the eyes of the Church, disbelief in the occult was tantamount to atheism.

Walking the razorblade of heresy, the physician stood accused.

"I cannot be certain that it is false," Groza conceded, "but I believe the second scourge is a malady with a *physical* rather than spiritual explanation—an origin found in this world rather than the next. If it is a hitherto unknown disease, then we must understand it on those terms. I believe it thus, Monsignor."

"That is your belief, which is most welcome." Bellori looked at Toth. "What is yours, Master Toth?"

Having committed the folio to memory over the past three weeks, Toth opened the documents to a field report, and he trailed his finger to a precise passage. It was testimony from a woman named Cili in Drunstall.

"I have no belief yet. Unlike my colleague, I don't form a belief and search for evidence to support it. However, the words of this young woman struck me as an especially important place to begin. This is testimony recorded by Sergeant Wallhausen."

"A worthy man," Melcher said.

Groza leaned over and spied the words. He left a cloud of lavender in his wake.

"Delusional girl," he muttered.

Toth declined the opportunity to spar with the tiresome physician.

Leaning against the shelves, Melcher said, "Go on, Master Toth."

"According to Wallhausen, Cili spied her brother in the forest. She saw him walk. She saw that his eyes watched her, but his mind did not recognize her. When called, she saw him flee rather than engage. And all this a month *after* his death from the pox. All this after he was interred. 'He is, at once,' Cili says, 'inside of his tomb and outside of it.'"

"Delusional with grief," said Groza.

Toth closed the folio. He drank wine.

"In other words," he said, "a revenant."

"It is, admittedly, jarring testimony," said Melcher.

"I'll begin with her sincerity."

Melcher sighed. "There's an addendum to make to the report, I'm afraid."

"What's that, Father?"

"Cili is deceased."

"How did she come to die?" Toth asked. "Pox?"

"By her own hand," said Melcher. "She damned herself with suicide."

Soberly, Toth bowed. "Then," he said, "I'll begin with Cili's grave."

"Disinterring corpses is not heathen?" Groza asked. "Gypsy, will you dig her out with your claws like a jackal? Lord save us."

The Monsignor eyed Groza, considering. He turned to Melcher. "He'll need a letter of permission from von Thun for disinterment. Can you supply a letter on short notice, Father?"

"I'll send a messenger immediately," Melcher said, and he started to the Stairs of Reconciliation.

The door opened and shut. Melcher's footfalls faded through the tower.

"This village, Drunstall, what happened to its priest?" Toth asked.

"Father Haas, yes. According to Wallhausen, he fled rather than face the onslaught of pox. Country priests are unpredictable, as you know. Haas is either dead or defrocked."

"Has a priest replaced him?"

"No, and there are no immediate plans to do so. In a month, Drunstall will be nothing but a plague pit."

"If I wished to request an audience with Wallhausen," Toth asked, "where is the sergeant at present?"

"The sergeant is deceased, Master Toth, and he is interred in Vienna."

"That's two you've missed," said Groza.

"How did he pass?" asked Toth.

"Smallpox."

"I see."

"There's one more matter. Will both of you be traveling alone?" Bellori asked.

"My assistant, Andreas, will travel at my side," said Groza. "If Toth is going to Drunstall, I'll begin with Karnstein."

"And you, Master Toth?" Bellori asked.

"I'll be traveling with my greyhound, Monsignor, but no other companions."

"His mutt," said Groza.

"Very well then." Bellori stood. "I'll keep both of you in my prayers, as will His Holiness."

Groza pushed together the documents of his folio.

Toth faced the physician expectantly.

"Shall we go down the stairs together?" Toth asked. "To strengthen our bond of friendship, Kaspar? To meet in the middle?"

The physician glared at the wall of books, but the Monsignor betrayed his emotion again, grinning at the corner of his mouth.

"I suppose not," Toth said. He finished his wine. He wiped sweat from his brow.

"The two of you will be but a couple leagues distant from one another. Despite your misgivings, it will be a blessing to have one another close."

"A blessing," Groza repeated.

"Regardless of what either of you believe, it's clear what the people of Drunstall and Karnstein believe. They're convinced a brood of ghosts plagues them." He eyed Groza. "Convinced," he repeated.

"As were the people of Babylon," Groza said. He looked at Toth. "I'm sure that passage is written on your heart, Revelator."

"'Babylon the great is fallen, and is become the habitation of devils, and the hold of every foul spirit, and a cage of every unclean bird'," Toth quoted.

"Yes, that one," Groza said. He sighed. "Bravo, gypsy."

III

CAPITULUM

In a Styrian wood near the village of Drunstall, Annalise Bergmann sat on the edge of a bridge, playing
with rosary beads that were strung like ornaments
above the water. The stream snaked below her feet,
jetting down a slope, frothing where water met stone. The
shadows of twilight brought the forest closer. Trees overhung
the bank. Crickets and beetles swelled into a chorus above the
rush of water.

As she had for six months, Annalise thought about Merrick, the man to whom she was once betrothed. She brooded
and remembered. To her left, the path led to the Voitsberg
road. To her right, the path funneled into Drunstall. If Merrick were to return, it would be by the path to her left. He'd
cross this bridge, just as he crossed it when he departed. His
return was a fantasy so timeworn that she could pick up the
tale at any point and carry it to a climax. Annalise envisioned
Merrick lugging the burdens of a soldier, metal clinging as he
strode, beaten-postured but bright-eyed.

It was a vision of the unreal, pernicious rather than thera-
peutic.

Annalise picked at a splinter, prying a sliver loose.

The unbearable truth was that Merrick Weltz was deceased, lost, damaged, mangled, bled out. Merrick was not coming home. He died fighting Turks somewhere in the Balkans. At least he had not suffered the pox.

No, pox is easier. Pox is closure.

It was the *somewhere* that never loosened its grip on her pain—Annalise couldn't find comfort in knowing the location of her fiancé's grave. Whether the grave was a trench smoothed with mud or a field of stone beneath the sun, she couldn't say.

No matter how much she needed Merrick, he was gone.

The old bridge creaked when Annalise stood. Curiously, a raven responded, gliding down from a tall hickory. The night bird was as large as a cat and equally curious. It landed on the bridge, planting talons and tucking its wings. The raven walked the planks, clacking, shivering its feathers. The great beak parted to caw, but the night bird was voiceless. Coal-black eyes with an oiled sheen regarded Annalise. The bird tilted its head. The beak opened in silence.

Ravens were not unique to the wood, but Annalise had never seen the birds exist in the hordes that had arrived over the preceding months. The ravens had appeared in spring, and their number grew through summer until the village was inundated. The birds proved inescapable pests, for they were not only ubiquitous but also curious and watchful. Ravens perched on homes like gargoyles and lined paths like sentinels. Their black eyes filled the forest. Ravens proliferated like cicadas released from the ground.

Large, beautiful birds though they were, the infestation inspired anger rather than wonder. The ravens were creatures of the gallows, eaters of the dead, and pox called them like the *Lorelei.*

Annalise stomped at the raven to chase it away, but the bird offered a turned wing and dropped gaze, nothing more. The beak worked, opening and closing in silence. She stomped again, and the bird pivoted to watch the current.

Under the bridge, the buzz of insects mixed with jangling rosary beads. Angered by the stomp, wasps exited a nest and swarmed a rock in the stream. Their number was not impressive, but their synchronization was extraordinary. Despite the frenzy of wings, the wasps gathered in the air, tightening into an orb. Annalise watched with growing dread. The distinct noise of their wings drew closer and closer, beat by beat, until the drone of the orb was a collective drone, a single voice. The noise was at once disturbing and pleasing, uncanny and harmonious. When the sound of the current passed through the drone, a voice that approximated that of a man emerged.

At first, there was no language in its music, but when language surfaced the voice solidified into a tone that Annalise knew.

The voice of Merrick Weltz emanated from the vibrations.

In concert with the voice, the chirping insects of the forest calmed, making room for the delicate speech to travel.

You're losing your good sense, Annalise thought.

Regardless, she listened.

It's a returning memory, she cautioned. *You're making sense of sound like one makes a face from the clouds.*

The raven wobbled to her feet, staring up with eyes of black.

Be reasonable, Anna. Keep your sense.

Like a fragrance on the breeze, water carried Merrick's voice from the wasps to the bridge.

Annalise was torn between sprinting free and remaining to hear. Dread competed with desire. The voice was unnatural, an intrusion, but the shade of possibility was beguiling. Stranger things than this had occurred in Drunstall.

Be reasonable. Keep your senses.

What if—?

—What if? was the key to open the box.

Annalise peered down. No one stood beneath the bridge, and no one stood on the muddy shoreline, but thin tendrils of mist rose from the water. The mist interwove with the wasp orb, coating it, growing around its core.

Merrick's voice said, "Stay where you are, Anna. Let me see you. Sit down."

"Merrick?" Annalise asked. Her voice was a peculiar sound, as though someone spoke in her place, spoke for her, as her.

Annalise stepped to the edge of the planks. The wood was slick, with only a slender ledge to prevent falling. A shape in the mist focused her attention. It was a manifestation to accompany Merrick's voice, but the shape was small, childlike, and feral—a thing rather than a man. The wasp orb was visible in its stomach. The shape moved as the water moved, never the same form twice. Annalise saw through the shape and inside of it, and she saw the water on the other side.

"Sit down," the thing said in Merrick's voice.

The desire to obey was strong.

As the shape neared the bridge, it left the water and gained the shoreline.

"Do not run," it warned. "Be reasonable, Anna. Keep your senses."

The thing hovered over the mud, leaving no prints. It was nebulous and chimeric, with features that shifted as air passed through its mist-like flesh. A multitude of faces materialized inside the figure. The wasps, tightening at the core, were the only constant.

As the shape came nearer, terror gripped Annalise by the spine. If there were many faces, there could be many voices.

"Do not run." The voice assumed character, tone, and emotion. It threatened with more urgency.

"Merrick is dead," Annalise managed to say.

Breath caught in her throat. Her eyes weakened. She balled her hands into fists.

The raven watched, working its maw, crinkling its tongue.

Ambiguously, the shape said, "I am."

"Merrick died in the Balkans," Annalise said, and it occurred to her that she didn't understand what that meant. It was a phrase soldiers used. *Far away.* That's what *somewhere in the Balkans* meant. Merrick died far away.

"Close your eyes and hear me," said the figure. "If you cannot see me then hear me."

Annalise inched from the ledge. She kept her eyes wide. She recognized the folly in trust, but the voice dammed inhibition.

The shape grew firmer, decreasing in size. The form, the size of the raven then, scuttled up the muddy bank. It moved like a river rat with a dragging tail. The figure stopped in the road, separating Annalise from the village path.

"Close your eyes," it ordered.

The mouth did not move when the thing spoke. The voice emanated from wasps in its stomach, droning through its throat. Air moved around the shape like heat distortion from a flame. With each movement, the figure disturbed the night.

Annalise looked at the open path to the Voitsberg road. In that direction, safety was leagues distant. Certainly, she could run, but the dread of angering the shape was immense. The feeling built inside her, leaving her anchored. Running was a hopeless cause. She could flee, but how far? To what end?

The night bird will watch you go. The night bird will follow.

The voice in her mind was not her own. This, too, was Merrick. The voice invaded.

Be reasonable, Anna. Keep your senses.

In all the terror, behind it, was the reassuring voice of her fiancé. It *was* his voice. It was difficult to pierce the emotions that came with hearing his voice after so long. The mere thought of Merrick's presence made her weak. She had prayed to God many times that news of his death was false. She had prayed about Merrick on the bridge tonight.

"Turn me into anything you desire," said the figure.

The possibility weakened her further. Without trying, she imagined Merrick. She saw him like he'd only left her bedside. She saw his thin, tall, boyish frame. She saw the Levantine face, the dark and thoughtful eyes, the curled blond hair, the turned mouth. She saw his long hands, the fingers fit for music rather than labor. She experienced the heat of his proximity. Smelled the scent of his skin.

Annalise wept.

The shape changed. The rat devolved into tendrilled mist, losing any semblance of the rodent, losing the semblance of anything tangible. Wind moved off the water and over the bridge, thinning and expanding the mist.

Annalise imagined the breath of God and the weight of abomination.

Faces formed in the mist. Faces she had seen and never seen. The mist concentrated into an arm, then a shoulder, then the lines of a neck. The face, Merrick's face, materialized. The face wavered a moment, and then the features were solid.

In a moment of lucidity, Annalise thought, *The Devil makes faces with glamour. Dead is dead.*

"What are you?" she asked.

The thing did not dignify Annalise's question, but it walked forward. With each step, the form became denser, firmer. When it stopped in front of Annalise, the figure was Merrick. He touched her wrist with fingers cold as clay. Yet, flesh met flesh. The hand did not pass through her own. Merrick caressed her thumb.

He said, "Go home, Anna. I'll follow you there."

The illusion was incomplete because his mouth did not move. The voice came from the hive in his stomach.

"The voice is here," Merrick said.

He brought up his hand (the very hand she remembered so well) and touched his chest. The wasps rumbled there, trembling bones. Merrick's fingers trailed to his stomach where the drone was most intense. He wore the buff coat of a soldier. The garment was neither scarred nor bloody. The garment had never seen battle. The buff coat looked as it had upon his departure from Drunstall.

"The voice is here," Merrick repeated. He urged Annalise to lean closer.

His proximity lessened her will to resist. His disturbed air moved through her aura. She did as he asked.

"It takes a very long time," Merrick said, "to become whole again. Go home, Anna. I'll follow you tonight. I'll find you. You'll wake up by my side."

"Why not walk with me?" asked Annalise.

Merrick had walked her home many times from this very spot.

He moved aside, no longer obstructing her path. He said nothing more.

Annalise reached for Merrick's hand, but this time her touch broke the illusion and scattered mist. The stench of musty earth and nightshade penetrated—something from a story she knew in childhood. Her father told how the Devil grew a garden of nightshade, that he created and nursed the plant for ill, and that he always carried its scent wherever he traveled. The Devil did not stink of brimstone. If he were so obvious, life would be simple. It was a parable for the tempted. The bitter perfume and purple flowers of nightshade masked lethal poison.

Merrick watched Annalise. His gaze darkened.

"Do not follow me," she said. A tremor removed the threat from her words.

Merrick turned to the water. His shape grew less distinct.

Annalise sprinted homeward. She didn't know what else to do. The raven on the bridge lifted and flew above the trees, keeping pace.

Annalise ducked around the barn, running breathlessly toward a line of stone domiciles against the hillside. With curfew fallen, a torch hanging at the church burned, but it was the only light yet to be extinguished. Moonlight coated shuttered homes. Drunstall was quiet and motionless. Unsleeping ravens waited in the thatch of rooftops, alert to her presence. The night bird from the bridge joined its fellows.

Annalise passed the alehouse where rain dolls dangled from the trees. The ornaments hung like a mobile, swinging in the dark. Pigs behind fences and dogs huddled between houses watched Annalise. Other eyes peered from creased shutters.

Her father's home, surrounded by a short fence of unpainted staves, was yellow with light at the seams. Annalise pushed through the gate, knocking it back with violence. She shoved the door but found it barred.

Annalise pressed her head against the wood, dropping to her knees. She cried with exhaustion. When a chair scraped the floor, relief swelled inside her. Her father was not, as was his custom, taking a midnight walk in the wood.

When the door opened, Matthias's bearded face, bathed in candlelight, showed in the crack. His skin was sallow and pitted. Veins ran through his tired eyes.

Annalise bowed her head. Her back heaved.

Matthias set the candle aside. He helped his daughter from the ground.

Within, from a mat on the floor, her brother cried out. Air breathed over Bertram's scabbed hide.

Matthias led his daughter to one of the beds that anchored the room. The rope lattice holding the mattress creaked.

The home was not one of success and wealth, but it was humble, and it fit with the other domiciles of the village. Matthias, a widower who had buried a wife and two children in a life that fell short of sixty years, moved a book aside. He had been reading the Gospel of Luke to Bertram.

Annalise watched her brother with great pity. His face was contorted. The festering sores of smallpox covered the young man's flesh, from his scalp to the soles of his feet. The sores were drying, his skin stiffening into a brittle shell. Bertram groaned with torment, deliriously passing between sleep and wakefulness. Luke failed to comfort him. He lay on his back, prostrate, to keep his skin from bunching and cracking. The scent of death was on him.

"Be still, child," Matthias told Bertram. He looked at Annalise. "Do you see what you've done?"

Wind from the mountain moved the thatch and quaked the walls. The hut of mortared stone possessed two windows, both shuttered against the night. Timber columns, knotted and gnarled, braced the rafters. A yellow glow washed stacks of books. The open hearth and cookery were cold and dark. A soiled mortar and pestle waited on a shelf.

"You should have been home before nightfall," Matthias said sternly. He stood over his daughter. "You should've been present to read Luke to your brother."

Hypocrite, Annalise thought, breathing deeply. Her mind rushed. She didn't call attention to the many nights her father wandered the forest, disobeying the curfew he imposed, leaving her to watch Bertram.

"I didn't hear the church bell," she said.

"The bell rang at its customary time," Matthias countered. "You must've traveled far, child."

Annalise wiped mucus from her lip. As she caught her breath, she watched Bertram. The calmness that follows pain was in his eyes.

"Your face is swollen," Matthias said. "What happened?"

Annalise's chin bunched. She ran her hand over her temple and cheek. Indeed, her face was puffy and welted.

The wasps, she thought. Had the wasps been stinging her all along? How had she not noticed the pain of their barbs?

Matthias lifted a mechanical beetle from the table between the beds. The beetle was an automaton of brass that doddered when wound. Making his hands busy with the small machine, Matthias sat beside his daughter. He stopped short of wrapping his arm around Annalise. Regardless, she planted her face against his shoulder. Matthias played with the beetle's wings until the crying slowed. Only then did he speak again.

"What troubled you?" Matthias asked.

"Merrick," Annalise said.

"I know what it means to lose a loved one," said Matthias. "The pain will dull, child, but it will never leave."

He wound the key on the beetle, tightening the screw.

"I *saw* Merrick," said Annalise.

Her tone brought a chill to the room. She watched Bertram. The boy was gaunt and skeletal. Shadows crossed his face.

"How do you mean?" asked Matthias.

Annalise turned with vehemence. "You know how I mean. I'm not the first. Merrick stood on the bridge." She hesitated, testing a thought, then added, "I touched him. He was there, father. Like the others. He was real."

Matthias placed the beetle on the floor. The mechanical legs propelled it into the dark. The metal scraped. Matthias bowed his head and prayed.

"Father?"

"Yes?" he breathed.

"Is Merrick dead?"

"You know he is, child."

"No, *you* know he is. Tell me how."

"Merrick died in the Balkans."

"*Somewhere* in the Balkans. He died *somewhere* in the Balkans. How can you be certain of that?"

Matthias stood from the bed. He walked to a corner of the room and retrieved a book from a recess in the wall.

"Try to sleep," he said. "I'll be awake for a while, and I'll keep watch."

A buzzing by the door caught her ear, and Annalise spun with such intensity that her father was taken aback. The book dropped to the floor. With a bloodless face, Matthias looked to the door, as if he expected Merrick's cold flesh to fill the threshold.

"It's only a wasp," Matthias said, gathering himself. He picked up the book. "It's only a wasp that trailed you inside, child."

IV
CAPITULUM

win horses pulled a cart along the dirt trace that connected Drunstall to Voitsberg. As the horses beat dirt and stone with fury, three drums rattled in the bed. No one witnessed the intrusion except ravens and straying sheep in fields beyond the road.

The cart came to a jarring stop near a bridge. Crucifixes, crudely hewn, and rosary beads hung from the planks, suspended over the water. Heavy foliage around the bridge blended in the dark of night.

Grau and Toader traveled with a new companion. The Lieutenant, as Grau dubbed him, rode in the back with the casks. He had grown significantly since the night he was spilled from brine at the guardhouse. When the horses stilled, The Lieutenant shuffled like an unbalanced animal from the rear of the cart. Grau and Toader stepped to the road. The trio started toward the bridge, leaving the steaming horses behind.

The Lieutenant walked to a bank littered with sandstone. He made a search along the edge, kicking through leaves, climbing over stones on all fours, overturning rocks.

Toader crossed the bridge, jangling beads that dangled on the edge. He cut through a patch of bramble on the other side.

A moment later, he grunted. With his keen eye, Toader located a pale creature coiled in the mud. Weak from exertion, the creature crawled on its belly, trembling. The creature grunted at Toader, mimicking him.

An angry wasp barbed The Lieutenant. The soldier shrieked.

"Quiet," Grau ordered. From his stance on the bridge, he shot a look at the bank. "You cretin." He turned back to Toader. "Did it respond to you?"

Toader grunted.

"How long's he been out?" Grau asked.

Grau waded through the weeds, pushing aside thorns. When he reached Toader, he looked at the creature in the mud.

The skin on its back waivered, changing color with veins of red. The veins snaked until the skin assumed the pink hue of Toader's flesh. Its trunk was corpulent as a rat, and its arms, with which it pulled itself, were long and spindly.

Toader gripped the creature's neck, lifting it.

Grau studied the form. He ran a knife-like finger over the coarse back, a grafted square of pink. Bones had yet to develop inside the sack of flesh. It was young, despite its proclivity for mimicry and its intelligence.

"Quite the catch, friend," Grau said. "Come."

Chewing a strip of skin, breaking the pox scabs with his teeth, he led Toader to the cart. Grau removed a barrel lid. The brine was empty. The moon shone over the dark liquid.

"Throw him in," Grau ordered. "He's a baby yet. He'll grow."

Toader stuffed the foul glob inside. The arms struggled, splashing. The giant fastened the lid.

The Lieutenant came ambling from the shore, battling another wasp.

"How does it...know what to...become?" The Lieutenant asked. His speech was slurred, thick, and gurgling. A pool of liquid from his gut stayed at the back of his throat, and he spoke through it. Thick bubbles formed on his lips. His language was a pidgin of Bavarian and another tongue—perhaps Bulgarian—that had lodged in his dying brain. He moved to the occupied barrels. "How do these...know what shape...to become?" He tapped the foremost cask with a dark fingernail lined with moss.

Impatiently, Grau said, "You wouldn't understand, cretin."

"I…would understand."

Grau eyed Toader. "A matter of what he sees before we catch him and stuff him in the brine. The sooner we catch it, the more we shape it. This one's already been changing. We stole you right out of the grave, so perfect it isn't. You rot so fast you're going to be a pool in your boots one day."

The Lieutenant stood in the moonlight, contemplating his breastplate, ignoring the long-winded Grau. He was uncertain how he had come to be dressed in the garb of a soldier, although Grau had related the story of the militia watchman more than once. The Lieutenant had no memory for details. Grau said his brain was growing mushrooms and turning to sauce. The Lieutenant was skeptical.

"What *imprinted*…on Toader?" The Lieutenant asked. He wiped sap that leaked from his eye sockets. If Grau was correct, the ooze was his rotten brain. His body excreted sacks of filth.

Grau laughed. Shielding his mouth with the edge of his hand, he said, "Some joker went and dropped a rat in his barrel. Wanted him to look like my son."

"Did…somebody drop a rat…in your barrel?"

Disapprovingly, Toader watched from the shadow of his cowl.

"Why don't we…throw…something good…in this barrel?" The Lieutenant asked.

"Like what?" asked Grau.

The Lieutenant dug through a pouch of skin, rumpled like a scrotum, at his waist. The sacks formed on several points over his body. He utilized all of them for storage. He retrieved a pair of bird talons, black as onyx.

"I've been…saving these," he said.

Grau brought his hands to his chest. He shrugged.

"Throw 'em in the stew. See what happens."

The Lieutenant smiled.

With a grunt of disapproval, Toader returned to the high back seat behind the horses. The cart tipped to one side when he climbed up.

In went the talons—claws stripped from a dead raven.

"It's...looking up...at me," The Lieutenant said. "He...looks...like me. He's mad."

Grau peeked into the barrel.

"Damn smart one," he said. "Let him marinate."

The Lieutenant replaced the lid.

"Why...is he mad?"

"He wants to roam free," said Grau. "He's already found something he wants."

V
CAPITULUM

The road, rising toward the hazy mountains, lanced through fields of grass and stone. Dorin Toth and Vinegar Tom had encountered no travelers on the artery from Voitsberg to the Stubalpe range. Three days since the last manned checkpoint, three days since Toth offered a soldier the letter from Bishop von Thun, and not a single wagon, horse, or man on foot passed in either direction. Tom was undisturbed. He enjoyed the solitude, running through fields and marching up stones, chasing birds and lording over sheep. Toth found the emptiness unnatural and portentous.

Where the dead abandoned this corner of earth to nature, wilding occurred. Weeds grew in the road. Although travelers decreased to nil, the curious presence of ravens increased tenfold. Clusters of birds filled the pines that edged the way. Nests marked high joints and outcroppings of stone. As the forest grew primeval, it became a world of dark eyes and oily wings.

Portents, Toth thought.

For the superstitious, a single raven croaking on the gable foretold death.

What do a thousand death birds foretell? he thought.

With Drunstall drawing close, woodsmoke and the foulness of life arrived on the breeze. Toth welcomed the change. The squalor halted Tom's exploration, and the dog scaled a boulder to sniff high. He was a fine animal in the sun: strong, lean, and proud. Tom peered at his master, distant where the road curved into a bank of shadow. When Toth released a piercing whistle, Tom leapt from the rock, stretching to his full length in a sprint through the grass.

"We'll rest and sup before entering the village," Toth said. He pointed at the greyhound. "I want you to be on your best behavior, young man. No posturing. No fighting."

Tom shook his coat and panted.

"Come," Toth said. "Let's find a seat in the shade."

Tom stopped midstride. He cocked his head and closed his mouth, straightening his spine at a noise in the forest.

Toth followed the greyhound's eyes to a swath of darkness beneath the trees.

An enormous white dog appeared under the canopy of a pine, parting weeds as it emerged. The animal's coat was long, and its head was wide, ringed by a great ruff like a mane. Drool tanned the neck. The trunk of the dog was as large as a barrel. Despite the intimidating frame, the face was frightened rather than cruel.

A guardian of the sheep, Toth surmised, *at least at one time.*

"A goliath, isn't she?" he said to Tom. "Like a bear."

The white dog stared, uncertain and wary. The animal was too curious to be feral. She was either abandoned or orphaned. Pox scourges left many dogs to wander, so that was not unusual. Her demeanor betrayed no sign of rabies. Whatever her station, she suffered neglect. Prickly burrs decked her knotted coat. Dead leaves clung to her plume of a tail. A bevy of gnats crowded her rump.

Chien de Montagne des Pyrénées, Toth thought. *A Pyrenean Mountain Dog.* He last saw the breed in Aquitaine, where the Pyrenees guarded chateaus in addition to sheep.

Toth whistled gently. When the Pyrenees leaned forward in response, Tom leapt in anger. The white dog bolted from sight, cutting through the undergrowth, beating her massive paws.

Toth managed to grab Tom by the collar.

"Behave yourself," he chided.

Tom struggled.

"Tom, behave!"

Reluctantly, Vinegar Tom quit his fight. He scanned the forest manically, and he growled and barked for good measure.

"You're a hard one, Tom," Toth said. "The poor thing lost her master."

The greyhound looked up, his snout scrunching to show incisors.

"Doesn't that stir your cold heart?"

A pleasant thought struck Toth then: a vision of the Pyrenees leaving Drunstall beside the greyhound.

Another companion, he thought, watching Tom. *Won't you be displeased.*

"Pray I don't find her again," he said, "because I may well keep her."

When Toth freed Tom, the greyhound sniffed where the Pyrenees had been. He marked the pine spitefully.

Toth walked a trail to where the shade deepened. The undergrowth opened onto a flat with ancient trees, vines, and nests. The curious scent of sulfur infused the air. To the far right of the clearing was a staircase carved into hillside bedrock. Near the center he came upon a lattice of briars that was so abrupt in placement, so isolated, that the barrier resembled a manicured wall. Once, the lattice surrounded a garden of flowers, he presumed, but the flowers were gone. Behind the thorns was a large circle of mud. In the center of the mud a substantial hole opened, a cylindrical shaft that sank into the earth.

There was something distinctly pagan about the lattice, circle, and hole. Toth was reminded of rituals in which men and women passed through apertures, either to the benefit or detriment of their health.

The magic circle, so prevalent in folk magic. He wondered if this was the work of an individual, or if the villagers of Drunstall had regressed.

Tom quit his search for the Pyrenees, joining Toth.

Air escaped the hole with force, funneling upward in a column, venting brimstone. The leaves of an overhanging hazel had shriveled and died. The ropes of briar vibrated.

Unprompted, Tom entered the circle, sinking paws into the muck. After a sniff, he hopped into weeds on the opposite side.

"Don't be a fool, Tom," said Toth, walking the contour. He reached his hand into the air escaping the shaft, and he withdrew it as quickly. Even through his glove, the heat was intense, as if a fire burned in the belly of the earth.

Tom barked, startling Toth before he could contemplate the anomaly further. He looked down to find a creature furrowing into the back of a toppled scarecrow, once part of the garden. The thing buried its head in the effigy's tattered coat. Pale to the point of translucence, the creature was bred in total darkness, with a hide so thin that tendons connecting undeveloped eyes to a kernel of brain were visible. Moss dotted its back.

The thing is a Boschian nightmare, Toth thought. *Shrieking Hell.*

His heart quickened. He grabbed Tom's collar before the dog pounced. When Toth stepped back, he spotted another being of similar design, this one coated with mud. No larger than a rodent, the thing lay on its back, nestled. The underbelly looked like a pig intestine with a wad of stomach inside.

Revulsion was Toth's first reaction—primitive and hot. He nearly stomped the devil, but he refrained.

Neither creature threatened him. Neither reacted to his presence. Both had a lazy air, so stationary that ants crawled over their slug-like hides. The one near Toth's foot ate a wasp from the mud. With webbed claws, the creature stripped the insect's wings. The other fed on roaches traveling through the scarecrow.

Toth wiped at his mouth and slowed his breath. The urge to vomit left him bloodless. The pit smelled of sulfur and the creatures stank of decayed flesh. When he could handle no more, he turned his back. He found no relief. Another confounding sight deepened his bewilderment.

A figure stood near the stairs, silently watching.

Hell is seeping from the ground, Toth thought, *distorting this land.*

Tom's fur stiffened into a ridge along his spine.

Toth dropped his grip on the collar, freeing the greyhound. Tom leapt at the hunched figure, breaking into a sprint. Toth charged after the dog, his satchel slamming against his hip. Limbs scraped and ripped, and the world blurred.

"Ho, there," Toth yelled, slugging for air. "Ho, there!"

VI
CAPITULUM

With the first spasm of Vinegar Tom's shoulder, the figure darted, fleeing through a thicket toward the stairs. It was a useless endeavor, attempting to outrun Tom, but the voyeur persisted. He ran twenty yards before the greyhound—hackles raised, teeth bared, tail rigid—cornered him.

Toth, much slower, followed.

The intruder, the watcher in the woods, was nothing more than a boy. The child's chin quivered, and his eyes darted with terror. He cowered against stairs that led to the top of the hill. Soil and leaves partially buried the stone behind him.

"Down, Tom," Toth shouted. "Down."

The youth shrank against the steps.

Winded, Toth pushed through limbs, angering a nest of wasps, but the insects flew high rather than low.

The greyhound relaxed his posture. He began to pant.

"You're safe, boy," Toth said. He inhaled deeply.

When a knocking caught Toth's ear, he searched the trees until he spotted a windchime in the branches of an acacia. The tree was ancient and massive, rising higher than the stairs. The chime was dead sticks wired together, hanging from a limb.

Toth patted Tom's ribs and eyed the youth. He tightened his fist to press the tremble from his bones.

The child was ten years old, maybe less. He had auburn hair and eyes of brown. A harelip and the fresh scars of smallpox marred his face. The scars were red. He was no less a stray than the Pyrenees. A child of dirt and toil.

Toth pulled a pipe from his satchel. The bowl was etched with stars, the Canis Major and Orion constellations. After filling the bowl with a pinch of tobacco, he bit the stem.

"This dog won't harm you," Toth told the boy, "unless I tell him to do so."

"What do you want?" asked the child. Mud streaked his face and hands.

Tom sat on his haunches.

Toth retrieved a contraption from the satchel, a droll machine for lighting when no flame was handy—a device constructed from flint rock and hemp. With a flick, it sparked. The rope smoked. He lit the tobacco.

The boy watched, curious.

"Have you ever seen something like this?" Toth asked.

"No."

"Good to have on hand when you need fire. I picked it up in Nuremberg."

"What do you want?"

Toth swatted at a tenacious wasp. In the acacia with the chime, another large nest, grey as an old barn, sagged. The insects were angry.

"We're traveling to Drunstall," said Toth. He put away the lighter. "We came by way of Graz and Voitsberg."

"No travelers are allowed here," said the boy. He straightened with indignation. Despite fear, there was a fire inside him. "Pox."

Toth exhaled smoke. "Yes, I understand you've suffered greatly from pox. Boy, what were you doing back there? Why were you watching us?"

The child said nothing.

"What's your name? Are you from the village?"

The boy nodded.

"And your name."

"Sebastian," he said.

"Very well. I'm Dorin Toth and this is Vinegar Tom."

"That's a strange name for a dog," Sebastian said.

"He's a strange dog."

"He looks mean."

"He *is* mean."

Sebastian monitored the animal. "Why are you on the road if no travelers are allowed?" he asked. "Why do you travel by foot rather than by horse? I watched you walk in."

"Is that your duty? Are you a watchman?"

"Maybe I am."

Toth drew on the pipe. The aroma was welcome. Brimstone from the pit clung to his senses.

"Bishop von Thun in Graz sent us. We arrive with special permission. Have you ever visited the city?"

Sebastian hesitated. "No," he admitted.

"The Bishop has a church as large as this forest with a ceiling high as these trees. Your eyes wouldn't believe it. Will you tell me something?"

Sebastian continued to watch the greyhound. His breath slowed.

"What were you doing back there?"

"No travelers are allowed, Bishop or not," said Sebastian.

"When did that hole in the earth appear?" Toth asked. "It's spewing something noxious. Has it always been thus?"

The child shook his head.

"It hasn't. From whence did it come? Pray tell, boy. You aren't slow-witted. Stop behaving thus."

"It wasn't me," said Sebastian. He paused, considered running, and then said, "All those things come out of there."

"The slovenly creatures?" Toth asked. He blew smoke from the corner of his mouth. "What are they?"

Sebastian turned, placing his bare foot on the step. Earth was removed to the bedrock, and from the stone twelve stairs were carved. The rock bore the scars and uneven lines of a chisel. Judging by the worn indentations in the center of each step, the work was carried out ages prior. The stairs were used heavily once, but now a mix of winnowed leaves, roots, and soil obscured their prominence. A breeze came through the forest, blowing leaves along the mound, moving the chimes, rattling wasps.

"Do you see the creatures often?" Toth asked.

The child nodded. "They're monsters," he said.

In the distance, a raven called, abrasive against the backdrop of swallows.

"Lead on," Toth said.

Vinegar Tom passed Sebastian, eager to be the first to ascend the steps, eager to be free of the clearing. Impatiently, he crooked his neck to see if his master followed. Sebastian went next, and then Toth.

Toth didn't deny the hesitancy that overtook him. Dread colored his expectations about what waited at the top of the hill.

When the trio mounted the final step, however, Toth stood astonished. He gazed around, taking in a stone garden, overgrown with weeds, wildflowers, trees, and graves. A medieval cemetery arched the hilltop. Lines of graves—some with simple stones pushed into the earth, others with erect crosses painted black—sprawled for an impressive distance. Over a thousand plots peeked from weeds.

It takes centuries for a tumbledown settlement to amass so many graves, Toth thought, *plague or not*.

A squat fence, constructed with layers of stone, marked the perimeter. In one section, the fence was toppled, a rotten tree having fallen, crushing rocks beneath its bulk. At the far right corner stood the ruins of a chapel. Most of the building was dismantled, leaving only a façade and foundation.

The shadow of finery stoked Toth's curiosity. Drunstall was important to someone of means a millennium ago.

Tom scurried through a row of black crosses, his nose to the ground.

Sebastian pointed in Tom's direction.

"Please don't let your hound hurt them," he said.

Indeed, Tom moved toward two women at the far end of the cemetery, kneeling in prayer at the foot of a grave. The women were so absorbed in their task that neither noticed strangers in their midst. Garmented in robes of brown, the pair made a tranquil decoration in the ruins.

The greyhound ruined the moment of serenity. Irreverently, he barked from deep in his gullet.

"Please don't let him hurt them," Sebastian implored.

Toth removed his pipe, scowling. He put his fingers to his mouth and whistled.

Tom ignored the call.

The women, hooded despite the summer heat, rose. Unlike the boy, they were unafraid of the greyhound. One of the women disarmed Tom with a sweet greeting. Ceasing his attempt at menace, the dog wagged his tail. The woman scratched his ears while he sniffed her cloak.

The behavior irked Toth. Tom had been away from civilization too long. His manners were slipping.

"He isn't the menace I painted him to be," Toth told the boy. "Don't worry your mind."

He trailed Sebastian through the knee-high grass. The women raised their hands in greeting. Toth returned the gesture, while Sebastian kept his eyes to the ground.

The boy said, "These are my sisters, Floris and Blancheflor."

The women were twins, and they were senior to their brother.

"I apologize for the animal's manners," Toth began.

Blancheflor knelt by the greyhound. She scratched his neck and throat. Vinegar Tom side-eyed his master, raising his chin, allowing the touch. He kicked at the air, shutting his eyes with pleasure.

"Say no more of it," Blancheflor said. "He's a sweet, charming boy. Look at that leg. That feels good, doesn't it, little hound?"

The sisters wore austere cloaks of mourning.

Floris pulled back her coverchief, revealing her face. She was a youth, despite assuredness and poise. A shock of red hair fell past her shoulders, reaching the small of her back. She was fair, Celtic rather than Germanic, with prominent ruddiness at her cheekbones. Freckles bridged her petite nose.

Peculiarly, Floris bent and lifted what appeared to be an infant from the grass. The way she cradled it, Toth at first thought the baby genuine, but the thing was a wooden doll in swaddling clothes. A painted eye was visible through the folds.

Sebastian watched the doll with disdain.

Toth drew on his pipe.

"Who are you?" asked Blancheflor. She frowned and withdrew her hand from the dog's muzzle. "Drunstall is under quarantine, sir. As is Karnstein. No travelers are allowed in these mountains. Not for any reason."

Toth replied, "I've been sent by the Bishop in Graz. I arrive with a letter of permission with von Thun's seal."

Blancheflor stood. She, too, dropped her coverchief. Unlike her sister, she had flowers through her braided hair and a diadem of purple and white petals atop her head.

"Show the letter," she demanded.

Toth clenched the pipe stem with his teeth, and he removed the satchel from his shoulder. He rummaged through its pocket. As he did, he introduced himself.

"I'm Dorin Toth, a Doctor of Theology at the University of Vienna and an investigator for the Order of Saint Guinefort. I come by way of Graz."

"What is the Order of Saint Guinefort?" Blancheflor asked.

"A monastic order of friars," Toth said. He retrieved the document that Father Melcher provided. He handed the letter to Floris.

Floris held her doll closely, tucking it against her chest with one arm. She held the letter with her free hand.

"The dog is Vinegar Tom," Sebastian added.

"What a brute he is," Blancheflor said. She scratched his chin. "Is he a member of your order, too?"

Tom wagged his tail.

"In fact, he is, yes. You'll find the seal on his collar."

Blancheflor smiled. "I was only joking, Master Toth."

Floris scanned the letter, and then she handed the document to her sister.

"Can you read it?" Toth asked.

After a moment, Blancheflor admitted that she could not. Her smile turned sheepish. There was kindness in her features that contrasted with the coldness of her sister. "Did it seem like we were reading? Were you fooled, Master Toth?"

Toth laughed politely, but his eyes stayed on the wooden doll. There was something uncanny about the eye, animus in the hide. An ant crawled along the nose.

"Why do you handle that plaything like a child?" Toth asked.

Blancheflor handed the letter to Toth. He folded it and tucked the document into his satchel.

"You look like a gypsy," Floris responded. "I'll overlook your insolence."

"That I am. I'm of the Romani."

"I thought your people traveled in packs. The red scarf won't court you favor here, you know."

"It never has in your country, but surely someone in Drunstall can read this letter. Is that not so? Surely someone literate named you. Floris and Blancheflor are names in an old French tale. Although," he added, "you might as well know Floris is a man in that story." He smirked.

"And the pair are lovers," Blancheflor said, "which we decidedly are not. So maybe that person isn't quite as literate as you believe."

"Point made," said Toth.

"I know someone that can read it," Sebastian offered. He rubbed his harelip and looked to his sisters for approval. "We have to take him to the village, though."

Blancheflor and Floris nodded.

"The peril is mine, isn't it? Not yours," Toth said.

"It's certainly yours," said Floris.

Tom stood, put his nose to the earth, and began exploring. He wandered into the field of graves, crosses, and ticks.

"I don't mean to mar the welcome," Toth said, "but I must tell you I spotted something quite strange at the base of this hill. There is a hole in the ground, and it releases heat, and there are pale creatures, like those in a cave, in the mud." He pointed to the stairs.

"—and it had wasps crawling into its mouth," Blancheflor said.

Toth hesitated. "Yes," he said. "One was eating a wasp."

"Forget it, gypsy," Floris muttered. She rubbed the nose of her doll. The wood was pliant. It rumpled.

"Begging your pardon, *Fräulein*, but I won't forget it. That is why I'm here." Toth looked at Sebastian. "You saw it, did you not?"

Sebastian didn't answer.

"Indeed, you saw it," Blancheflor said. "We don't doubt that. Did moss grow on the hide?"

"It did."

"We're infested with them. They come and go through those holes. Go back, and you'll find that they're already gone. They crawl in and out as it pleases them."

"You've seen them, too, then?"

"We have," Floris and Blancheflor responded in unison. What color they held in their cheeks faded. The sisters looked ill.

"What are they?" Toth asked.

"*Le meneur de loups* brought them out of the ground," Sebastian said.

Puzzled, Toth turned to the child.

"*Le meneur de loups?*" he asked. "A wolf leader."

Le meneur de loups was a name applied to conjurors, but it was a phrase Toth hadn't heard since his student days. It certainly wasn't in common usage outside the most provincial corners of France.

"Who taught you French?" he asked. "Was it the same literate soul who named your sisters?"

"It was," Blancheflor replied.

"I'd like to meet this person, as well," Toth said.

Blancheflor shook her head. "She died a month ago." She gestured at a mound of earth. "This is her grave. She was our mother."

Three blank stones marked the plot. The rocks had only begun to settle.

"My apologies," Toth said. "*Requiescat in Pace.* What was your mother's name?"

"Cili," said Floris.

Toth bowed. "Cili," he repeated.

She damned herself with suicide, Father Melcher had said. If she were buried in consecrated earth, her children didn't believe this. Either that or Cili was buried without permission. The priest, Father Haas, was gone from Drunstall, so the latter was possible.

Toth bore another letter in his folio, one that would devastate the siblings. In it, Bishop von Thun granted permission to exhume Cili's corpse. The fresh dirt and sunken stones were more poignant to look upon then.

How do I broach such a topic with children of the deceased?

"This hasn't been the ideal way to make your acquaintance, I'm afraid," Toth said. "How close is Drunstall, pray tell?"

"But a short walk, Master Toth," said Blancheflor. "There's a trail beyond the trees. We'll lead you there."

"I must retrieve my hound first," Toth said.

"You must search for those pale slugs, you mean," said Floris. "You don't believe us about their proclivity for retreat."

Toth did not argue.

"If you take the road," Blancheflor continued, "it forks. The left path leads to Drunstall. The right leads to Karnstein Chateau. The signs were dismantled by order of the lords of Styria."

"Thank you for the guidance," Toth said. "We'll speak again soon."

"I suggest you take neither path, gypsy," Floris said. "Return to Voitsberg. Your medicine won't do any good." She rocked the doll with both arms.

"I'm not here to bring medicine, Fräulein," said Toth. "Your battle with pox isn't my concern."

"Then what is your concern, gypsy?" asked Floris. Her mouth tightened.

"To begin, *le meneur de loups.*"

Floris turned away.

Blancheflor stopped momentarily, having more to say, but then she followed her siblings toward the stone fence. Solemnly, she lifted her coverchief back in place, hiding the flame of her hair, hiding flowers. Passing through the cemetery, the image she cast was grim.

Toth whistled for Tom, and then he returned to the stairs that led to the clearing below. A breeze stirred the trees.

"Brought from the earth by a leader of wolves," he said to the greyhound. "*Le meneur de loups.*"

When Toth and Tom reached the wattle of briars, the creatures were gone from the mud. The writhing wasps remained, one wingless, half-consumed. Heat jetted from the earth with a low roar. Dissatisfied, Tom explored the scarecrow where one of the devils had lain, but no scent caught his interest, and the prominence of roaches left him disgusted.

Toth stared through the distorted air, drawing on his pipe, thinking. The hazel with withered leaves, he noticed then, held more wasps, as if they huddled on the bark. The insects were unmoving, so he stepped closer. A pile of dead wasps lay at the base of the tree, while those on the trunk had their barbs imbedded, stabbed in wood.

Toth studied the lines. Collectively, the wasps formed a shape. One end resembled the transept and apse of a cathedral, while the other end was an unintelligible mass, a crisscrossed abortion. Unfinished. Or confused.

A sigil, a rune, or a trick of the eye? Toth wondered.

"So it begins," he said.

nnalise skirted the alehouse, joining a track that led to the tithe barn. Her mind was busy, her thoughts intrusive. In search of an engrossing chore, she balanced a spade on her shoulder. She passed chickens hunting weevils in the shade. She passed Dragoslav, the old man who owned The Cock's Foot, and two of his sons leaning on a battered fence. The men greeted her with lascivious stares.

"Say, lass, you want real a chore?" said the old man. "Do me a kindness and wrap those legs around me."

His sons snickered. His cat, perched on a fencepost, licked its paws.

Dragoslav picked at his teeth, and he smiled with lips the color of bruises. His face quivered.

The thin layer of decorum that had existed in the village was dead, Annalise decided, so she responded with a *Rotwelsch* gesture that her father, in wisdom or amusement, taught her. The formation of finger and thumb amounted to a stretched asshole.

It was a language of thieves, so Annalise assumed Dragoslav was intimately familiar.

"I can do that any time you want," Dragoslav said.

The sons erupted in laughter.

"Let me show you."

"She'll come around when she's in heat," one of his sons said, "and that shovel handle ain't satisfying her anymore. Won't you, Anna?"

Dragoslav smacked the fence, wheezing.

Annalise gave no more energy to the men. She brushed through hanging rain dolls, leaving the alehouse in her wake.

"Maybe her old man satisfies her," Dragoslav was saying. "Or maybe the scabbed dick of her brother. That Matthias, you know, he—"

She heard no more. She gave another *Rotwelsch* gesture over her shoulder.

More laughter.

The barn, in an alcove on the hill, loomed over the domiciles, corrals, wells, pastures, and river. A deep wood enclosed the barn on three sides. The crown of foliage left the building in perpetual shadow, so that moss and mold grew like fur on its surface. With its steeply pitched roof and half-timbered exterior, the tithe barn existed to serve the needs of a priest, but Father Haas was gone, having abandoned his flock when the first pox victims were buried. Haas left without a word, which demoralized Annalise more than she cared to admit. Since the Church sent no parish priest to replace Haas, or since no priest was willing to step into the jaws of a scourge, the barn was repurposed, the tithe discarded.

Rather than housing produce, the building sheltered the dead awaiting burial. The transformation to charnel house was as gruesome as it was shameful. A stave over the door, balanced in metal cradles, barred scavengers. Except river rats, roaches, and ants, nothing went inside.

As she approached, Annalise thought, *one more precaution to keep plague wolves at bay.*

There were additional safeguards. A sack of consecrated hosts hung from the stave and a witch ball of rosemary sprigs was suspended above the door.

Flies and wasps covered the seams of the barn, where the fetor of dead flesh leaked. On hot days, the decay was unbearable, blanketing everything down to the river. There were nights, when the wind changed, that the odor invaded sleep.

The smell of corpses haunted Drunstall. The chain from death to the grave had faltered when manpower declined, but the excuse was weak. While cemetery earth went undisturbed, the dead accumulated, carcass by carcass, layer by layer. Fourteen men, women, and children occupied the barn. Ignominy festered like a sore.

It was solely because of Annalise that work progressed on a burial pit.

Whenever she possessed the strength, she worked a spade, digging until curfew drove her home. No one else showed interest in seeing the barn emptied. Young men, what remained of them, preferred the distractions of Dragoslav and The Cock's Foot.

Annalise gripped the shovel and moved around the barn. A busybody raven walked the edge, following her, opening its mouth with a mute caw. Seven more ravens lined the barn's ridge.

There's nothing to fear in the light of day, thought Annalise. *Listen for the church bell. You'll never be out after dark if you listen for the bell.*

Cold streaked through her chest, regardless.

Merrick is out there, she thought, *with wasps in his gut. He's waiting for me.*

Merrick is dead, she countered. *He died in the Balkans. He died fighting the Turks. He died a soldier. He died somewhere in the Balkans. He died somewhere.*

Merrick didn't come home. Who is to say that he is dead?

If not Merrick, what did you see, Anna?

Annalise freed herself from the barn's shadow, holding her breath in defense against miasma. At the rear of the building, a scarlet crucifix was painted crudely over the timbers.

You'll never be out after dark if you listen for the bell.

At the tree line, the plague pit opened as a V-shaped trench that stretched twelve feet in length and three feet deep. A bout of storms turned the dirt into mud, glazing the stones. An ever-growing mound of earth and rocks waited at the edge of the pit, scaling high on the trunk of a yew tree.

Annalise dropped into the trench. A chorus of insects sounded from the muggy forest. She plunged the spade into earth with violence. Out went a load of mud and gravel, raining against the mound. She repeated the process, slamming the spade with anger, allowing her thoughts to coalesce around the action, until her back ached. Sweat poured in runnels down her face. The sun was behind the trees.

Labor made her thoughts wrathful. In her mind, she saw Dragoslav and his sons in front of The Cock's Foot. Four other young men huddled on the tavern's porch, drunk on ale and wine, laughing. These were able-bodied souls. They were not ill, like Bertram and so many others. They were not dying. They were the strength and blood of the community, but rather than work where needed, they drank and gambled at jacks. With no priest to admonish them—*God damn you for leaving us, Father*— the men shunned duty. Their lethargy was infuriating and infectious. Daily, the lethargy spread. Men and women fell victim to the urge to give up, hide, sleep, and wait, to blame and pray.

Although Annalise was reluctant to call attention to the fact, even her father was guilty. He used Bertram as an excuse to retreat from life. His vigor had waned. Annalise could just as easily read Luke to the boy, fetch his water, clean his messes, and pray. She could endure his moans of agony. She could—

—Annalise buried the spade with a hard thrust, slicing into mud. Breathlessly, she gripped the handle and pressed her sweaty scalp against her fist. Her chest heaved.

She could do those things as easily as Matthias could dig. The scourge changed him. The death of her mother changed him.

Footfalls in the deeper wood, a busy shuffling through undergrowth, halted the barrage of thoughts. Annalise's fury backstepped. She looked over the lip of the trench, searching between trees for a source. Shadows grew toward the pit. The forest trilled with insects. Wind moved the branches above, and the wind whistled.

It was not only Merrick that she feared. The curfew had as much to do with wolves as it did with the evil of men. The fear of a pack down from the mountain was constant. The bounty of pox dead in other villages had kept wolves distant, but their eventual arrival was as good as a promise.

Plague, like war, makes wolves greedy and brave.

The saying was, Matthias claimed, repurposed from a heraldic motto. Regardless of the source, the wisdom of the phrase endured: scavengers hunt the grounds of tragedy. This was the promise of plague wolves.

When the shuffling ceased, it was not baying animals but a man's voice that issued.

"Anna, Anna, Gravedigger Anna," he said. After a moment of pause, he sang again.

Sweat erupted on Annalise's palms. Mud coated the roots of her tongue. She searched the shadows, but no shape appeared in the darkness. Dread swelled. Sweat was cold against her neck.

"Anna, come closer. Anna, crawl to me. I'll follow you, Anna. I'll follow you home."

It was the voice of Merrick.

Annalise fought for composure. She fought for reason.

Merrick is dead. He died in the Balkans. He died fighting the Turks.

How do you know? How can you be certain?

She placed the spade on the ground. She lifted herself free of the crumbling wall. Annalise advanced toward the trees, each step a test of will. She stood in the grass, searching.

Without a body, how can you be certain he is dead?

The desire to see Merrick, as she saw him on the bridge, was undeniable. It was inhuman to not *need* such a thing.

"Show yourself," she whispered.

The beating of wings from the barn caught her off-guard, and Annalise jumped, startled. One of the ravens lifted from the roof, alighting in a nearby tree.

"Enough of your games," she shouted. Her chin trembled. "Show yourself, Merrick." She balled her fists. "Show yourself."

A lengthy silence held sway. Miasma enveloped Annalise where she stood, seeping into her clothes and hair. When she returned for the shovel, determined to flee, she saw that her arms shook.

"Anna the Gravedigger," the voice said, amused. "Anna the Daughter, Anna the Wife. Anna the Sister, Anna the Friend, Anna with the peasant spade in her hand."

"Show yourself," she demanded.

"Crawl to me," said Merrick, and the voice was no longer distant. The voice was at her side. A finger rough and cold as hoarfrost ran along her neck, lifting the collar of her blouse, tracing her sweat, moving to her spine.

Tears swelled, ringing her eyes. Bile threatened her tongue.

"Anna," Merrick whispered, and chilly breath stroked her ear.

From the church in the bottom, the bell clanged with great force, flooding the valley, flooding the moment.

The curfew, she thought. *You'll never be out after dark if you listen for the bell.*

Steeling herself, Annalise moved from the voice. She rushed around the barn. She refrained from sprinting, although the desire to run was strong. She refused to give Merrick the pleasure of seeing her flee in terror.

Merrick is dead.

Merrick is dead.

Merrick is dead.

The voice stayed near the pit as Annalise, shaking, stepped onto the trail and into the open light of day.

The bell, she realized, was too early to signal curfew. The sun was high. Nightfall was distant.

Again, the peal moved through the valley and up the hills.

Gather yourself, Annalise demanded. *Merrick is dead. He died fighting the Turks.*

The press of the freezing digit endured on her neck, running ice through her bones.

Gather yourself.

At the third ring, Annalise gripped the crucifix on her chest and prayed.

Ave Maria, gratia plena. Hail Mary, full of grace.

Control yourself, she finished. *God willing, control yourself.*

With a shuddery breath, her gaze went to the road that once deposited travelers into the mouth of Drunstall. For two months, the artery to civilization was empty. Grass sprouted through its center. The village gate was unguarded, hanging on its hinges.

A man and his dog walked brazenly past the watchhouse, defying orders of quarantine and restrictions of travel. He crossed into the main thoroughfare where the quartered fields of wheat and buckwheat rose at his shoulder.

Men, women, and children exited homes, the church, and the alehouse to slake curiosity. A crowd gathered outside The Cock's Foot.

The traveler did not slip into Drunstall under the cover of night. His purpose was not that of a thief. His posture was straight and trained. Although he had the bearing of a lord, he wore the ornamentation of a gypsy. A curious swath of red proclaimed his origin. Gypsies were barred from traveling freely here, quarantine or not, yet the man moved without deference.

Annalise glanced back at the barn. The ravens were curious about the intruder, as was, she assumed, the voice in the pit.

Merrick.

No, it isn't Merrick.

The traveler arrived like a storm.

Covered in mud, Annalise started toward the golden wheatfields.

Plague, like war, makes wolves greedy and brave.

Wolves hunt. Wolves descend.

A scavenger and his hound, thought Annalise, *reaching the quarry of their hunt.*

Anger colored her fear like a conjoining stream.

When Annalise entered the muddy lane, the traveler was speaking to a child near the rain tree. The boy pointed toward huts that lined the hillside. The stranger bowed. He looked over the crowd of onlookers, ignoring Annalise's approach. The dog, however, a greyhound of brindle made, eyed her with distrust. Unlike the mutts that roamed the wood, the dog was abnormally self-assured and alert. It didn't look away. Annalise wiped sweat from her face.

When the crowd tightened around the stranger and dog, the man rummaged through a satchel. He, too, was alert with intelligence and sangfroid. There was something noble in his manner. He retrieved a folded document, brandishing it high, waving it as a flag.

Indeed, he had the dark skin and hair of a gypsy. His eyes were dusky, his nose Greek. The garish red scarf of silk wrapped his neck. His clothes were finer than what she'd seen with other men who traveled without a horse. He wore breeches and a justacorps, of which the cloth was not coarse. Bands of lace touched his wrists, and gloves of fine leather covered his hands. A black cap, the antiquated *chapeau à bec,* covered his head. Although he was not decorated with jewels and a wig, his clothes would not be out of place on a journeying lord.

It took courage to tempt highwaymen thus, and it took courage to approach superiors without reverence.

"Is there anyone among you who can read?" he asked, raising his voice above the crowd.

The stranger spoke Bavarian, but his voice was heavily accented—an accent Annalise didn't recognize. Something from the East, she assumed. Something from the Balkans, perhaps. Merrick, she thought, would know the accent.

When no one volunteered, Annalise said, "I can read."

The stranger mirrored his hound, eyeing Annalise with distrust.

"I beg your pardon, Fräulein?" said the man.

Annalise returned the look. She collected her strength, although she was pale with exhaustion and fright.

"I can read the letter," she said.

A murmur went through the crowd. Dragoslav, leaning on his fence, wheezed.

"Very well, Fräulein," said the stranger. "Very well. Thank you."

The foreigner bowed with aristocratic grace.

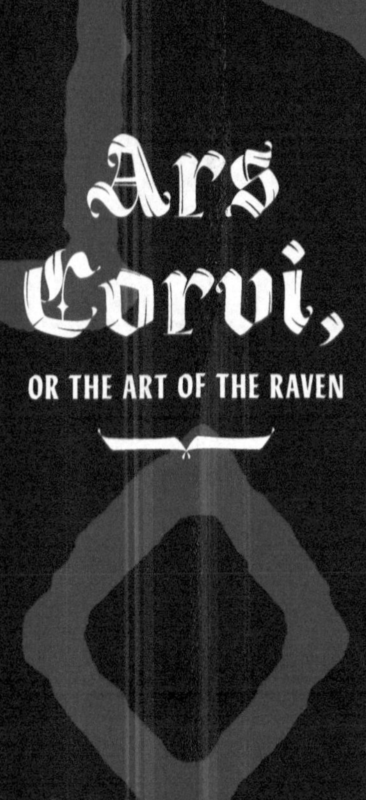

Ars Corvi,

OR THE ART OF THE RAVEN

A bowlegged cat, high white with a cape of grey, ripped the carcass from the teeth of his companion and rushed from the grave. A tabby gave chase. The felines navigated the field of weeds and stone deftly, and then they darted into the forest. In their wake, the hunters left an array of ebony feathers and a pile of intestines. The remainder of the raven was gone.

The Lieutenant started to follow the cats, but Grau snatched him by the buff coat. The soldier's helmet rattled. He swung his elbow, jerking loose, agitated. His face glistened.

"The bird's no matter," Grau said.

Gripping a lantern, The Lieutenant stared into the tenebrous corner of the cemetery.

"I…collect talons," he said, demoralized. "And beaks." He demonstrated by shaking the pouch of skin at his waist. The sack hung like a goiter, stuffed to brimming with bird carrion. "Treasures. Cat beasts don't…eat the beaks…or feet."

"You were shot in the head, weren't you?" Grau asked.

"No."

"That's how you died. I'm sure of it. Someone shot your brain to pieces, left it jelly."

"I was...never dead," The Lieutenant countered.

Toader shook his head. He grunted.

"You're an imbecile," Grau said.

Toader lowered his bulk, kneeling by the grave. Three stones covered in moss and lichens, three stones without carvings to identify the deceased, marked the dirt.

"How do you...know...one of them's in there?" The Lieutenant asked. Dejected, rattling his pouch, he gave up the desire to chase. Such jaunts never ended well for him. He was as uncoordinated as he was slow: a pitiful, leaking specimen, full of cancer. A run through the forest left his arms and legs in ribbons.

Grau peeled a strip of skin from the soldier's arm. He put the flesh in his mouth and chewed.

"Your little treasures point the way," Grau said. He worked the skin like a cud.

The Lieutenant smiled, cracking glaze at the corner of his mouth. Stems of fungus grew from his bottom gum.

"Birds always hang about. A new one out of the grave makes ravens dizzy, and that's what lets those cat beasts pounce. You follow the cats to the ravens and the ravens to the dirt."

The Lieutenant pivoted. "Cat beasts," he said. "Maybe...I'll collect...paws."

"Too much life in cats. You could barely handle a dying one."

The Lieutenant started toward the fence.

Again, Grau grabbed his buff coat.

"Bring the lantern closer," he ordered. "Hold it steady over the dirt."

The Lieutenant extended the light. Reluctantly, he knelt beside Toader. He ripped a piece of skin from his arm and rolled it into a ball. Meticulously, he began to fashion arms and legs, pinching the flesh into shape.

Grau went to his knees. He combed through grass at the side of the grave until he spotted a hole. The indentation was narrow—a cavity a burrowing snake might leave behind—with the circumference of a gulden. Dirt ringed the hole, earth pushed out rather than in, a mark of emergence. Grau jammed his finger into the shaft. The walls were smooth clay.

"Too late with this one," Grau said. "It's already out."

"How long?" The Lieutenant asked.

"Could be days."

"What happens…when we don't…catch 'em?" The Lieutenant asked.

Grau tucked the wad of skin into his jaw.

"We don't catch most of 'em," he said. "Fortunate to snag what we do. How many times I gotta tell you that? They've got no sense when they're fresh. Unless they have the brains of our friend that's stewin' back there, they follow their bellies. They crawl about, imitate what they see, and then skin starts growin' thick on 'em if they can get inside the Lord's belly. Most of 'em don't grow enough to matter."

"They…stay globs," The Lieutenant said. With his fingernail, he cut cloth under his right arm. He freed a sack that was causing his shirt to tighten. Mildewed flesh dangled free.

"Some of 'em get trapped in creeks like frog shit." Grau laughed. "Then," he said, grinning, "they imitate the shit. They stay there like a lily pad until they starve. It's waste that doesn't please The Lord."

"What if…they imitate…a tree?" The Lieutenant asked. "Eat the sun…until they starve?"

Grau sighed. "As soon as the one we got grows bigger than you, I'm going to have Toader kill you. Sooner, if you don't stop with the questions."

The Lieutenant straightened his smile. He played with the skin in his hand, fashioning a head to go with the arms and legs. His mouth shook.

"He's going to cook you and eat you."

Grau pulled the flesh from his mouth. He rolled it between his claw-like fingers. "Or I'll do it raw." He popped the morsel and swallowed.

The Lieutenant placed the lantern on the dirt. He crouched. His helmet trembled as he sobbed.

"One more time," Grau mouthed to Toader.

Toader stood.

"Why don't you show him the barrels again? That'll cheer him up."

The Lieutenant turned, hopeful. The tears around his eyes were thick as sap. The tears crystallized, glazing his face. With the lantern under his chin, the soldier shone like glass. Eventually, he'd have enough sap on his face to resemble the craggy hide of a tree, which was fitting since a forest grew inside him.

With a webbed hand, Toader lifted The Lieutenant, helping him to his feet. Grau took the lantern.

At the rear of the wagon, Toader opened a cask. He guided The Lieutenant closer.

Until the hide thickened, the creatures were fragile as motherless chicks. Of Grau's three recent catches, only one had survived to grow. Two had withered, drowning and pickling. The survivor, whom Grau called The Stripling, developed with astonishing speed. The left hand had the shape of a talon: three spikes and a dew claw. The rest was humanoid with a toddler's legs, arms, and oversized head.

Stormy thoughts churned behind the creature's paper-thin skull. There were times when The Stripling's thoughts escaped the drum, pricking at Grau, teasing The Lieutenant, tempting Toader. The Stripling mimicked everything, so that its appearance changed as much as a stream. It was a mirror to anyone who faced it.

The idea that The Stripling was an incarnation of The Lord had occurred to Grau, but he couldn't form the accusation, let alone utter it.

The Lieutenant looked in the brine and smiled through a varnish of tears. He picked a crystal from his eyelid and dropped it into the mixture.

"He's…gone," said The Lieutenant. "He got out…again."

Grau peeked into the barrel, curious.

"Son of a bitch," he hissed. "My Lord won't be pleased."

Toader grunted.

"He can't have gone far," Grau said, "not without ripping himself to pieces."

"I can…go far," The Lieutenant said.

"I wish you would, cretin."

Grau carried the lantern back into the wood.

"How does he…get out?" The Lieutenant asked, trailing behind.

"I'm beginning to think he seeps through the staves, mimicking the brine."

Grau searched the trees. A storm moved over the wood, swaying branches. The sky darkened.

It was in the joint of an acacia that Grau found The Stripling. The creature was perched on a limb between two ravens, stone-faced, shivering, and wet, staring into the night, entranced.

"He's projecting himself elsewhere," Grau said. "Toader, get him down."

The giant reached up to the limb and grabbed the pale, wet form.

"Get one…of the birds," said The Lieutenant.

"Forget the birds. Let's get him back," Grau said, relieved. "He's got growin' to do."

"He'll be…a good one," The Lieutenant said.

Grau flicked the soldier's helmet. "You're a scholar. That's the brightest thing you've said all night."

The Lieutenant gurgled with laughter. He took the ball of skin, now a crude figurine, and propped it upright on the branch.

"What is that?" Grau asked.

"It…is me."

"You're an artist and a scholar."

"Yes."

As Toader carried The Stripling to the wagon, Grau said, "Toader needs to feed or he really will eat you. We'll make our way into the village tonight."

Toader cradled The Stripling in one arm. With the other, he dropped his cowl. The face, pinched and rumpled, twitched. He grunted approval.

"Down you go, troublemaker," said Grau.

Delicately, Toader dipped the entranced creature into liquid.

IX

CAPITULUM

The wind changed, and the quality of the darkness changed, heralding rain. Corpse rot traveled down the valley, unmistakable and raw as a battlefield. Ravens bated, exchanging seats, preparing for the storm rather than sheltering.

While Vinegar Tom rested in grass, Toth waited at the entrance of a hovel, speaking to a sorrel-headed man named Matthias Bergmann. Like most men in Drunstall, he wore a beard of mourning. Matthias was the father of Annalise, who read Toth's letter of ingress aloud in the common. Annalise sat within the hovel, reading the Gospel of Luke to a sibling ill with pox. Every inch of the young man's flesh was hard with scabs. He lay in sweat on a floor mat. Death eddied in the room.

Annalise stopped reading, watching Toth through the doorway. When Toth bowed, she returned to the text.

Matthias was an elder. His education garnered respect from certain villagers, although not all. In the absence of a priest, Matthias had assumed the responsibility of Christian rites. The man was something of a self-taught polymath, with stacks of books and curious machines in his home. Presently, he demonstrated the use of a mechanical beetle, an automaton device with a key to twist.

Toth held the beetle in his palm, moving the wings with his finger. Clock gears turned inside the belly.

"Whence did you come by this?" Toth asked. "Did you make it?"

On this point, Matthias was vague.

"Peddlers and soldiers travel through," he said. "They sell and trade things."

Toth had his doubts. He returned the beetle.

Matthias ratcheted the key, and the automaton lumbered from his palm to his fingertips. The old man smiled satisfaction.

"I have a Jacob's staff for measuring stars," Matthias said. "I understand you're an astrologer in addition to other pursuits. Would you like to see it, as well?"

"Mayhap another time," Toth said. "Are you a student of astrology, Herr Bergmann?"

"Oh, I dabble in everything, friend," said Matthias.

The old man's amicable manner was welcome. Matthias made no fuss about Toth's Romani heritage, which was uncommon for a man of rural sensibilities. He made no complaint about Toth's request to use the church for a gathering.

"I want to show *you* something now," said Toth.

He pulled the pipe and pouch of tobacco from his satchel. He stuffed the bowl and handed it to the old man.

Matthias admired the constellation etched in the wood. He smelled the tobacco.

"Spanish?"

"It is."

"What a luxury, friend."

Toth retrieved the lighter of flint and hemp. He demonstrated how the device worked, and the rope smoked.

Matthias lit the tobacco with a grin.

"If I had money, I'd buy that from you," he said. "Maybe a trade, friend? I have a few things inside that might interest you."

Toth laughed. "Quite rare, these," he said.

"I see. I might put my own together then."

"If you made the beetle, it certainly isn't beyond your skill."

Matthias smoked the tobacco. The bouquet worked to mask the stench of the wind.

"Anna," he called inside, "Master Toth and I will be at the church."

Annalise didn't halt her reading. She droned through the passages of Luke.

"Come," Matthias said to Toth.

"Tom," Toth said.

After the greyhound rose and stretched, Toth followed Matthias into the lane.

Matthias gripped the beetle as he walked. Smoke trailed from his nose.

"Although it's hidden in these times, Drunstall was once recipient to the Archduke's grace," said the old man.

"With such a fine church, I believe it," Toth said.

Matthias took a draw. "The Archduke kept a hunting lodge near in the mountains. He came through this settlement twice a year. His entire entourage in a train of wagons that stretched a Roman mile. His Grace had the church built as a personal chapel."

"An impressive legacy, Herr Bergmann. An honor and distinction."

Tom stepped blithely through the mud, watching the storm brew above.

Bitterness crept into Matthias's tone. He stuffed the beetle in his coat pocket.

"His Grace brought prestige, but that was two hundred years past. Princes no longer build in Drunstall, and the Karnstein family prefers to believe we don't exist. When we lost royal favor, the village went back to sleep."

"There's nothing you must do to lose the favor of a prince," Toth said. "Nobles move on to new playgrounds."

Matthias stopped in the road. To his left, fronting a line of homes, was an alehouse named The Cock's Foot. The smell of yeast crossed the yard. The tavern was situated in a copse of trees, pens, and corrals. Pigs, chickens, and horses clustered around the trunks. A midden of dung rose at the rear. Torches burned at the door, casting fluttering rings of light. The Cock's Foot bustled. An angry exchange came through the walls.

"They're discussing you, Master Toth," Matthias said. "You must understand they're distrustful of a stranger, especially a foreigner."

Toth checked Tom. The greyhound watched the alehouse, but he made no move.

"That's abundantly clear," Toth said, unruffled. "Let's pray that drink doesn't stir them into a mob."

Matthias waved at the air. "They know nothing of action. Words will be the only venom you suffer tonight."

Of the trees in the tavern's fenced yard, one overhanging the road had Toth's attention. Ornaments decorated the squat hazel. He stepped nearer. Hanging like myriad ghosts were rain dolls of calico and twine. Toth made a quick count of fourteen effigies. The breeze teased their skirts. The rain doll was an old charm of farmers, a protector against drought. Little crosses of red, painted where a face should be, offset heathen origins.

Toth held one of the dolls. There was nothing fine or careful in its construction.

"Not only a distrustful people," Matthias said, "but superstitious."

Thunder punctuated the din of the alehouse.

"Who's to argue with what works, Herr Bergmann?" Toth asked.

Matthias smiled. "That's not something a man of the Church would say."

"My Order is a peculiar one."

"Yes, I know of Saint Guinefort."

"You do?"

"Yes, your business is occult matters."

"Indeed, it is. You're a learned man. Why the distrust here?" Toth asked. "Does the seal of Bishop von Thun carry no weight in these mountains?"

Matthias drew on the pipe stem. He started in the direction of the church.

"The Bishop isn't accustomed to sending his best, is he? His priests only diminish in quality. Our most recent was illiterate, Master Toth. Or nearly. Haas was his name. I knew the Bible better than he."

"Priests aren't what they once were," Toth admitted. "What happened to Father Haas? That's unclear to me."

Matthias nodded philosophically. "Pox scared him," he said.

"Did you know him well?"

"Quite well, yes. The coward fled at the first sign of trouble. The very first. He left his Book of Rites, left everything."

"I assume, Herr Bergmann, that his departure wasn't due to something nefarious. That much is certain?"

Matthias stared over the fields at the river, the skin of which rippled with the wind. "You're plumbing for rumors, friend," he said.

"Were there rumors about Haas?"

Matthias smiled. "*Every* village has rumors."

"Some carry more weight than others."

"Do they?"

"I met a child at the cemetery this afternoon. A boy. His name was Sebastian."

Matthias scoffed. "One of Cili's brood," he said.

"Yes. Her son."

"Or her brother. Or uncle. Incestual lot, they are."

"Why do you dislike this family, Herr Bergmann?"

"The storm would come and go before I finished that tale," Matthias said. He laughed, but another storm brewed in the depth of his eyes.

"Sebastian suggested that your troubles are brought on by *le meneur de loups*. A leader of wolves, as it were. That's an old phrase. Do you know it?"

"I don't, friend," Matthias said. He exhaled a cloud of smoke. "It sounds like dirty French."

"It *is* French. It's a poetic way of saying 'conjuror'. A conjuror in the old style. A man who, through summoning, commands nature, even the dangers of wolves."

Matthias removed the pipe. "Don't tell me, friend, that you believe my beetle an act of sorcery."

"Not at all, Herr Bergmann."

"Are the rain dolls witchcraft?"

"No."

"Then what *are* you getting at, Master Toth?"

"I want to know if that description fits Father Haas. Of everyone, he would have the mechanisms and knowledge to conjure. His disappearance doesn't bode well. I find the idea of him fleeing out of fear less than satisfactory."

"The description does not fit him, friend," Matthias said flatly. "Haas was feebleminded. He was a weak man in every respect."

"A conjuror would not be a weak man?"

"He was weak because he—"

"—Abandoned his parish," Toth finished. "Yes, I know."

"Precisely, friend. He abandoned his flock."

"Why would a child say something like that? That certainly isn't a thought that originated in the boy's mind. He can't even read. Is there a rumor here of conjuration?"

Matthias exhaled a cloud of smoke. His manner had gone cold.

"Sebastian's mother, God rest her soul." He laughed bitterly. "That's why Sebastian would say it. No telling what else Cili planted in their heads. What did the girls tell you, friend?"

"Not enough. They were closed to me. Would you say, Herr Bergmann, that *le meneur de loups* fits anyone in Cili's family?"

"It fits no one better than Cili herself. She's in Hell for a reason, Master Toth."

"In Hell? I suspect you don't mean suicide."

"That," he said, "and more."

"What more?"

"You know, one day the river will sweep away Drunstall," Matthias commented. He gestured at the settlement. "If Cili's rain dolls do their job, that is. And her other work." He smiled.

When he and Toth arrived at the church, Vinegar Tom sat in the grass and yawned.

"I'll put you to bed soon," Toth promised the dog.

"Do you always speak openly to the hound?" Matthias asked.

"Certainly. How else would I communicate with him?"

Matthias shrugged. He looked up at the church. Dark clouds swirled above the spire.

Rather than a wooden meeting house, a building of carved stone, replete with a belltower and bell cast from bronze, flanked a crop of buckwheat. An orb and crucifix on the tower, atop which a raven balanced, was the highest point in the settlement, visible from a mile distant on the road. A mural decorated the façade, a *memento mori* of skeletal devils in blue. The minions of Pluto gripped a prince. The mural was weathered, leaving lacunae in the tale it told.

Equally artless was a Latin phrase marring the walnut door. The words read: *dat deus incrementum. God gives growth.*

Princes give growth, Toth corrected. *Dat principes incrementum.*

"It is a fine church, isn't it, friend?" Matthias said.

As the old man finished the tobacco and fell into contemplative silence, Toth looked at the river. Beyond fields under cultivation, the dark Lavant flowed, a tributary of the great Drava. A muddy shore girded with sarsen stones extended to a forested bend. A millhouse stood amidst the monoliths. Within the touch of lapping water was the carcass of a gnarled tree. Ravens covered the limbs.

Matthias noticed his curiosity.

"*Ars corvi,*" said the old man. *The art of the raven.*

"Why do the ravens congregate here?" Toth asked. "Even for a plague, there are too many carrion birds about."

"Devils," Matthias said. "Jackals. They feed on the dead and wait for the dying."

"Not all these at once," Toth said. "Not so many."

"Cili opened their cages when she got to Hell."

Matthias stepped around Toth, and he gestured to the lane.

"Here they come," he said. "Their council is finished."

Toth's heart quickened at the mass of humanity. Two men with torches exited the alehouse, leading a crowd of thirty from The Cock's Foot. The crowd proceeded so silently that the roar of torches was audible above the slop of footfalls.

Toth had requested that all able-bodied men, women, and children gather so that he could address them at once. His request bore fruit. He gave the pox-sick leave to remain cloistered in their homes with a guardian. Toth wanted no part in increasing their suffering.

Watching the mob's approach, Toth understood the weight of his task. He must give hope without making promises. He wondered if Kaspar Groza encountered similar hostility at Karnstein. He wondered if the villagers would rather face a man of medicine than an occultist.

Matthias watched with nervous energy of his own.

Thunder moved through the valley, growing closer, louder, and more intense. The first raindrops fell. The wind gusted, chasing ravens from the belltower.

"Will we stable your hound?" Matthias asked.

"He stays with me," Toth said firmly.

"Even in the church?"

"Even in the church, Herr Bergmann," Toth said. He eyed the greyhound. "Come, Tom. Up."

Matthias grimaced. "How about that white mutt the size of a calf? Shall we invite it inside, too, friend?"

The stray Pyrenees, her mane and tail blown wide in the wind, waited by a barn on the hill, watching.

Matthias made light. "Did you not see the behemoth? She made a circuit around the fields, watching you and your Tom. Conceivably, I daresay, a guardian in disguise, friend."

Toth admired the shock of white in the darkness. "I didn't see her."

Matthias emptied the pipe. He handed it to Toth.

"Thanks for the tobacco," he said. "That pleasure was a long time coming."

"Come, Tom," Toth said.

Tom stood and stretched his front legs. After a look at the approaching throng, he preceded Toth and Matthias through the doorway. He bristled in agitation.

"Does the thunder frighten your hound?" Matthias asked, entering the nave, splitting rows of walnut pews. His footsteps echoed.

"Very little frightens Tom," Toth said. He lifted the satchel from his shoulder. "Many things anger him."

"Got a little wolf in him, eh?"

The dog's nails clacked against the floor. He shook off the rain that had touched his coat.

"He certainly believes it so."

X

CAPITULUM

oth joined Matthias at the altar and looked out at the assemblage. The broken stares and impotent anger of refugees greeted him. Thirty souls within the confines of the church made a more formidable group than thirty in the open street. From front row to last, the pews were full.

Elevated two steps above the floor, the platform upon which Toth stood held the furnishings of a working church. A table and tabernacle for the Eucharist gathered dust, while twelve candlesticks, each alight, lined a shelf. Above the altar, recessed in the stone wall, was an enormous crucifix. A distressed lectern fronted the stage. The wood was scarred where an anxious priest scratched the pedestal.

The interior was simple and sparse. Torches hung on each side of the entrance, casting a trembling glow over the nave. Smoke gathered at the vaulted ceiling. Except for the finely carved pews, regalia was largely absent. In each sidewall, plank doors rattled with the storm. Rattling, too, were the arched windows, empty of glass, shuttered poorly and fastened with rope. Rain beat the roof, walls, and belltower. One badge of prosperity struck Toth: a niche in the left corner held alabaster figurines of the Apostles. The figures were not the work of a whittler. The art was as fine as that encountered in Vienna.

The villagers talked among themselves and watched Toth.

Vinegar Tom guarded the righthand door. He watched the people as intently as they watched his master.

When Matthias raised his hands, a hush fell.

Toth surveyed the faces. Of the assembled, he recognized Floris, Blancheflor, Sebastian, and Annalise, but no others.

"This man is Dr. Dorin Toth," Matthias began. He raised his voice, projecting to the back of the room. "The Lord Bishop von Thun in Graz sent Dr. Toth here to—"

"—deliver us," someone shouted. A man. "To rescue our poor savage souls."

Scattered laughter followed.

"—to *investigate*," Matthias said carefully. "To investigate the reports submitted to Sergeant Wallhausen in the spring of this year."

"To mock us more like!"

"They work fast in Graz," said another man.

"They send us a gypsy when they can't even send a priest," another shouted.

Each call stoked anger, and each speaker emboldened the next.

"Pass around your hat, gypsy, and we'll fill it with gold!"

"And send you back with more paper!"

"We'll hear from Graz again in six months!"

Matthias looked at Toth apologetically.

"Enough," Toth said. He moved to the lectern where his satchel waited. He raised his hand to silence the crowd. "Enough!" he shouted. He slammed his fist against wood.

Tom's ears perked.

"A gypsy with a devil dog," a man said, but his voice was weaker.

While wind rattled and rain pounded, a beat of hesitation passed through the congregation.

Sternly, Toth introduced himself.

"My name is Dorin Toth. I am a Doctor of Theology at the

University of Vienna, and I am an investigator for the Order of Saint Guinefort, which finds its chief patron in Rome."

He scanned the room. Saint Guinefort brought no looks of recognition. Despite Matthias's knowledge, Guinefort was a hidden service of the Church, and when one knew it, they were usually in a position where they wished they didn't.

Matthias stepped from the platform and took a seat in the front pew.

"The Order of Saint Guinefort exists," Toth said, making every effort to smooth his accent, "to investigate claims such as those reported by your people." Seeing doubt register, he added. "I am not here to correct or ridicule you. Or to interrogate you. I am here because someone in the Church—not everyone, you know this—but someone of rank took your claims seriously. I, as well, take your claims seriously. I've read the reports submitted by Sergeant Wallhausen, and I believe I can help."

"What does the Church care about pox?" It was Annalise who spoke. The dark-headed woman rose to ask the question.

Toth eyed her. "My presence has nothing to do with smallpox, Fräulein. My concern is that an additional plague, one of the spirit, has come unto you. My concern is," he paused, looking around, "of an *occult* rather than medical nature."

A murmur went through the crowd.

"He's here to burn witches," a man said. "I knew it. He'll drag out a hag and put the blame on her. Watch him."

"Then twenty more besides!"

"I want to be clear," Toth said. "I do not believe that any shortcomings angered God and caused this. I am not here to preach fire, and I am *not* searching for witches. I am here to find the cause of your troubles and then provide a remedy."

"If not witches, gypsy, then what are you looking for?"

Toth swallowed his anger. With the matter wrapped in grief, he wanted to treat it with delicacy, but such an entreaty would sink unheard. He had to prod the wound. He unsheathed the reports and held the folio aloft.

"A cause. That you are seeing your loved ones after they are dead and in the grave. That they are coming unto you and speaking. What is the cause? *That* is why I'm here."

The mood changed. Tension and disquiet fell over the crowd. The subject was taboo even among those who had experienced it.

"And you," Toth said, pointing at Floris and her siblings. "Your mother, Cili, did she not see her brother before she perished? Her brother, who was deceased, walking in the forest. Do you not desire to know what caused the apparition? Did your mother not commit suicide from the despair the encounter wrought?"

Blancheflor stood, red with anger. "She did not commit suicide, sir! How dare you!"

Toth shot a quick look at Matthias, who was stone-faced.

"Mayhap, she didn't," Toth said. "Do you not want me to find what happened to her then? I trust that her place in the cemetery means that many here do not believe that she damned herself. Take your seat, Fräulein."

Blancheflor gripped the pew. "We know what happened to her, Master Toth."

"Oh, come now," a man said.

"I believe you, Fräulein," Toth said. "Take your seat."

Reluctantly, Blancheflor sat.

"Is there anyone else who has seen a loved one after they passed?" Toth scanned the crowd, searching the torment on several faces. "There were two pale creatures crawling from a shaft by the cemetery today." He jabbed at his chest. "I saw them, and then they were gone. The phantoms were there, and then they were not. I believe you. I am not here to ridicule. Now, again, who here has witnessed the dead free of the grave? You must cooperate if you wish me to trace the root."

A hand went up, that of an old man. "I saw my son," he said simply. He left the matter there.

"Note these names," Toth told Matthias.

Matthias nodded.

A moment passed. Annalise rose and freed herself from the pew. She stepped into the aisle.

"My fiancé appeared to me," she said. "His name is Merrick." She advanced toward the pulpit to make a testimonial. Her eyes were red from crying.

"How many times have you seen Merrick?" Toth asked.

Annalise stopped before reaching the platform. She looked up at Toth. She had no aim in her walking, save for drawing closer to Matthias in the front row. The old man swiveled in his seat, watching his daughter. He gestured for her to continue.

"Three times," she said.

"And you will show me where this occurred, Fräulein?"

Annalise nodded. She looked at her father.

Matthias stood. He looked over the crowd.

"Confess what you've seen to this man," he said. "Confess it."

Another hand went up. And then another.

"And you," Toth said, finding Floris and Blancheflor in the commotion, "will you show me where your mother spied your uncle?"

"I'll do you one better," said Blancheflor.

"Quiet!" Toth said, shouting down the growing calls and raised hands.

Blancheflor didn't explain her meaning.

It was as Toth pointed to another woman, opening the floor to her testimonial, that a cry of agony overcame the storm and pierced the stone walls.

The crowd stilled, turning to the entryway. The cry was more than one of pain. It was a scream for help.

Vinegar Tom bolted, cutting between the torches, and striking the door of splintered walnut with his front legs. Unlatched, the door gave with his second assault, and the hound was off into the night, stretching his great length for speed.

Toth leapt from the platform and pushed through the crowd.

XII
CAPITULUM

When Grau caught the scent, his mouth twitched, and he salivated over his dark lips. With skillful patience, he tempered the gnawing hunger. To rush, and to be exposed, would drive his prey into hiding. He didn't have the numbers to be cavalier.

Once he decided on a path, Grau rose from the river, surrounded to the waist by the rushing current. He motioned for Toader and The Lieutenant to join him. His companions advanced through the water, emerging from their concealment. Toader's scalp shone with a flash of lightning. Thunder shook the muck around their boots.

Ahead, the village waited, dark with points of fire dotting the gloom.

Toader sniffed the air, flaring his broad nostrils, and The Lieutenant imitated his action. Rain drummed the soldier's helmet and kicked up the water.

Grau's mouth trembled.

"Ripe?" he asked.

Toader grunted.

Hunkered, Grau led his companions to the shore. The Lieutenant struggled against the water, fighting for balance.

The current was strong, moving with a roar and reaching the sarsens on the bank. Toader grabbed The Lieutenant and pulled him by the waist until he was free.

Through the lashing rain, Grau, Toader, and The Lieutenant trampled through a field. On the other side, the church stood before them. There was life within—a multitude. An aura of anger and fear hung over the place.

Grau watched the building with interest. He took the cap and wilted feather from his pocket and placed it on his head. Cold water ran over his ears and down his back.

"They're gathering," he said, amused. He smelled to be certain. "Gathering without their sick."

Toader grunted with satisfaction.

Grau started from the church through a row of homes, trailing the scent he'd discovered in the forest. Slopping through mud, he proceeded, and he no longer admonished The Lieutenant for gratuitous noise. He no longer hunkered, and he no longer worried about inciting a mob of hunters.

"*Keine Wächter*," he said to Toader. He rasped a thin laugh. *No watchmen.*

Only the animals of the village, feebly sheltered beneath canopies, watched. Among these, an enormous dog of white on the hillside was interested. Within the tree line, the dog stooped and kept pace.

"Kill the dog beast if it comes near," Grau said to his companions.

He approached a stone hut. The home waited behind a short fence—a domestic touch that flamed a memory in the pit of Grau's brain. The thought, elusive, distant, and sweet, faded to nothing.

Toader threw his leg over the slats before Grau unlatched the gate. Hunger exposed the giant's impatience. This close, Toader could not be denied. When The Lieutenant began to follow Toader's deft motion, Grau pulled him through the opening. A thin path led to the front door.

Candlelight filled a crack in the shutters like an eye opening from sleep. A gust trembled the thatch. Three ravens waited on the roof, wind in their feathers.

Toader moved to the window. Pressing his rat-like face against the shutter, he emitted the low whimper of a wounded deer. It was mimicry he'd practiced, a timbre of pain the giant perfected. With eyes shut, Grau couldn't differentiate between Toader's cry and that of a broken-legged fawn. Toader placed his burned-off ear on the boards.

His entreaty elicited no response from within.

Grau moved to the opposite window and peered through a fissure.

Toader whimpered again, louder, more urgently.

The Lieutenant worked his mouth in imitation, practicing.

Inside the room, on a mat between two beds, lay the miserable form of a young man. Without a guardian, he was alone, defenseless, suffering, and afraid. Although the whimpering fawn woke him, he possessed no strength to investigate. He lacked the strength to look around the room. He stared at the ceiling, motionless except the rise and fall of his chest. Pox scabs, rough as stone, covered him like scales. His hands looked like they were steeped in tar and dried. He worked his mouth to loosen the flesh, cracking skin around his lips.

When Toader whimpered once more, the young man released a hoarse groan.

Then, with great effort, he called, "Anna?" The weak muscles of his tongue muddled the name.

"Quite ripe," Grau whispered. Eagerness and hunger worked him into a frenzy.

Toader stepped to the entrance. The door was unfastened and ajar. Toader pushed the slab inward, and candlelight stretched over the threshold. The giant stooped, turning sideways to enter. With his head in the rafters, a flash of lightning illuminated his presence in the cramped room. Grau and The Lieutenant entered next. The domicile smelled of mildew, woodsmoke, and the skin rot Grau had detected a league distant.

The man was on the verge of death, weak as a broken bird. He drew a quick breath and his eyes darted, the only signs that the intrusion startled him, the only signs of a desire to resist. Desire did not translate to motion, so Toader mocked him with another deer whimper.

Grau advanced through a room of books, metal, and wood. A flame flickered on a table beside the front door of the hovel, illuminating the wall and casting an arc on the floor, spreading to the mat. The fat burned low, piling.

Grau sat on the edge of a bed.

"Who left you so alone?" he whispered, locking eyes with the face of suffering.

The man's sclerae had gone yellow and red. His spirit stared.

Toader and The Lieutenant stood at his blanketed feet.

The man pushed air through his lungs, but no word formed. With a last surge of strength, he rose. He lifted his back from the mat with a primal thrust, his intentions obscure. As he bent at the waist, he released a tortured scream that rimmed the village. He had risen, but his scabbed back, a full layer of skin, remained fused to the floor. The shriek cracked scabs on his face into fault lines that reached his fevered ears.

While Toader rushed to lift the man, to snatch his body and flee, The Lieutenant dropped to his knees in hunger and lust, crazed by the horror. He fell forward on his hands, his breastplate striking the floor, his helmet rolling free onto the boards, and he ate the scabs, drizzled with pus and maggots, from the mat. He lapped like an animal.

Although the man still lived, he fainted cold from agony. The air against his skinless back was too much sensation. Toader threw him over his shoulder. The body rustled and cracked like a mud-caked bag. In seconds, Toader was out the door.

"Up," Grau said to The Lieutenant. "There'll be plenty of time for that."

The Lieutenant hesitated, greedy as a hound with meat. He scraped his clawed fingers through the gore, gathering another mouthful. Awkwardly, he rose and loped outside, following Grau and Toader. Behind him, the entryway was a yellow rectangle cutting the black of night. Behind him, too, his steel helmet rattled on the floor. The Lieutenant rushed into darkness toward the river.

As Toader escorted the quarry into the safety of the current, Grau waited between sarsens, oscillating his gaze between the errant Lieutenant, who stopped in the field to eat from his hand, and a crowd spilling from the church, fighting rain with torches. A lone dog barked angrily, which spurred other dogs, and this was the cacophony Grau left in his wake.

He strode into the river.

XII

CAPITULUM

inegar Tom stood in flowers, aiming his muzzle at the doorway. Candlelight from the interior reached the greyhound. Rain soaked his coat, accentuating the thinness of his face and form. Tom snapped off three barks, which set off a chain of baying dogs. The curious Pyrenees waited outside the fence, joining the chorus with her deep wail. Soon the racket of animals, mixed with thunder, wind, and rain was disorientating. The hue and cry echoed through the hills.

Toth slopped through mud with a surfeit of fortitude. Many villagers stayed in the shadow of the church, confused and unwilling, but Annalise dashed forward, joining Toth in the dark lane. The woman said nothing. She neither asked for permission nor cared to receive it. Toth sensed great strength in her, and he sensed the turbulence of rancor beneath the surface. He'd have to earn Annalise as an ally, he realized, or suffer her as an enemy. Good or ill, she'd be a force in his investigation.

When Annalise spotted Tom at the home of Matthias, she ran ahead.

"Bertram," she shouted. "Bertram!"

At his son's name, Matthias broke from the crowd. Two men accompanied him.

Lightning cast a white pall over the fields, and Toth witnessed a lean figure standing among the stalks. The shape emerged like a scarecrow, watching, lashed by rain, mesmerized by the fury of the dogs. The man wore the breastplate, bandolier, and buff coat of a soldier. Wind bent the stalks around him. Rain hammered his armor. Startled, Toth halted, staring through the corral. Copper reached his throat. Cold rooted in his chest, deeper than the chill of rain.

Why a soldier? he thought. He questioned his senses.

The pale face had a sheen like ice in sunlight. It was a face of glass.

Following a crack of thunder that cowed the dogs into momentary silence, the soldier turned. He darted through the wheat, retreating to the river like an untethered effigy. He scurried with ungainly motion, as though shopworn limbs were sewn to his trunk. Matthias's mechanical beetle came to mind—the gracelessness of an automaton.

The vision was so bizarre that Toth questioned its reality.

A scream of horror, that of Annalise, drew him outward, and Toth moved from locked torpor to a sprint. Annalise's scream was not directed at the fields. She and Tom were in the domicile.

Toth passed through tufts of rain-beaten flowers. He passed into the interior where mold and rot held sway. Instinctively, he lifted the scarf to cover his nose and mouth. He glanced around the room, girding himself for the shock of carnage. His head buzzed. The image of the soldier, and the ubiquitous violence of militaries, remained in his mind.

Annalise stood between the beds, partially hidden by a timber pillar. She gripped her skull until her hands were bloodless, and she stared at a soiled mat on the floor. Color had drained from her face and neck.

"He's gone," she said. Terror gave strange rhythm to her words. "Bertram's gone."

Toth approached, dropping his scarf. He grabbed the greyhound's collar.

"Back, Tom," he said. His heart hammered.

The dog ignored his command.

Annalise's back trembled, as did the bones of her hands. She gripped the bedclothes, crumpling wool, and she vented an agonized cry, a tortured moan that withered Toth's heart. He knew the sound well, had heard it too often for a single lifetime. It was long suffering, disbelief, and blackness spreading in the soul—all compressed into a moment. Annalise dropped to the mattress, sobbing. Her face disappeared into the blanket.

"Plague wolves," she muttered.

Toth didn't counter the claim. He stepped to her side, touching her shoulder. As Annalise cried, Toth stroked her raven hair and studied the gore on the mat. A necrotic layer of skin—a jagged square a foot long and equally wide—was fused to the pad. The sight, the violence and pain of it, staggered Toth, but he was not a man weak of stomach. He kept his head. Five lines, the crescent drag of claws, ran through the flesh, piling it at one side. The scrape of teeth, two incisors like those of a rat, shaped the edges. Maggots and ants wriggled in the meat.

Tom sniffed the hem of Annalise's skirt, peering up at her hidden face. He put his paws on the mattress and lifted himself. He coiled at the woman's side, pressing wet fur against her thigh, and pushing away a leather Bible with his feet.

"Down, Tom," Toth said.

The dog looked away in refusal.

Outside, Matthias shouted for his children. Toth's stomach knotted. This was Matthias's moment before knowing, the instant before truth ripped him apart. The man's voice grew louder.

"Get out of there, mutt," Matthias shouted at the Pyrenees.

Toth searched the floor around the mat. There was no blood, and there was no sign of struggle. However, just beneath a mattress, half-shadowed, lay the upended helmet of a soldier. A ring of water surrounded it. The helmet was a steel burgonet, battle-beaten, with a sharp comb that ran front to rear. It was a cheap piece of equipment, open-faced, undecorated, the secondhand gear militiamen of no means possessed. Flat spots in the metal suggested combat use.

Toth stooped and lifted the piece. He held the burgonet in the light, turning it over. A stench came from the metal, an odor more concentrated than that of the hut. A muddied glaze, thick as tree sap, lined the edges where steel touched flesh. The substance stank with the force of a dead, gaseous stomach. Toth rotated the helmet until its sheen caught light.

The face of glass, he thought.

"Did this belong to Bertram?" Toth asked. He held out the helmet for Tom to sniff.

Annalise raised her head. She wiped her eyes and narrowed her gaze. Finding the breath to speak, she said, "No. Bertram was never a soldier."

"Nor your father?"

She shook her head.

"This helmet is unfamiliar to you?"

She said nothing to that.

The soldier wasn't a phantasm, Toth thought. Dread darkened his manner. The man's ambulant dissonance returned, and Toth imagined it simple for such a creature to shed equipment when acting in haste. Bertram's cry had caused the soldier to rush. The soldier was not carrying Bertram, so either Annalise's brother was in the field or the soldier did not act alone.

Matthias and two men passed through the door, filling the room.

Annalise did not rise.

"We must find him," she said miserably. Then, with force, she looked at Toth and said, "*We must find him!*"

Matthias dropped to his knees. He tried to reach his daughter, but the strength to make it across the room was not in him. The empty mat went through him like a bullet. Matthias braced himself, palms against the floor. The silence of his pain was disturbing. He did not gasp, heave, or cry. He assumed the position, absorbing the moment.

Annalise looked from her father to Toth.

"Merrick was a soldier," she said.

"Merrick, your fiancé?"

"We must find him," she said.

Toth held the helmet for Tom to sniff again. He wanted the scent inside the dog's head.

"Where is Merrick buried?" Toth asked.

Annalise furrowed her brow. "If he's no longer in the grave, what does it matter?" she asked weakly.

"What of Bertram?" a man in the doorway asked.

Toth turned. "Organize a search," he said. "And make haste."

The man jogged into the rain.

Deliriously, Matthias shouted at the floor, rattling about the First Rider and the First Seal, of pestilence on white horse-flesh, and of Cili the Witch.

"Cili did this," he shouted. "Cili did this. If you want to know, Toth, Cili did all of this."

To the man who remained, Toth said, "Help me get this poor soul into a bed before he loses his mind."

Together, they picked Matthias from the floor.

"Cili did this!"

Annalise, gripping her skull, dashed into the night.

XIII

CAPITULUM

oth shouted, but the storm swallowed his voice.

"There was a man here!"

Tom tunneled through the wheat, turning circles in search of a scent.

The world was against locating Bertram. The torrent increased with relentless storm clouds swirling above. Rain pooled in the mud, bending and drowning the wheat. Lightning flared each second, a chain reaction that cast the world white. A squall broke the spine of a tree on the hillside. The river, growing angrier, abraded the shoreline, covering the sarsens. Choked with debris, the current roared.

Four men and Annalise, bearing extinguished torches, moved toward the tithe barn. Matthias was not among the meager party.

Toth splashed from the field with Tom at his heels. Near the alehouse, Toth spotted the Pyrenees mirroring his movements, running through the darkness, muddy at her undercarriage. He whistled for her to join, but the dog preferred distance. When Toth reached the search party, the men spun like he and the greyhound were wild animals on the attack. Terror wrapped their hearts like vine. Duty rather than courage had pressed them into service.

"There was a man in the field," Toth said, gasping for breath. "A soldier." He gazed at Annalise through the rain. "I suspect the helmet on the floor belonged to him."

One of the men, young with a matted beard, pushed his companions aside and faced Toth. He equaled the Hungarian in height.

"What do you mean by 'a soldier'?" he shouted over the storm. Rain smacked his ears and neck. Even at this proximity, it was difficult to make out every word.

Lightning cracked, casting the pit, the barn, and the forest pale.

"He wore a breastplate," Toth said. "Unmistakable. He stood in the field, watching."

"Was he alone?"

"Yes, but I suspect there are more of his kind. He wasn't carrying the boy."

"Raiders?" another man, the one who'd accompanied Matthias to the domicile, asked.

"He was no Turk," shouted Toth.

Impatiently, Annalise broke from the throng and stepped across a dark trench. On the other side, a trail opened and led into the deeper wood. She stopped at the mouth of the path where trees rippled. The men were reluctant to accompany her. Toth parted them to be at Annalise's side.

With the prospect of the forest, verve drained from the searchers. The wilderness pulsed with darkness, shuddering like the walls of an open maw. The path waded into blackness.

"It's too late now, Anna," one of the men said. "He's too far gone."

"We couldn't find him in this mess," another agreed.

"If there's anything to find," said another.

Annalise, soaked to the bone, clenched her fist.

"We can pick it up in the morning, Anna."

"You're cowards, all of you," she said. "What if it was your brother, Veit? Would you wait until morning? Would you let the storm stop you?"

Veit dropped his eyes. The club in his grip fell to his side. Rain pricked his scalp.

"What could we do against soldiers?" he said.

"Come on, lads," said his companion. "Let's get outta the rain. We'll recover Bertram in the morning."

The action of one gave permission to all, so the four men retreated from the track. Without haste, the men started toward the alehouse, leaving Annalise and Toth at the head of the trail.

"I hope the flood drowns them," Annalise said. Her glassy stare ended in another land, another time. "Worthless whore-sons, all."

"We'll accompany you into the wood," Toth said.

"You and who else, Master Toth?"

"Tom will lead the way," he said.

Annalise studied the path of rainswept trees. With another strike of lightning, bark glistened. Thunder quaked the earth.

"Bertram's dead, isn't he?" Annalise said.

"There's always a chance that he isn't." Toth took Annalise by the arm, his gloved hand gentle. "There's always reason to hope," he said.

"Are you afraid, Master Toth?"

"Yes. In that, you're not alone."

Determined, Annalise nodded.

"Come," she said.

Toth and Tom walked on either side of Annalise. Toth kept his hand on the dagger at his waist, although to wield the blade would be to do so blindly. The path was broad to begin, but the trail shrank to a slender footpath as it sloped. The ground was treacherously slick. The forest closed in, tightening into a dripping tunnel of foliage.

"Where does the trail lead?" Toth asked.

"The cemetery," said Annalise, "and then the Voitsberg road leads south."

A wall of steam undulated where the trail leveled, bleeding into the trees.

Toth stopped. He put his hand through the warm, almost tropical mist.

"Wait here a moment," he ordered. "We'll walk ahead."

Annalise looked back at the barn. Hair matted her face.

The greyhound watched his master with trepidation. Identical to the pit near the cemetery stairs, a gaping hole opened in the earth, breaking the path. Air rushed from the orifice, steam billowing like fog. Stones sizzled at the lip.

Toth continued forward, keeping the greyhound in his shadow. He squelched into the hot mud, losing balance when the ground shifted. His heel connected with a mass of fat and brittle bone, and his leg kicked out. Toth fell hard on his elbow, and his stomach struck the mud. Searing filth splashed his face, burning where it touched. A rush of steam engulfed him. As Tom barked in alarm, Toth rolled into the weeds at the side of the path, freeing himself from air that burned like flame. He wiped muck from his face.

Drawn from her stupor, Annalise jumped after him.

"Don't go near it," Toth shouted from the ground.

A lightning flash granted Toth vision of the cylindrical shaft. He heard nothing above the hissing steam. Breathless, he moved to a kneeling position, wiping his gloves. He looked to the ground where he'd lost balance. A pale form as large as a cat lay prostrate on its back. The hide was like an intestine scraped clean. The creature collected rain in its jagged mouth. Toth's boot had smashed its stomach, cleaving downward to a severed spine. Rain and gore filled the cavity.

Toth pushed himself to standing. With horror, he watched the broken creature: sap-like ichor oozed from its chest; the creature showed no sign of expiring, no hint of pain. Its throat rippled as rainwater descended the tiny gullet.

Toth moved from the roar of the shaft. His ears rang.

He asked, "What are these things?"

Annalise was neither surprised nor frightened by the opening in the earth, although she maintained a cautious distance from the heat.

"Holes like this run through the hills," she said.

"And that?" Toth pointed at the unmoving thing in the mud.

Annalise wiped her face.

The creature gave its first indication of pain, closing its mouth. A cry with less force than a whistle vibrated the throat.

"They travel through the shafts," Annalise said. "My father says they're goblins." She hesitated, remembering. "Father Haas said the same. He was the first to find one."

The creature's throat stilled. The cry ceased. The crushed thing had bled out.

"Your priest found them?" Toth confirmed.

Annalise raised her voice. Thunder punctuated her words, and wind dispersed them.

"He brought one back," she said. "My father killed it, but they're harmless things."

"I quite seriously doubt that, Fräulein," Toth said, "pitiful as they seem."

Annalise turned, disgusted. She started to the barn. The search had advanced less than fifty yards into the wood.

Toth wiped mud from his sleeves.

"It's futile," shouted Annalise. "God doesn't want us to find Bertram."

The greyhound sniffed the creature. Toth grabbed Tom when he opened his mouth.

"No," he said. "Don't bite it."

A goblin, Toth thought. *Why would Haas bring one back? Who would be anything but revolted by their presence?*

You would, too, he countered. *In fact, do.*

Swallowing his disgust, Toth pulled a kerchief from his coat. He took the goblin from the mud, wrapping the creature in cloth. The flesh was warm to the touch.

"Come, Tom," he said. Toth stared through the steam.

And you, too, he thought, searching for the unseen Pyrenees that, Toth was certain, hid in the brush, surveilling.

XIV
CAPITULUM

When the search for Bertram ended, Sebastian and another child, Nikolaus, led Toth through the church to the vestry, where it was agreed he would quarter. No family received Toth as a guest. Even the idea of a "gypsy" sleeping in the church upset men at the tavern.

Does your kind not prefer a roof of stars? Savages feel restless and trapped when they encounter four walls. You must have nature and open spaces.

Toth didn't push the matter, for his mind was on Bertram and his family.

The nave was dark and silent except for a drip from the ceiling. Vinegar Tom walked through the pews, slump-shouldered, spiked wet, and exhausted. His thighs shivered.

When Sebastian opened the vestry door, he looked to Nikolaus for courage and said, "Bertram would be alive if you hadn't made us come here." The condemnation was sincere. He locked eyes with Toth and grinded his jaw. Cow-eyed Nikolaus agreed with a nod.

It was sentiment on the minds of many. In the light of morning, when chaos settled, blame would be at Toth's door. Conceivably, even Matthias and Annalise considered him guilty.

Weren't the sick to be left with guardians?

Toth had advised caution when he requested the gathering. For Bertram to be alone was a mistake, yes, but it was a mistake that belonged to the boy's family.

Toth left his defense unspoken. Arguing with a child achieved nothing, especially with a boy who possessed the anger of Sebastian.

Matthias blames your mother, child, Toth thought.

"Thank you for the escort, gentlemen," he said.

With Tom's zeal for confrontation depleted, the greyhound stepped into the room and explored the scent of Father Haas's belongings.

Sebastian left the remainder of his accusations bottled. The boy nodded curtly, and then he and Nikolaus, unsatisfied, returned through the nave, two small figures in muddied garb. Two frightened children.

As the boys reached the pews, Nikolaus muttered, "A whoreson gypsy, he is." The child stopped short of spitting, although the urge puckered his face.

"*Le fils d'un loup,*" Sebastian said. *The son of a wolf.*

The door closed, leaving Toth alone.

After retrieving his satchel from the lectern, and removing the pale creature from his coat, he moved into the vestry. He lit a candle and shut away the world, closing he and Tom inside. He placed his satchel, the slimy cadaver, and the burgonet on a scarred desk. Then he vented his rage.

"*Az Isten verjen meg,*" Toth shouted. *May God beat you.*

He grabbed needlework from the wall, a silk-embroidered flower, and he smashed the frivolous decoration against the floor. The frame splintered into pieces.

Toth cursed again, stomping the flower.

Cautiously, Tom watched from the corner.

"I'm sorry," Toth said to the greyhound.

He breathed. He inhaled and collected his thoughts.

"I'm sorry, Tom."

Toth kicked the needlework and frame into a pile.

The storm had abated, so he opened the vestry shutters, allowing night air into the cramped space. He filled his lungs.

When his heart slowed, Toth stripped his heavy, wet clothes. He wrung them out the window, and then he spread his breeches and gloves over the back of a wooden chair. He hung his shirt, coat, scarf, and hat on the vestment hooks. He placed the dagger and sheath on the desk.

Tom shook his coat, spattering the wall, and then he curled up in the corner for warmth. He trembled at the ribs. Toth stripped a wool blanket from the cot, and he placed it over the dog. He gently dried the greyhound's face and ears.

"I'm sorry, Tom," he said again.

He placed a handful of feed on the floor. Within moments, Tom was asleep. His breath deepened until he snored. The food went uneaten.

With a candle in his grip, Toth walked the contour of the vestry, trying to calm himself. The room was no larger than a closet. It held a cot, a crate of candlesticks, a wooden desk and chair, and a shelf of tomes coated in dust. As wind braced the open window, Toth ran a light along the spines. Haas's library didn't prove worldly. Alongside a guide called *A Chrystall Glasse for Christian Women* were Augustine, Aquinas, the Vulgate Bible, and other texts of the Roman Rite. One book stood out as a curious relic, however. Haas possessed a worn copy of the *Malleus Maleficarum, The Hammer of the Witches.* A fevered wet dream, the book was a Dominican manual for examining, torturing, and trying practitioners of black magic. Toth pulled the *Malleus.* The other texts slumped against a pewter bookend. The manual's pages were well-thumbed.

At one time, he thought, *there was witch hunting in this place of misery and squalor.*

Toth sat at the desk, situating the candle for reading light. A yellow orb pulsed against the wall. From his satchel, he pulled another book to join the *Malleus Maleficarum,* a grimoire text titled *Hieroglyphs of Ba'al.*

Vinegar Tom murmured and twitched, dreaming under the warmth of the blanket.

The creature from the pit lay on its back, stinking offensively. Its dead eyes were locked with the ceiling. The flesh glinted like wet kelp.

When Toth was certain Tom would not wake, he opened *Ba'al* to a commentary on the "Seventy-Two–Fold Name of God" and the seventy-two adversarial spirits that corresponded to this hidden name. An idea hot from his anger spurred him: the troubles plaguing Drunstall emanated from a single fount. One source connected the phenomena.

The *Ba'al* commentary drew from Kabbalists and another grimoire titled *The Book of the Office of Spirits.* The handwritten manuscript, one of three extant copies of *Ba'al,* contained sigils for each of the seventy-two adversarial spirits, demonic forms in the language of the Church. The sigils were carefully drawn, dividing the "demons" into kings, dukes, princes, marquises, counts, and knights of Hell. Toth possessed his own ideas about adversarial spirits, and he didn't give credence to a Hellscape populated with feudal manors, but an idea had grabbed him. He thought back to the dead wasps impaling a hazel, branding the bark with the unfinished cathedral. The image was never long from his mind because it was familiar.

Toth traced through rows of angelic geometry, searching for a similar design. He landed on the adversarial spirit numbered forty, whose name was Old Räum, a Great Count of Hell. Räum's sigil had the appearance of a cathedral diagram, too, outlining the nave, apse, and transepts. A diamond marked the fore.

Old Räum, Toth thought. *The wasp sigil could very well be the same as this, albeit a primitive attempt.*

He produced a vial of ink and a quill from his satchel. The third book he opened was a journal with notes he'd compiled in Luxor and Graz. He traced Old Räum's sigil in the margin. Then he traced it again. The scratch of his quill filled the vestry. His damp hand shook with cold.

Chewing his mustache, Toth read the *Ba'al* commentary. He jotted notes in the journal. He found no mention of wasps, but the overabundance of carrion birds matched Old Räum. Adversarial spirits—whether one labeled them demons or not—were ancient and powerful beings. Although quite varied across the spectrum in intention and ability, the spirits had one behavior in common: they boasted. The canvas of their work always held a signature. If a God in the heavens defended man, this was one of His gifts: adversarial spirits were victims of hubris.

Find the signature. That was a lesson instilled in all investigators for the Order of Saint Guinefort. *Find the signature and the seal is cracked.*

Are wasps the ink of Old Räum? Toth wondered. He tapped the quill. *And what is the purpose of the ravens?*

Concerning ravens, *Ba'al* contained a passage plagiarized from *The Book of the Office of Spirits* that read thus:

Räum Comes est magnus: ut corvus visitor.

Räum is a great count: he is seen as a raven.

The raven was the preferred form of the spirit, and a conjuror, *Ba'al* claimed, could bind him to this form, render him weak.

"*Räum is a great thief of treasures, a lover of baubles, and a dispenser of wealth,*" Toth read aloud. "*He has military pride and duty, commanding thirty legions of demons in Hell.* Oh, I'm not so certain of that part, Tom. Don't despair. Unless the wasps comprise his legions." He eyed the cadaver. "Or these sluglike devils. *Before the Fall of the Angels, he was of the Order of Thrones, a warrior angel of God Almighty.*"

Toth twisted his mustache.

"Take that last part with a pinch of salt," he said to the sleeping dog. "It's a poor man's understanding."

Tom rolled onto his side, kicking down the blanket.

Toth lifted his quill. He balanced his chin on his fist, thinking. The idea of apocalyptic angels and demons was simple-minded, grandiose, and desperately literal. It was an idea for men who feared the moon, and he believed nothing of the sort. Old Räum, however, like many of the seventy-two spirits, traveled the edge of truth, shaded into truth, even if his existence on the page was a distortion of reality.

Mayhap, there is an adversarial spirit that attracts the carrion bird and commands legions of wasps. Giving it the name of Old Räum grants a face to disordered thoughts. The ravens and sigil are his signatures. That is the thing.

"Call it Old Räum," he told Tom. "Or call it Hellequin of the Wild Hunt. Or call it Odin, flanked by Huginn and Muninn, ravens of thought and memory."

Odin's no less grandiose than apocalyptic angels riding chariots, I'm afraid. We'll call it Old Räum.

What of the pale creatures? he thought then. *Matthias's goblins?*

There he had no answer. Frowning at the cadaver, Toth retrieved his pipe. He lit the tobacco with the candle flame, and a tendril of smoke curled into the darkness, wreathing his head. He turned the leaf in his journal. Studying the monstrous form splayed before him, Toth drew its features on the page with a trained hand.

The legs, shaggy with moss, were without bone or cartilage, weak as empty sacks. The thin arms stretched longer than the legs, as if the thing moved by dragging itself. Mud-encrusted claws held nails translucent as the skin. The bulbous torso was absent of genitalia. Of the face, two clouded eyes dominated the visage, while other features were underdeveloped. A conjoined hole marked the nose. The mouth was thin, a gash without lips.

Toth unsheathed his dagger. With the blade, he pried open the mouth. The creature was stiffening, resistant to movement. Toth cracked the tiny jaw, breaking bone. A hideous row of teeth, carnivorously sharp, lined the front gums. The back was absent of molars. Veins of blue crisscrossed the roof of the mouth.

Next, Toth churned the abdomen with his dagger tip. The organs protruding from the chest were identifiable—a stomach and minute coil of intestines. The transparent stomach contained bits and pieces of wasps. Ants, still living, crawled the inner walls.

The creature was not an animal of this world. That much was certain.

Toth noted these details, drawing an approximation of the creature. The face in the portrait disturbed him. The eyes disturbed him.

A final detail caught his attention. Surrounding a cavity at the side of the skull—an ear, he assumed—were three sprouts of brown hair and a sliver of human skin. The patch of flesh was an additional growth, not unlike the moss. Toth shaved the hair and skin with his dagger. He examined the fibers in the light. The strands were thin as gossamer, fine as spider webbing. The skin underneath had a pinkish hue, like that of an infant. He brushed the detritus to the floor, wiping his hands.

The creature was growing, he thought. *Or changing. Into what? An imitation of man?*

Picking up the "goblin" by way of the dagger through its mouth, Toth paced to the window. He slung the thing into the muddy lane for ravens to devour. It wasn't long before one of the death birds descended.

Toth sheathed his blade and moved to the cot. He sat on the edge, and he exhaled a cloud of smoke. The movement didn't disturb Vinegar Tom. When the immense fatigue of the day gripped Toth, his thoughts became as nebulous as the smoke.

Le meneur de loups conjures Old Räum. Father Haas? Cili? Räum hides, grows, and distorts.

Old Räum, Toth thought, *might have been worshipped in these mountains when the world was pagan, when augurs read his signature of birds, when sarsens on the shore served a purpose other than catching river debris.*

What of the burning holes in the earth? Maybe Räum is large enough to connect the shafts. Maybe they're the burning antra of Old Räum's gut. Even the earth below us is his body.

What of the goblins? What of the soldier in the wheat? Is the glaze on the helmet the same that oozes from the wounded devil? Are the creatures connected?

Toth leaned against the wall as his mind drifted. He drew on the stem, and he stared out the window at the night until the pipe failed. A rustling outside pulled him from the precipice of sleep. He rose and padded once more to the window.

A man shuffled through the mud like a somnambulist. He was on the incline that led to the barn. It was Matthias, disheveled and wet from the storm.

"*Hexe,*" he spat. "*Hexe.*"

Witch.

"Herr Bergmann," Toth called.

Tom darted awake at the change of tone.

The old man faced the church. His eyes testified of a lost mind. Behind the glow of a torch, he said, "Keep your distance, gypsy. You've done enough damage."

"Where is it that you're going?"

"To find my son," Matthias said, and his voice was fraught with madness.

"Will you not take anyone with you?"

Matthias trundled to the barn. "*Hexe,*" he said. The torch burned in his grip.

No one shadowed him into the dark wood, not even Annalise.

Tom put his chin against the ground and sighed.

"*Hexe,*" Matthias shouted, distant now. "*Hexe.*"

Toth watched until his light was a dot in the forest. He looked at the *Malleus Maleficarum,* and he doubted the manual had belonged to Haas.

"*Hexe,*" came the voice once more, and then, like the light, it was gone.

XV
CAPITULUM

The fortress was in a state of abandonment, a bastion of crumbling stone that dated to the Third Crusade. Perched on an outcropping, the walls of the fortification were unstable, made to sag by copious tunneling. Rows of jagged teeth topped the defenses. The fortress was a scar on the highlands, a relic of the Turkish power for destruction.

Open sores allowed the moon inside Schloss Greinberg, and its light silvered a tapestry above the tunnel to the portcullis. Within the castle walls, the drip of rain and the movement of three figures echoed against stone. The business of troops—grating sword belts, clasping muskets, weariness, alarm, and mirth in turn—were long past, swung into darkness by the fire of Turks on the road to Vienna.

Cathedral doorways lined the hall. Some of the doors had been stripped and repurposed, while other slabs hung askew. Large raven nests filled the rafters and joints above. The hall was rancid with their feces. The floor, once checkered black and white, was a sheet of mud and shit.

While Toader lugged a full barrel, hugging the drum against his chest, Grau cast a withering glare. His eye fell on

The Lieutenant, who shuffled in the wake of his compatriots. The disobedient imbecile lost his helmet during the hunt, carelessly leaving his mark. To Grau's rage, he'd proven himself a fool once again. The Lieutenant was beyond redemption.

"A malformed cretin," Grau lamented, shoveling abuse.

The Lieutenant lowered his eyes. He swallowed what remained of the skin in his mouth, and then he threw a gnawed finger bone to the floor. This was the last of the boy's bones, scattered over miles. The Lieutenant offered no defense. He understood his deficiencies.

Toader stopped at an open arch. He placed the barrel on the floor.

To the left was a room that had been the quarters of an officer. To the right was a glowing stairwell of cut bedrock that descended into the bowels of the fortress, a cavern used in turn for ammunition, beer, grain, prisoners, and as a crypt.

Lighting the descent, stuffed into the arched recess of the wall above the steps, was the pox-scabbed, plague-blackened corpse of a man. Grau did not know the origins of the cadaver. The man had always been, so Grau refrained from consuming the meat. Hair fell like corn silk over black skin. The hair was the only thing that stirred when air belched from the stairwell. Heat mummified his flesh, and his broken jaw was wrenched into the shape of a perpetual scream. His eyes were gone, his tongue chewed to a stump, pilfered by ravens and rats. His heart was an empty hole in the chest. His stomach was slit wide with a pocket of coals replacing the innards. The coals burned with a force Grau neither questioned nor understood. He had never put flame to them. The glow lighted cracks in the man's scabbed hide, running through his form, orange against black like the fault lines of cooling lava.

Grau turned from the human lantern.

"Remove The Stripling," he ordered.

Toader detached the barrel lid. Then, as The Lieutenant held back the sleeves of Toader's habit, the giant reached inside, submerging his arms to the elbow. As he pulled up, gripping with webbed hands, The Stripling reached out willfully, touching the sides of the barrel.

"Careful," Grau said. He hovered over Toader's work. "We don't want him to turn out like our simpleton officer here."

Frowning, The Lieutenant reached in to help, securing the emerging legs so that the barrel didn't spill down the stairs.

"What did you...do...to me?" The Lieutenant asked.

"Toader dumped you out the back of the cart onto your head," said Grau. "It bruised you like a fruit."

When The Stripling was free, he emitted a mandrake shriek of confusion and pain. Toader cradled him like an infant, calming him, and then he offered the creature to Grau.

The Stripling inspired pity and revulsion, but there was vast intelligence behind the eyes. The face was the well-formed visage of a man, with aquiline nose, thin lips, and blond hair. The eyes were pits of black water. The right hand was human, with four fingers and a thumb webbed by membrane. The left hand had three digits and a dew claw for balance. Each digit possessed a thorn-like nail, black as obsidian.

The Lieutenant swept through the liquid until he found the raven foot. Self-consciously, watching Grau for reprimand, he lifted the talon. He dried the claw on his pants, and then he stuffed it into the pouch at his waist.

Grau took The Stripling into his arms, slick, naked, and stinking, and he cradled the creature as Toader had cradled him. Grau experienced a lurch of pride. When he began down the stairs, The Lieutenant attempted to follow, but Toader restrained the soldier. Grau did not look back. He gripped the body, his capture, his success, and his harvest, and he stepped down to the crypt below.

On the final stair, where Grau had chiseled in his infancy, were the words *Dominus et Miles. Lord and Knight.* The phrase covered the ceiling like graffiti.

Another light emanated from around a bend on the uneven dirt floor, but this was no corpse piled with coals. The glow was the mark of Grau's Lord, his creator, and he approached with proper deference.

Grau recited *Dominus et Miles* to balance his distress. His vocals shuddered with terror and awe. An aura passed through him like flame heat. With The Stripling in his arms, he stepped into the heat of the tomb.

The Stripling shrieked, clawing at Grau's shoulder.

XVI

When a spade striking dirt caught his attention, Toth rose from his knee in the stalks.

The morning was humid and windless. The village was still, save for the frenetic business of insects traveling inland from the shore. Toth's examination had turned up no military accoutrements. With the field an indecipherable maze of impressions, further crawling was futile. Tom had already grown bored with the task. The dog walked through the sarsens, brushing against the watchful Pyrenees. The poor white dog still wouldn't come close to Toth, but she sniffed Tom with bemused interest.

The spade work came from the barn, contrasting with the lethargy hanging over the village. Despite the late hour, most people stayed inside, neglecting chores, neglecting squealing pigs, whimpering dogs, and yawling cats, and ignoring hundreds of additional raven pests that painted Drunstall black.

Toth walked from the field and passed through the corral beside The Cock's Foot. When he whistled for Tom, the dog came trotting. The Pyrenees maintained a safe distance, but she followed.

Tufts of moss grew over the barn's timbers, and human decay seeped from its pores. It did not require imagination to conclude that the unburied waited inside. Black flies, wasps, and millipedes crawled the exterior. Seven ravens gripped the steep roof. As Toth and the dogs approached, an array of beady eyes turned.

Toth approached a door barred by an axe handle and purse of sacramental bread. Large ants issued from a tunnel in the dirt and advanced up the door and through the copious flies.

Vinegar Tom disengaged from his master and walked ahead, taking a path around the barn. The Pyrenees shadowed his movement. Unable to stomach the charnel miasma seeping through the door, Toth moved, too. When the shoveling ceased, Tom's tail wagged. The Pyrenees hung back, so that Toth came nearer to her than he ever had before. The dog didn't run—a good sign.

Tom's partial to you, Annalise, Toth thought, bewildered by the fact. The greyhound was not one to ask for attention, especially after he'd eaten. Yet, here he was, coquettish as an alley whore.

Behind the barn, under a canopy of trees, stretched a gash in the earth, long and wide. Annalise stood at the center, the walls rising high as her waist, while Tom waited at the ledge. He leaned down for the woman to scratch his snout. Annalise obliged.

Somehow, the stench at the back of the barn was more concentrated than the front—it burrowed like a migraine, but Toth composed himself.

He asked, "Has it always been this way with the ravens?" He crunched through a bed of stones, approaching the pit.

The Pyrenees retreated into the woods.

Annalise looked like she hadn't slept, which, considering the ordeal of Bertram and Matthias, was unsurprising. With eyes ringed red, she worked to punish herself, sweating like a flagellant in the sun. Mosquitoes crawled her arms and neck. Trauma left her gaze flat. She wore night clothes, and her feet were bare, sinking into mud.

"Do you often wander out here alone?" Toth asked.

Is this where your fiancé appeared to you, Annalise?

"It's an infestation," she said. "Some of the boys hunt the ravens with slingshots, but it does no good. When one bird goes down, another takes its place."

Toth edged the burial pit. Mud clods crumbled beneath his boots.

Shameful and wanton, he thought. *Scraping the dead into a hole as though this were a battlefield.*

Toth offered Annalise a hand.

She looked at the deerskin glove, considered rebuffing his gesture, and then she took hold. Her grip was hard and strong. Cords of muscle lined her forearms.

Toth pulled her from the trench.

In a gown of undyed calico, Annalise stood at his side. She was as tall as Toth's six feet without shoes. Seeing the woman in a state of undress was improper, and Toth understood the danger of someone finding him here. With the skin of her shoulders and back visible, Toth would not be forgiven the transgression. Annalise's hair, Slavic in its darkness, was uncovered and unpinned, falling down the length of her spine. Mud covered her feet and the hem of the gown, spotted her arms, spotted her neck and face. There was beauty in her strength, unmarred by toil.

A hunger inside him stirred, but he denied it.

Toth pondered what Annalise would have become if born in Vienna rather than the highlands. He knew the anchor that isolated village life was to a child. Toth had experienced the same grip in Hungary, where his siblings remained, living the old way. He found it enlightening that Annalise's fiancé was a soldier. It showed a desire to experience the world, or at least a desire to attach to someone who had. She was a woman with aspirations. Eventually, the village would kill those dreams.

"Ravens increase by the day," Annalise finished. She brushed her hands on her gown, rippling the fabric.

Toth experienced a touch of guilt for his lust, but his temptation surged. He turned his gaze to the forest where his eyes were harmless.

Tom sniffed Annalise's leg.

"The ravens are migrating here by the hundreds," Toth said. He started around the contour of the pit, stuffing his hands in the velvet pockets of his coat. His clothes were damp and heavy. Although he suspected the answers, he asked, "What's in the barn, Fräulein? And what's the purpose of this trench upon which you work so diligently?"

"May God grant you better sense if you really must ask, Master Toth," Annalise said. She crossed her arms and frowned. "Or is it that you deny your good sense to make me squirm? Some of the boys say you're an inquisitor looking for witches, looking to burn like those men who traveled during the war."

Toth watched a raven, gargoyle-like in its stillness, on the ridge. The raven watched him in return. Toth gave no credence to the ridiculous accusation of witch burning. He'd made clear he was no witchfinder. Those traveling charlatans existed half a century prior. Such activities were unheard of now, even in the remote highlands.

"Your father is more concerned with witches than I am," Toth said.

Annalise stared.

"I saw him come this way last night when the storm ended. He had the word on his lips."

"Every inquisitor requires an assistant, Master Toth."

"He said he was searching for Bertram. Did Matthias return last night?"

"No, he didn't. He hasn't."

"Are you not concerned?"

"It's not unusual for him to wander off in the night."

"It isn't?"

"He'll be back. In time."

"You don't sound certain."

"He'll be back," Annalise said, "although not with Bertram."

Toth circled the pit. He brushed through a low hanging acacia.

"Would you prefer Tom and I search for your father?"

"Don't bother. He'll return. He always does."

"Are you the only one here willing to bury the dead?" Toth asked. "Why is the cemetery no longer in use? The grounds are beautiful there, if overgrown. The dead would be out of sight."

"The grounds aren't trusted there, Master Toth."

"That's a curious thing to say. Why aren't they trusted?"

"You talk rather than act," Annalise said, "so the reason doesn't matter." She gestured at the line of homes. "The rest sleep rather than talk or act. Someone must act. That burden fell to me."

"I see that. It's an unfair burden, but it's not unusual for people to give up during tragedy. It happens often. However, I can assure you I do more than talk. Mayhap, when the time comes, I'll surprise you, Fräulein."

"You didn't surprise me last night, Master Toth. You retreated at the first sign of trouble."

"That's untrue."

"You're too soft." Annalise pointed at the ditch. "That spade can defeat you. You'd be bloodied after a day in that hole." She smirked.

"There's no virtue in peasant labor," Toth said, growing irritated.

"That's the character you desire to portray, isn't it? The Lord in velvet, deerskin, and silk. Fine. That's fine to hear, *my lord*. For what purpose do you pull me from this peasant labor? What is it that you'd like to *speak* about?"

"I—"

"—And don't you *dare* waste breath with platitudes, condolences, and inane questions to which you know the answer. I'll have no more of it."

When Tom wagged his tail, Toth glared furtively at the animal.

"Fair enough," he said. "Fair enough, Fräulein. I want to know about your fiancé, Merrick."

"A simple matter simply solved then, because I don't wish to speak of Merrick. I don't wish to speak of him ever. Now go on your way."

"Last night you were willing to talk about Merrick."

"Stop saying his name. It doesn't belong to you. Obviously, things have changed since last night."

"Yes, they've worsened."

"No thanks to you. Or shall I give you sole credit?"

Toth chewed his mustache. A moment of silence passed.

"Before we found that Bertram was missing," Toth said, "I saw a figure in the fields. He was adorned like a soldier. The helmet inside the house matched him. Your fiancé was a soldier."

Annalise set her mouth in a hard line. "I recall you saying as much. You saw him, and yet you gave no chase. Was it the lightning that scared you from doing so? Or the dark? Or is it that you're a conspirator?"

"It was good sense," Toth said. "Bertram was not on his person. The baying dogs had the soldier's interest, so he didn't spot me. I didn't want to make my presence known yet."

"You *are* important, aren't you? If it saw you, I imagine, the entire village would be obliterated in fear of Master Toth."

"I said nothing of the sort, Fräulein."

"What use are you then?" Annalise patted Tom, who brushed against her leg. "Your hound would've chased."

"He would've, yes. But if you credit Tom's decisions, then you don't value sense at all, I'm afraid."

"Perhaps, I don't. I receive too much 'sense' from my father."

Toth completed another circuit of the pit, returning to a spot beside the woman. He pushed down his frustration, and he looked at her with sincerity.

"I want you to begin by telling me where Merrick is buried. Is he in the barn with the others?"

Annalise looked to the ground. "He isn't here," she said. "Merrick never made it home."

"And his grave?"

"Somewhere in the Balkans where he was killed. In a pit. Or he's bleaching in the sun, a trophy of the Janissaries. He died fighting the Turks. They're heathens who have no respect for the dead. They look like you. They probably speak your garbled tongue."

"Yet you've seen Merrick in the flesh."

"I've done more than see him." Annalise met Toth's gaze. "I touched him. I was as near to him as you are to me now. And I touched him as plainly as I touched you when you pulled me from the hole."

"Was his flesh cold?" Toth asked.

"It was cold as clay," Annalise said.

"*Similia similibus*," Toth said. "Like engenders like."

"What?"

"The dead imitating the dead," said Toth. "If his body is not here, and yet he appears, it bespeaks imitation, a fluidity of form. He could be the imitation of your memory. I spotted another case of mimicry last night."

Your goblins, he thought.

Toth wondered at the depth of possibilities. The imitation of an image in Annalise's mind was curious. A mirror made flesh. If this were possible, it didn't matter if Merrick were alive or dead as long as Annalise believed him dead.

"Will you take me to where you saw him?" Toth asked.

"I've heard Merrick twice, and I've seen him once. Both times I heard him, it was here, by this pit." She pointed into the wood. "He was in there. I asked to see him, but he refused to show himself."

"You *wanted* to see him?"

"I was tempted, yes."

"What did he say to you?"

"He mocked me for digging. He told me to drop the shovel and crawl to him."

"And when you saw him?"

Annalise gestured at the path that led between the trees, the muddy trace wild with disuse, the same path she and Toth abandoned the night prior.

"Once you get beyond the cemetery, there's a bridge that crosses a stream. It was on the bridge that I saw Merrick."

"Will you not take me there, Fräulein?"

Annalise considered, then she shook her head.

"I haven't returned since it happened," she admitted. "I have no intention of returning now."

It did no good to push the matter, Toth decided. "Very well," he said.

"Master Toth?"

"Yes?"

"About what you said of imitation. I saw the thing *before* it became Merrick. When it came from the water, it was shapeless. It was small as a rook, and it was pale like the thing, the goblin, you killed last night."

"Do you imply the creatures are changelings?" asked Toth. "I've suspected as much."

"It grew skin, and it grew larger, until it took the shape of Merrick."

"Merrick as you remembered him? Not Merrick in death?"

Annalise began to cry. "Yes," she said. "As I remember him."

"I wonder if the soldier, too, is an imitation," Toth said. "The pale creatures change and grow."

Annalise wiped her eyes.

"Did the changeling remain in the form of Merrick?" Toth asked.

Annalise swallowed. "When I turned to go, he lost shape."

"Tell me this," Toth said. Delicately, he touched Annalise's shoulder. "Were you thinking of Merrick before the changeling appeared from the water? Do you recall?"

Annalise nodded. She grabbed Toth, pulling him close, and she buried her face against his chest. The woman sobbed. Her back heaved.

Toth comforted her, allowing his questions to die away.

Tom stepped into the pit and paced its length. His hackles were raised. A scent escaped the spell of effluvia, catching his nose, drawing his attention.

Annalise pulled back and rubbed her eyes.

"I must go, Master Toth," she said.

She looked at the spade, but a change came over her, like that of waking from a dream, a moment of clarity. Turning her back, Annalise started around the barn. Her shoulders trembled as she went.

"I'll find my father," she muttered. "I'll send him to you when I do."

XVII
CAPITULUM

The ravens and Toth watched Annalise go, but Tom had his eye on the forest. The dog leapt from the pit and inched toward the footpath.

As Toth joined the greyhound, his mind buzzed. Whatever the source of Tom's curiosity, its artless movement was audible. There was no effort to be stealth. Tom growled his displeasure.

"Hold," Toth said. He grabbed the dog's collar, restraining him.

Tom bristled.

"What do you plan to do, Tom? Really now?" He shook his head.

The trail was not the menacing portal of darkness that it had been the night before. In the light of morning, the path was ordinary. The dripping leaves ceased to be portentous. Shapes in the shadows proved to be matrixing trees. In the far distance, safely away from the ravens, a pleasant chorus of swallows emerged.

An ordinary morning exists somewhere out there, Toth thought, which he found reassuring.

Ignoring the trail only extended Toth's appointment in Drunstall, so he released Tom and started toward the disruption.

Toth's heart quickened as he descended the first slope.

What he imagined to be a fifty-yard jaunt in the night turned out to be much less. The barn was still in sight when Toth reached the burning antrum that opened in the trail.

Tom probed, circling the shaft, tripping over his feet in excitement. He looked up at Toth, panting.

Heavy rain erased prints in the mud, washing away signs of violence. Myriad wasps navigated the muck, buzzing their coated wings, unable to free themselves. Ants marched on the paralyzed wasps.

Toth picked a dead leaf, limp with rain, from the weeds. Out of curiosity, he released it into the jetted air. The column held the leaf aloft a moment while fire curled the edges, then, oddly, it drifted down. When the leaf entered the shaft like the insertion of a key, the flow dissipated, choked to nothing with a hiss. The foul stench of brimstone remained.

Curious, thought Toth.

Several minutes passed before the ground rumbled and the gaseous heat returned. Toth lifted an acorn and repeated the experiment. Once the acorn crossed the threshold, passing into the hole, the heat ceased.

Toth wasted no time. He went to his knees and, craning his neck, peered within. The mud was hot through his breeches. Tom rushed to his side.

The walls of the cavity were slick clay, marbled grey and brown, glinting where sunlight touched. The hole did not proceed straight into the bowels of the earth, disappearing into darkness. Rather, the shaft veered into a blind turn after several feet. The mud in the basin was tenebrous, but, shading his eyes from the sun, Toth saw, and he was absorbed. The elbow held two articles of interest: one that sparked questions and one that imprinted horror.

First, the tasseled cincture of a priest, a belt of rope, lay coiled and blackened against the earth. The hemp was charred and flaking. Mud partially buried the garment.

Father Haas, Toth wondered.

It was possible for a man of the correct size to enter the shaft—the opening was wide enough for one of narrow shoulders—but lunacy rather than curiosity would drive such an action. The priest, Annalise said, was the first to capture one of the changelings. Possibly, he was intellectually soft. Capturing a changeling and crawling into the antrum were behaviors suited to a child. Where did curiosity end and lunacy begin?

The second item was more grotesque. Initially, it appeared to be the corpse of a red squirrel, matted with rain, clouded at the eye, and receding to bone at the maw. The remains emitted no stench. If one were to spot the animal without context, there would be no thought except pity and revulsion, but it was curious that the squirrel was not charred.

Toth studied its form.

The right arm was not correct. A slash of white brought the image of bone to mind, but the arm was not reduced to bone. Rather, a claw and arm of pale, translucent flesh protruded from the corpse.

It's incomplete, Toth thought. *Unfinished.*

The skin that emerged from fur was familiar. It was the same as the changeling's.

In response to Toth's probing, the arm—four raw tendons twisted together—writhed like a wad of snakes.

The bone maw flinched, parting.

Toth and Tom recoiled. The dog growled.

An imitation of a corpse, Toth thought, astonished. *The changeling is in the process of mimicking a corpse. The things mimic what they encounter*, he reasoned.

Toth was overcome, and his mind convulsed at the idea. He restrained Tom.

The squirrel's claw wriggled.

Toth stood, and his timing was apt. A low rumble issued from deep in the tunnel. The heat returned. The column of air stretched high within seconds.

Do the changelings vary in intelligence? Toth wondered. *Is the one that imitates Merrick more gifted? Is the one in this antrum mindless?*

In Toth's moment of indecision and wonder, the church bell clanged to life, ringing a call to gather. The din moved up the hillside. The ravens shifted on the barn, turning their gaze from Toth to the river bottom. One of the birds lifted.

"Come, Tom," Toth said, eagerly returning to the barn. He rushed from the goblin taking shape like wax under a seal.

Tom ran ahead, curious.

Ravens circled above the belltower.

XVIII
CAPITULUM

The sight of riders at the gate made Toth's blood run warm, and then a lurid voice from one of the silhouettes ran it cold again.

He found Vinegar Tom at the bottom of the slope, watching commotion at The Cock's Foot. The hollow resonance of the bell moved over the scene. Dogs barked and pigs whined. Men, women, and children, those healthy enough to do so, drifted from their homes like ghosts, pallid and louring. Sunlight blazed their eyes.

"Why ring bells when your people die like cattle?" shouted the rider. Daintily, he covered his ears.

The voice erased any doubt in his mind. The rider was Kaspar Groza.

The man of doubt trailed me here, Toth thought. He balled his fist and cursed.

Through the open gate, Groza and his companion rode chestnut Haflingers, bone-weary animals with shocks of blonde mane. The mares were laden with saddlebags and small chests, equipment and clothing the physician didn't require. A puppy risked its life by nipping at the horses' fetlocks. The horses stomped and missed. The dog jumped back, yipping its dismay. Groza nodded his great-wigged head at his companion, a man whom Toth did not recognize, but who dressed in the same foppish style as the doctor. Like Groza, he kept his chin high.

Guiding the horse with the pressure of his knees, the man unscrolled a document. He lifted the parchment above his eyes with both hands until the sun shone through the fibers, and he bellowed with the brazenness of a town crier.

"We travel with the permission of his Lord Bishop Johann Ernst Reichsgraf von Thun in Graz and His Excellency, the Emperor of the Romans and Germans, Leopold of the Habsburg Blood, of the Royal See, Fortified in his Palace in Vienna, Bringing Great Death to Turk and Tartar, Being a Man of Blood, a Man of Learning, and Being Your Lord in All Matters—"

—The letter says nothing of the sort, Toth thought—

"—Stand forth and receive us with hospitality and gratitude. Stand forth for the imperial physician, the esteemed Dr. Kaspar Wenzel Maximilian Groza of Bohemia. Stand forth for his lowly manservant Andreas. Stand forth all and be counted."

"Bring out your pox victims!" Groza added shrilly, dissatisfied with the meagerness of the crowd, displeased with the lack of enthusiasm. The man wanted the dead to rise in parade. Ostrich fringe rippled in his cocked hat. "These souls, too, must be counted."

"An additional order of business," Andreas shouted. "An abode will be cleared for the use of Dr. Groza. You will vacate the premises and receive him thus. It shall not be a home in which death has recently occurred or that sickness has touched."

The villagers grumbled.

"The esteemed Dr. Groza will be fed at intervals of three meals per day. This room and board will be payment for the great service he is prepared to render unto your people."

Enough, Toth thought, and for a moment he was unhinged, free of decorum—for a moment he was prepared to strangle the physician.

"Why this intrusion?" he asked. "Why now? Groza!" Toth shouted, stamping through the soddened path. He passed Cili's children, and he passed Matthias, now returned, and Annalise and a bevy of men and women for which he had no names. "That's quite enough, Groza! Quite enough!"

Groza straightened in the saddle. With the sun behind him, his expression was lost, leaving him a silhouette. The physician was eight feet in the air. The sun shone through rings in his curls. He said nothing to show that he was surprised by Toth's presence in his shadow.

Groza turned to the throng at his side. His saddle creaked.

"You will no longer," he said calmly, "abide by or follow the gypsy who travels with a hound. He is an uneducated, Dark Age heathen who chases seraphim. He is a *witch hunter.* An *inquisitor.* He is unworthy of people even as lowly and miserable as yourselves. Check anywhere he's been for theft, and then start him on the road."

"It's in a gypsy's blood to steal," Andreas said.

Toth shaded his eyes.

Twin smirks spread across the faces of Groza and Andreas.

No one in Drunstall spoke in Toth's defense. Rather, most of the crowd appeared willing to offer obedience to the boisterous Germans. Protests stayed at the level of grumbling.

"Move, gypsy," Andreas said, nudging his horse forward, "or I'll see your mutt's leg broken."

"And I'll see you gutted," Toth said, and he experienced shame and the heat of anger at once.

"Is that so?" Andreas asked.

"He has violence in him," Groza said. "Primitive creatures always have violence in them. You must be wary, Andreas. Be warned of the savage." He looked down at Toth. "As my manservant politely advised you, gypsy: move aside. Your work here is complete. You may pack your baubles, beads, and decks, and depart at leisure."

Toth moved from the path of the horses so that Vinegar Tom would be unharmed. The yipping puppy followed Tom's lead, backing away.

"Bring out your pox victims," Andreas shouted, pushing his mount ahead. He pulled a bird-like mask from a satchel at his side. He hid his face behind it.

"Groza!" Toth shouted at the physician's back.

Slightly, Groza turned. Only his nose protruded from the edge of his wig. A velvet cape of purple shone in the sunlight.

"Why are you here?" Toth asked. "You were to begin at Karnstein. Why here?"

"I *almost* traveled to Karnstein," Groza said, "but I couldn't leave these poor souls in your hands, Stairs of Reconciliation or no, the Monsignor's disapproval or no. It had me weary with guilt, gypsy."

Like in Prague, Toth thought. *This is just as you did to that poor woman in Prague.*

"Bring out your pox victims!"

Slowly but obediently, the villagers pulled mats onto front stoops. The mobilization was grotesque and brutal. The ravens trilled, watching. The sufferers screamed in pain, shrieking with such vile brutishness that the sound cut the chorus of dogs and pigs. Tom flattened his ears with worry. Cruelty spread until twelve scabbed, miserable forms groaned in the light of morning. Twelve of the dying lay beside thirty survivors, everyone lined up for a military inspection.

Toth's gaze met that of Matthias, who had pulled Bertram's empty mat, still soiled, over the threshold of his home. *Bertram is alive*, Matthias was saying, *although we know not where*. There was blame in the man's eyes. Annalise stood at her father's side, fully dressed, her face and hands washed clean. She didn't look in Toth's direction. She stared at the dark river.

"—chases seraphim like old John Dee," Groza was saying. He laughed. The physician dismounted with cavalier flair at The Cock's Foot, with its tri-toed symbol burned above the door. Andreas closed his scroll and dismounted.

Groza ripped down one of the rain dolls. After a moment's examination, he threw the ghost in the mud.

"These will have to come down," he said, gesturing. "No need to tempt Lucifer."

"Someone stable the horses," Andreas shouted. "You, boys! Feed and water them properly."

Victims be damned, Toth thought. *To be counted, you'll have to wait until the doctor slakes his thirst.*

"Sun will do them good," Groza said. "God's light will dry them out." He paused, and then he faced the crowd. "I don't want them in these damp, moldy hovels. Turn your church into a hospital ward immediately. Open the shutters and let light in. Lay them down in the aisle and across the altar if you must."

Two boys hurried forth, grabbing the Haflingers by the reins.

Groza and Andreas pushed through the tavern door, full of bluster.

An old man and his cat trailed them inside.

Three women dashed toward the church.

"Vile man," Toth said. Ignobly, he unleashed a string of Hungarian curses. Save for bristling Tom, no one acknowledged his words.

Ars Goetia,

OR THE ART OF CONJURATION

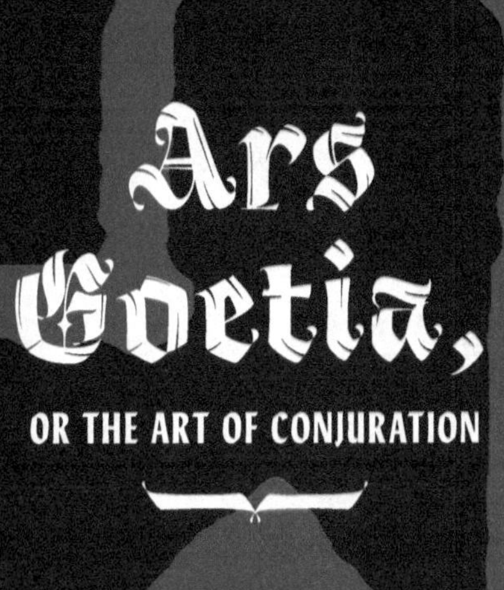

XIX
CAPITULUM

roza led a procession from The Cock's Foot to the church at noontide. With an open Bible in his palms, Andreas trailed in the doctor's shadow. The manservant read aloud from Isaiah, reciting Latin that was incomprehensible to the flock within earshot. He bellowed with a trained, inflective tongue, loosened by ale.

"Formans lucem et creans tenebras faciens pacem et creans malum ego Dominus faciens omnia haec."

I form the light and create darkness. I make peace and create evil. I the LORD do all these things.

"This I say to the Problem of Evil," Groza pontificated. "The Lord does all these things. This I say to men who blame devils, fauns, and elfshot for their woes. A good bleeding always accomplishes more than a good exorcism."

With Groza's marginalia complete, Andreas continued with the florid prose of Isaiah Forty-Five.

The villagers in a train behind Groza wore plague masks, replete with long noses full of smelling apple spices. Veit was among them. His beard protruded from the mask.

Groza brought masks to Drunstall as a prophylactic, and not an unwise one, but the mood they conjured suited Venetian plague shores better than the Austrian countryside. The image was discordant and surreal. With the addition of jester bells, the lane between tavern and church would be a carnival.

A masque to precede the bleeding, Toth thought.

The scene was theatrical enough to suit Groza's method. For all the insults the physician hurled, all the intellectual shaming he performed, his displays were no less an effort to reach God than a medieval morality play.

After collecting his notes and books from the vestry, and leaving the crusted helmet on a hook, Toth walked through the nave. He smoked his pipe, chasing decay from his senses.

Twelve bodies lay in the pews and aisles, stretched on woven pallets. No one argued about the heat of the church, which crept upward as the sun beat on stone. Against the walls, with heads bent in prayer, family of the sick waited for Groza. Nikolaus was there. The boy's sister was ill with pox, her arm shriveled, her lips parted for quick, shallow breaths. Her face was raw. Her eyes were wide with pain.

Of the twelve, the youngest was eight years old and the oldest was sixty. Regardless of age, all suffered. A few souls drifted closer to death, a few neared the return to life, and a few teetered between.

The torment was more than Toth could process. That the disease incubated in still more bodies, waiting to erupt, was unthinkable. Seeing the men and women arrayed thus, seeing the mass of flesh, surfaced his guilt for Bertram.

Toth would never give the physician the benefit of knowing, but Groza's blustering confidence wormed into his mind, leaving acute doubt. The physician pretended to know the world as one knows a map, memorizing its contours and pitfalls, while Toth's sense of the world amounted to groping through fog. In good times, secure times, Toth understood the errors of Groza's sophomoric folly, but in times of doubt he found the physician's manner oppressive, threatening, and superior.

Toth exhaled an aromatic cloud. The smoke drifted past his eyes like a veil.

A century prior, men like Groza had men like Toth trussed to poles and burned in public squares. That age was sinking into the sea, but periodically a high tide laid it bare. Sporadically, that type of thinking resurrected with force, especially in insular pockets like Styria. Groza had the air of wealth, power, and authority to leave a dull-minded villager in awe. He could mobilize old hatreds, revive old violence.

The church door opened, and Groza's procession entered, first the physician, then Andreas, then the masked converts.

Who are these people, Toth thought, *that gravitate to his side with ease?*

Among the sick, those who possessed strength swiveled their necks at footfalls over the threshold, and the motion occurred in horrible unison. The scrape of fracturing scabs, akin to twisted leather, filled the nave. The noise belonged in Hell. A collective groan of torment followed.

Toth's breath quickened around the pipe stem. Smoke drafted over his tongue and down his throat, thickening saliva until it coated his mouth. Nausea made him weak.

Groza, unbothered, glanced at Toth but offered no taunts. His mind went to the setup of a bleeding apparatus. Andreas folded his Bible neatly, set the book aside, and began to remove vials and tubes from a leather case.

Groza's indifference to suffering touched a nerve.

"A man of Galen, humors, and leeches calls me primitive," Toth said. "For pity's sake." He pushed through an empty pew to the main aisle. "Kaspar, these people are too weak to be bled."

The physician countered, but he spoke to the family members rather than Toth.

"This machine is from Paris," Groza said, matter-of-factly. Paris to the rural mind was as mystical as Atlantis—only great and terrible things flowed from that fount, nothing between. "From the physician Jean-Baptiste Denys, who not only removed blood but transfused it between animals. He pumped the blood of another creature into man. The restorative effects were sensational. I tell you this: Denys cured a madman of his ills. A man of the street and screeching mind. He cured him with the Blood of the Lamb. And quite literally!"

"Cured and then killed him in the process," Toth said.

Groza's face reddened. With wig askew, he stepped over a dying man, leaving Andreas to the machine. He stopped short of striking Toth, but the urge made his shoulder flinch. The physician was twenty years Toth's senior, and his advanced age showed when he was close. The black wig masked a head of grey, and streaks of tallow and egg white smoothed wrinkles around his eyes like plaster. Despite platform shoes, he stood four inches shorter than the Hungarian. When he shook his fist, he resembled a painted marionette.

In his youth, Toth would've stabbed his ample gut.

Groza lowered his tone and raised his eyes. "What you search for in devils, I search for in the blood. There's a madness in their blood, gypsy, and you're doing nothing but feeding it. This is a malady of the mind. You're simply another cancer here, a cancer attached to plague upon plague, sir, and I won't allow it." He shook his head. "God save me, gypsy, I'll never allow it as long as I live."

Toth released a puff of smoke. "As it was in Prague then?" he asked. "You spend so much time thwarting me that the answer crawls under your nose."

"I'd see you throttled and burned if the authorities favored it. All of you Guinefort people are perverted and ignorant. You're relics, and you only survive because the Church finds value in relics. And not only are you ignorant, gypsy, you're savage. You're a caravan-bred heathen who worships thieves and knives. I would give everything in my possession to see someone light you on fire. Along with your rotten fuck hole of a mutt."

Toth brushed off the tirade.

"Have you spoken to these people, Kaspar? Have you asked what they've *seen*? There's no madness here."

"I've no need to field confessions or preach another sermon. I *know* what is occurring here, gypsy. It's a madness of the blood, pure and simple. Whatever they see, it's imaginary. I do not need to know every detail of these hallucinations."

Toth removed his pipe. He considered his words, for Groza would only hear few of them.

"You saw something, didn't you? Is that what diverted you from Karnstein? There's no humiliation in fear, Kaspar. I saw it, too. Something frightened you, Doctor. Did you not want to be alone?"

Soul drained from Groza's eyes, and weariness manifested in the lines of his brow. He was too advanced in years for trials of the spirit. If it weren't for debts, he'd retire to grow old. His mouth hardened into a tight line, and the fat of his jaws quivered.

"You think you can intuit your way through the world, but you're delusional, Toth, and you're wrong. You are quite *wrong*."

Groza didn't allow a response. He returned to Andreas.

"Was it a soldier?" Toth asked. "Was it a soldier with a face of glass, Kaspar?"

A murmur moved through the family members amassed.

Andreas looked up, dropping a vial, shattering glass against the walnut pew.

When Groza refused to answer, Toth clutched the pipe in his teeth and walked to the nearest side door. The bright light of day outlined the frame, promising escape from the oppressive air and drone of prayers from the opposite wall.

Are phantoms infesting the roads? Toth thought. *Is the floor of the forest rattled with holes? Old Räum grows like a great system of roots.*

XX

CAPITULUM

rom within the church, a child screamed in pain.

Groza's bleeding them. Draining life from these weak souls and replacing it with what? The Blood of the Lamb, he said. The very idea is the essence of superstition, his Paris-wrought machine be damned.

Toth left the church and its agonies.

He spotted Vinegar Tom in the distance, confabulating with other dogs near the corral. Tom's conference was a curious sight for curious business. Orphaned animals—dogs, cats, sheep, pigs, horses—were abundant in Drunstall and the surrounding hills. When the village was finally consumed, the animals would form packs and scavenge the wood. Presently, Tom fronted seven dogs at the corral, allowing each to sniff his hindquarters. As the outnumbered guest, the greyhound lifted his tail, relaxing his ears, suppressing his combative nature.

Toth was pleased to spot the Pyrenees among the pack. Enormously strong at the shoulders and neck, the animal stood her ground, regarding Toth's approach with heedful suspicion.

Toth knelt in the street and urged the Pyrenees to come closer.

The dog, a head taller than Tom and head and shoulders taller than the others, panted in the heat. When a puppy in the group obeyed, wagging its tail, the Pyrenees surrendered. She stepped forward. When she did, the other dogs followed suit, ringing Toth.

To Tom's dismay, Toth retrieved a handful of feed from his satchel. He gave a mouthful to each dog in turn, and last of all to the Pyrenees. Rather than dumping feed into the mud, he offered the food in his palm. The Pyrenees smelled the offering, and then, not without reluctance, lapped with her broad, smooth tongue. Toth patted the white brow as she ate. With watery eyes veined red, the dog watched with distrust, but she allowed his touch.

Small victories, Toth thought. The dog relaxed his anger.

"I'll win you over yet," he said.

The Pyrenees stared. A single drop of drool fell from her tongue. She leaned in to have her ears scratched.

"Do you often speak to animals, Master Toth?"

Toth turned, startled by the intrusion. A shadow was on him.

The Pyrenees backed away, following the other dogs into the shade of the corral.

Voices and the stench of yeast wafted from The Cock's Foot.

Floris leaned against the rain tree with the doll in her arms. She wore a simple gown of flax rather than her mourning attire.

Toth stood in the lane, wiping his spit-coated glove against the leg of his breeches. Pyrenees drool left a streak of white. For the briefest moment, he thought he heard Floris's doll cry, soft but urgent, an imitation of the cries drifting from the church.

"More times than not, Fräulein, I prefer speaking to them," Toth said. The lace at his wrists trembled in the breeze. The stench on the wind was wrenchingly unpleasant. "To whom does the great white dog belong?"

Floris ran her finger down the doll's nose. The affection in her eyes contained an aura of zealotry. It was curious that "zealous" came to mind, but there it was—fanaticism—on her face.

"The white dog belongs to no one now, Master Toth," Floris said. "She won't let anyone near enough to touch her." She stroked the doll and rocked it. She did not make eye contact with Toth. "She's gone feral. We should poison her before she gets dangerous."

Quiet disgust settled in Toth's mind. If he'd attempted to like Floris previously, that ended with the threat of poison.

Tom, sensing his master's turn, walked toward the other animals, sliding into the shade. The Pyrenees struck him playfully with her paw. Tom stretched his front legs, bowing his head, and then he leapt. The dogs grappled at the fence line, disturbing the nearest Haflinger.

"The mutt's name is Greedy Gut," Floris said. "She belonged to my uncle, poor soul. Only he'd name a dog a terrible thing like Greedy Gut." She massaged her temple. "My uncle was touched."

You're touched, Toth thought, but he attempted a smile.

"So that's the path to her heart, is it? She loves to eat."

"She'd eat your hand, Master Toth. I doubt we could afford to feed such a beast. She'd need her own pigs. Better off poisoned, I say."

Toth swallowed. "What was your uncle's name?" he asked.

"Loring," said Floris. She gestured at the doll. "He, too, is named Loring, after his great uncle and father."

"I beg your pardon?" Toth said.

Floris relaxed against the tree. A living face peeked from the blanket in her arms. A rash on the pale cheek, the first stigmata of smallpox, made the face real. An infant slept where the doll had been. The chest rose and fell with breath. The nostrils flared with exhalation.

A touch of despair replaced the anger in Toth's heart.

Mimicry, he thought.

"I know you'll beg my pardon, Floris, but I must ask. Were you not carrying a doll in the same manner yesterday?"

"A doll?" Floris rocked the infant named Loring.

A single raven glided over the tavern. The shadow crossed Toth. The raven landed on the corral gate, behind which Groza and Andreas's horses milled about, and beside which Tom and Greedy Gut sparred.

Toth lifted a stone from the muck, and he tossed it at the bird. The dogs stopped, curious. The horses stopped. The raven beat its wings, dodging the rock, removing itself to a roof across the street. From the new perch, the bird glared. The feathers of its wing twitched with agitation. The beak opened and closed silently.

"Gargoyle," Toth muttered.

Floris frowned. "Why did you do that? After speaking highly of the dog, you abuse an innocent bird. Is this the mark of savagery of which the doctor speaks? A man unbound by reason?"

"The ravens," Toth said, "are too watchful to be innocent. Too abundant to be natural. I chased a set of eyes, not the creature commandeered to employ them."

Floris grimaced. "You have bizarre thoughts, Master Toth."

He gave a slight bow.

"In many ways you're a bizarre man."

"You really have no idea, Fräulein."

"As for this child," Floris said, "why did you think him a plaything?"

Toth maneuvered for a clear view of the infant. He suspected the blanket hid pale flesh like that of the changing squirrel.

"Did you lose a child from pox?" Toth asked.

The question didn't penetrate. Floris stared at the river. After a pause, she said, "I came here to apologize, Master Toth, for the anger Blancheflor and I showed you last night in the church, although you're not making the task of apology easy. We understand your purpose here. We don't scorn it, gypsy blood or not."

Toth tore his gaze from Loring. The hungry mouth disturbed him.

It was *a doll*, he thought. *This is not madness in the blood.*

"To be clear about last night," Toth managed to say, "I don't believe that your mother, Cili, committed suicide. I don't think anyone truly believes that. Even Sergeant Wallhausen was quick and unthinking in his remarks. He admits it is hearsay."

"Did he really?"

"Were you not given the report?"

"I'm unable to read, Master Toth."

"Forgive me. Yes, I forgot."

"Regardless of that, there are people here who believe my mother damned herself, if not through suicide, then certainly through witchcraft."

"Indeed? Who?"

"Matthias, for one."

"Why does he accuse Cili of witchcraft?"

"You'd be the last person I told, Inquisitor."

"That's not a good answer. Did Matthias harbor dislike for your mother?"

"Hatred more like. He thought my mother a heathen. He thinks all my family heathens. Matthias argued against her burial in the cemetery. He's the reason the barn is full. He made us stop using the graveyard when Haas left." Floris finally looked up, but she stared through Toth. "Matthias is not a good man, Master Toth. I can tell you things that will curdle your insides."

"Like what, Fräulein? Because he says the same of your mother."

Floris hesitated. She rubbed the infant's nose.

"He'll never say the same of her again," she said. "Of that I'm certain."

"Why not tell me these things?" Toth persisted.

Maddeningly, Floris said, "And this new man, Groza—he believes she committed suicide, too."

"What is it that you know about Matthias?" he asked. "It would help me a great deal to simply know what you know."

"The doctor found me at The Cock's Foot. I tend patrons there. He told me, in no uncertain terms, that you have the desire to unbury my mother, to exhume her. He said you procured permission to do it, even against Groza's protest. Is that so, Master Toth?"

Toth didn't shy from her stare. "That's the truth, yes, but it has nothing to do with suicide or witchcraft."

"Is it not sacrilege to unbury?" Although her tone did not alter, her jawline stiffened. "Do you wish to remove her to the barn?"

"Groza is looking to make enemies for me," Toth said. "He'll work on anyone willing to listen. Please remember that, Fräulein." Toth stepped closer, joining Floris in the shade. He removed his cap and wiped sweat from his brow. "My actions are not meant to disturb Cili's rest, nor will her grave be moved outside the cemetery gates. I assure you it will all be done with great delicacy. I've performed exhumations. I'm no stranger to it. Your mother won't leave her grave. She'll be returned to the dirt. She'll be covered. No one will even know an exhumation occurred."

"*We* will know."

"Yes, but no others. Not even Matthias."

"For what purpose if not to damn her?" Floris asked, and venom entered the voice. She rocked the infant too quickly, running blood to its head. The face grew scarlet with sickness and heat.

"I need to know how she died," Toth said, eyeing the child.

"Telling you how it occurred won't suffice?"

"I must see it."

"If we were to refuse? What then?"

Toth was silent.

"You'd proceed, regardless? Is that correct? You'd do it under cover of darkness if you must. Like a thief."

With humility, Toth said, "I would be forced to do the exhumation without your permission, yes."

"I won't grant permission, Master Toth."

Toth nodded.

"When do you plan to do it?"

"As soon as possible," Toth said. "Every hour matters."

Blood spread under the freckled skin of her cheek. The redness of the infant entered through her chest. A fiery tone replaced her paleness. She clenched her jaw, biting away insults that rose so naturally to her tongue.

Floris is, Toth concluded, *mentally ill. The madness in her blood is real. Was Cili, too, mad?*

When Floris turned to go, Toth mustered pity and said, "Your child is infected, Fräulein. Take young Loring somewhere cool and give him rest. He'll need your strength in the days ahead."

"What are you talking about?" Floris said.

"The mark on the child's jaw. The rash."

Floris peeled back the blanket, exposing the baby's face. There was no mark, no rash. The flesh was clean, save for glaze around the eyes that looked like muddied, imperfect glass. Sunlight glinted on the substance. Floris pulled the blanket tight, concealing Loring again.

"Fräulein, is this your child or not?"

Floris turned away. She gripped the infant, hugging him to her chest.

"He is mine," she said quietly.

"Did you birth him or did you find him?"

Floris gave no answer. She walked toward The Cock's Foot.

"God forbid if you found him in the wood," Toth said.

XXI
CAPITULUM

oth and Tom emerged from a stand of pines, halting where the cemetery stairs surfaced from the hillside. Despite summer heat that wrapped the forest with haze, the breeze from the mountain road was cool. Dead leaves scraped stone. Windchimes knocked in the acacia, pleasant notes intertwining with the business of wasps. The insects streamed from a grey nest, darting murderously as if the windchime was an intruder to be vanquished. It was lunatic combat. As the attack intensified, the clamor grew more musical.

Unlike the ravens, the wasps were antagonistic and hostile. The wasps did not surveil.

Perhaps, Toth thought, *my presence spurs their anger.*

The fancy was unwelcome.

Tom placed a paw on stone, but he hesitated, peering at the wasps.

Toth shared his reticence. With a spade leveled over his shoulder, he, too, was wary. Something as innocent as a vibration could unleash their barbs.

"On, Tom," Toth said, girding himself. "Up."

The greyhound moved along, two steps at a time.

Halfway through the ascent, Toth looked back. Sunlight broke through the treetops, sparkling in rhythm with the chimes. From this height, he spied the Voitsberg road that flanked the wilderness. Rugged peaks loomed against the sky.

The road urged Toth homeward, and at once he was ill with the fear of remaining in Drunstall and the hope of returning to Vienna. The urge to fold his investigation, to leave the plague matter unsettled, to abandon these people to Groza, grew stronger, spreading in his heart.

Whoreson gypsy, Toth thought, recalling Nikolaus's hostility.

Anger shadowed the gallant side of his nature.

Why risk your life in the face of contempt? Groza doesn't experience the same hatred and distrust.

Toth unleashed a torrent of Hungarian curses. Then, quieting himself, he cast a suspicious glance at the wasps. The insects were ambivalent.

The puzzle is the thing, he thought then, *not the people. Constructing meaning out of chaos matters. You'll leave these people and know them no longer. And they'll know you no longer. But you'll understand the thing called Old Räum. You'll define something hitherto undefined. You'll rewrite a chapter in Ba'al. That is reason enough.*

When he topped the stairs, Toth found Vinegar Tom halfway across the cemetery, sniffing a crucifix that rose from the roots of a young elm. Toth traced the greyhound's path, swishing through wildflowers toward the chapel ruins. He edged past the busy dog to Cili's plot. With a dread-engorged heart, he spotted overturned earth at the base of the back fence. Two mounds protruded from the weeds.

In his mind's eye, he saw Matthias marching into the forest with a spade.

Toth rushed forward. His dread was not unwarranted.

The peaceful grave of a day prior was a ragged hole in the ground. Toth's horror, disgust, and anger compressed into the moment of first sight, leaving him still and disturbed. The shovel dropped from his shoulder. The details of the abominable crime came to him one by one, layer by layer.

The three stones marking the grave were missing. The consecrated earth was thrown aside unceremoniously, with mud, rock, and root piled in haste. Cili's body was torn and exposed. Unprotected by a coffin, the corpse was desecrated with the offensive rabidness of jackal and vulture.

Toth's heart lurched.

A shroud that draped the woman's body was cut in twine, sliced clean, opening in a fissure that ran from the tip of Cili's skull to her chest. Her skin, which gave up the secret of her death, was burned thoroughly, charred black. Maggots writhed in the ridges of her flesh, while a gregarious raven worked to loosen the meat of her eye.

The violence to her corpse left Toth stunned.

He jabbed at the raven with the spade, chasing away the bird. A piece of the eye left with its talon. Toth laid the shovel beside the greyhound, parting grass. The animal panted nervously.

Toth knelt and removed his dagger from its sheath. He raised the scarf around his nose and tightened the silk. He calmed his breathing, steeled his nerves.

What anger drove you to do this? Toth thought. *Did you truly believe her a witch, Matthias?*

Toth cut the shroud to reveal more of the corpse. Matthias had attempted to cut Cili's neck to the spine, to sever the head from the body. With the job only half complete, the man abandoned the effort. The blade, with struggle and sawing, made it through the throat but no farther, opening the bloodless neck. A ball of roaches pulsed in the wound like a fallen poultice. The stench was that of wet earth.

Matthias did not stop at the neck. The left side of Cili's skull was opened to raw flesh by the strike of a spade. Auburn hair—red to match the locks of her children—hung in a flap over her blackened, shriveled ear. Behind the flap was an iron spike hammered through the skull with great force, fastening bone to earth.

Have you seen Cili out of the grave, Matthias? Toth thought. *Just as your daughter sees Merrick?*

Matthias's effort to restrain Cili went further. A wooden rosary bead lay on the woman's mouth, tucked in the crevice of her lips. More poignant were the wrinkled lily petals remaining in the folds of the shroud, placed at burial by Cili's daughters and son.

Overwhelmed, Toth sat in the grass. He had no desire to see more. He pulled the pipe from his coat. He sparked the rope and lit the tobacco. As smoke streamed from his nose, Toth watched Tom. The greyhound walked along the stone fence, marking.

As Toth pondered the motives of Matthias, commotion blasted his concentration. He craned his neck to find the source. The sound was like the wasps attacking chimes, only closer, as though the brood hunted a new target. When Toth located the cause, he instinctively drew back, prepared to flee. The locus was a portion of fence by the chapel crushed by a rotten log. Indeed, angry wasps clamored, but this colony was different than the previous.

A swarm moved from a cavity in the wood, slashing red and black. Once aloft, the wasps' mirrored flight formed a speckled orb in a lance of sunlight. Tom watched as Toth watched, wary as Toth was wary. One by one, wasps issued from the crumbling trunk, joining the ritual, until hundreds of red-scaled pests stabbed the air. The flight was coordinated with discipline. The orb grew to a vast size, swelling to the girth of the chapel ruins.

One of Old Räum's legions, Toth thought.

The insects hovered over the log, determining a target in which to drain their poison. The collective buzzing modulated like a voice, dipping and swelling as the orb pulsed, regulating until the notes synched. At the point of unison, the wave throbbed, sending out a pulse that unsettled Toth's mind, leaving him disoriented. The effect was paralyzing.

Toth maintained enough clarity to call Tom nearer. He did so, delicately, and the dog trotted to Cili's grave, watching over his shoulder.

The orb is every inch a ritual, Toth thought, *but there's something confused, something hesitant, lacking direction.*

The garbled signal amounted to stillborn choreography.

The throb in Toth's brain ceased, its reach too weak to maintain. Although freed, he made no movement to be seen.

When the orb was complete, the wasps darted from the congregation, planting their spikes in the flesh of a hazel fronting the chapel façade. This was the target decided by the assembly: a lone tree rather than the man and his dog. Many of the wasps smashed against the bark, were broken, and fell thrashing to the dirt, only to die. It was a cruel sight. Other wasps found weakness in the bark and planted barbs. The latter few writhed, clapping wings helplessly against the wood. For every wasp pinned, three fell, until a pile of dead insects rose in the shadow of a wriggling sigil.

Shrieking Hell, Toth thought. *They are, indeed, Old Räum's ink.*

He found only a crude cathedral in the lines of the design, but the effort to build the sigil was apparent. He wondered at the signature's failure to materialize.

Wasps moving in warped design, guided, misguided, and then left to reap.

Toth recalled a passage from a Puritan catechism. It was a tract about Satan's voice, wherein the Devil plants thoughts in the minds of man and animal:

I have known some which have been fearfully vexed and astonished in heart with horrible and blasphemous thoughts, which were Satan's injections, and terrors.

An injection of thought. Old Räum plants thoughts in inferior creatures to mobilize his will. The same energy that stirs ravens touches creatures with simpler minds, infuses and clouds them. Because they do not possess the intellect of the raven, the wasps do not have the sense to construct precise meaning from the pulse. The insects move as they're commanded, but they fail to understand the instructions. Albeit valiantly, the wasps fail.

The failure revealed weakness at the source. No omnipotent Devil was at the helm. Old Räum was no Prince of Hell, nor was he a god.

If weak at any point, the spirit can be rendered dormant.

Disturbed, Toth scratched Tom's neck, calming the animal. He had no desire to draw the insects' ire, lest they rise vampirically.

How many of these aberrations unfold by the minute? Toth thought.

Does the soul of man respond to Old Räum? Souls drawn from the grave as simply as wasps attack hazels. The man, the raven, the wasp—drawn, called, urged, ordered, all of one intention, all from a single fount.

Toth lifted the shovel. Before he turned attention to Cili, however, yet another intrusion impeded the task.

The rattle of hinge and chain arrived through the trees, distant on the wind.

Tom heard it first, and then Toth. Both swished through grass to the stairs. With great fatigue, Toth shaded his eyes against the sun.

On the Voitsberg road, a cart laden with passengers and a cargo of barrels raced around a bend. The clamor of metal-encased wheels cut through the chimes. The cart progressed, pulled swiftly by two ebony horses.

XXII
CAPITULUM

einforcements trailing Groza and Andreas, late to the gathering, Toth thought.

It was not out of character for the physician to hire *landsknechts,* vile mercenaries, to enforce his protocols. His means didn't preclude such an action. The idea set wrong, however. The more Toth watched, and the faster the cart traveled, a pit of warning grew in his gut.

The cart was too distant and swift to make out faces.

No one travels the road without purpose, and no one travels without permission. And not all permission issues from the Bishop in Graz.

Turkish raiders? No. Not even a vanguard of raiders travels so carelessly in the light of day, and with so few.

To Toth's dismay, the cart did not proceed to where the road split its destination between Drunstall and Karnstein. Rather, the driver worked the reins, slowing the horses when the road leveled. The cart stopped at the edge of the forest. Dust rose around the legs of the horses. The chests of the beasts swelled with fatigue. The sheep in the field opposite paid little mind.

Instinctively, Toth grabbed Tom's collar. Feeling the dog at his side was a jolt of courage.

Four men rode in the cart, each distinct in garment and poise.

The driver was a spot of grey behind black cloth. He wore an oversized coat with a large collar that obscured his face to the jawbone. A hat, topped with a starched feather and rolled at the brim, hid his brow. Delicate gloves covered his hands. He wore garments of winter.

The passenger at his side was an enormous man, a foot taller than the driver and possessing the girth of two stout lads. The brown habit of a monk obscured his face and draped his hands. The cowl was affixed to his head, tightened by rope at the neck. His posture was slumped, lethargic, and untroubled.

It was a passenger among the cargo barrels that unsteadied Toth's heart and tested his courage. Two shapes knelt at the rear of the cart. One figure was small and thin, with the diminutive profile of a child. He was scarcely taller than the barrels. Mismatching robes of burgundy and grey shrouded his form, and a lace ruff stained brown fell over his chest like a livery collar. A shock of blond hair sprung from his cave-born skin. Alien to light, the flesh was like the changelings from the pit. His eyes were slashes of lead, too large for the face, too sunken, like musket balls planted in snow.

The other figure, who rose, eager to be free of the cart, was the soldier from the wheatfield. There was no doubt in Toth's mind that the soldier was the same. His breastplate, with scars intricate as runes crossing the chest, glinted in sunlight. Metal sheets tied with twine covered the sleeves of a padded buff coat the color of calf skin. Free of his helmet, his dark hair, crystalized, rose like a tuft of weeds, and his face shone with the luster of glass.

Maladroitly, the soldier hopped to the dirt. His mechanics of motion were unnatural. His gait made his legs scissor, but pride kept the soldier aloft. When still, his spine was straight as an officer's.

There was no sign of Bertram. Unless, Toth thought sickly, his remains were inside one of the drums.

Tom was wise enough to stifle his barking, although he growled quietly. The fur along his spine was rigid, his shoulders tense. Toth held his collar. He stepped back from the stairs, and he knelt beside the greyhound. Wildflowers rose to his elbows.

"Keep calm," Toth whispered.

Toth forced Tom lower to the ground.

When the highway brood entered the forest, leaving horses and cart askew on the road, the wasps battling chimes reacted. Rather than continue their musical assault, the insects dropped several feet and retreated to their nest *en masse*. Gobs of vermillion covered the skin of the hive, awaiting entry.

Toth removed his bycoket. He tucked his scarf under his shirt. He jammed the cap and pipe into the pocket of his coat. He kept his breath shallow. He watched and listened until blood throbbed in his ears.

Clasping the amulet around his neck, a prayer to God Almighty crossed his heart.

The driver walked at the point, while the friar maintained the rear. Leaves swished with their advance. Standing, the friar was even larger than he seemed while seated. All his companions combined couldn't fill his robes. His size, and the strength it implied, gave Toth pause.

The ghoulish four walked to the wall of thorns and burning antrum.

The soldier was engaged in assisting his delicate companion, pulling materials from a sack at his waist and showing them, boasting of treasures. Toth could not determine what the soldier held, save that the artifacts were small. It was an effort at education, warranted, welcomed, or not. When the diminutive figure held out his hand to receive an offering from the soldier, Toth witnessed the monstrosity of his berobed shape.

Horror seized him.

The hand, although bound in skin, took the shape of a talon. The nails that protruded from each digit were blade-like and long, curving from a base of black to a tip of yellow. The protuberance was mobile, for the creature wrapped three fingers and a dew claw around an item the soldier gifted. The nails scraped together, keeping the grip loose.

What in God's name? Toth thought. *Is this what becomes of the changelings? What separates this abomination from the creature that imitates a dead squirrel? Or one that imitates Floris's child?* He deduced that the driver and friar separated the creatures, but how he could not say. Mayhap it was by the education he now witnessed. The changelings had to be nurtured.

This was not a shapeshifter of conjuration made. The descriptions of Old Räum in *Ba'al* surfaced. The talon was that of a raven.

A strange wonder of Hell, Toth thought, *these creatures of mimicry.*

At the pit, the driver lowered his collar and removed his hat. His skin was white, and his skull was bald as unadorned bone. His jaws were pitted and cadaverous. His mouth, fronted by thin lips of black, protruded with an overbite. His incisors were those of a rat. His eyes were pools of dead flesh.

When the driver spoke, it was in an archaic dialect of Bavarian. The voice was harsh and choked.

"Toader," he said to the friar, "keep the cretin on task."

In response, the soldier bowed his head, ashamed. He stuffed what looked to be a beak in the pouch at his waist. His gear creaked. Toth tried to make out words carved on the breastplate but was unable.

Toader, monolithic, said nothing. He offered no gesture. Perhaps his eyes shifted in the shadow of his cowl, perhaps not.

The smallest figure watched the driver with what amounted to reverence.

"Master Grau," he said. He did not possess the awkwardness of the soldier. The voice was clear and pleasant.

Of course, Toth thought, *the soldier would be the one who left pieces of himself at the scene of Bertram's abduction. He's malformed. The soldier is their weakness.*

Grau went to his knees in the mud, inching toward the heat of the shaft.

"The mad woman tucked the old fool in here," he rasped.

The mad woman? Toth thought. *And what old fool?*

It was then that another voice emerged from deeper in the wood. It was the voice of a woman. She called a name with great pathos.

Toth straightened. *Christ no,* he thought.

Tom stirred, craning his neck.

Grau ceased what he had planned for the pit, and he lifted his face. He returned the cap to his head. He stood. His arms went to his chest in fetal glee. His mouth, with concentration, shuddered with a nibbling motion, and his nose wrinkled and flared. He sniffed the air like Tom.

He, too, Toth thought, *has an animal inside. Not raven but rodent.*

"Merrick," the woman called. The name rang through the forest, stilling the wasps. A long hush followed.

Annalise approached on the path from the tithe barn.

Grau gestured at the smallest of his brood.

The creature lifted his chin, aiming his voice at the trees, and called out in a dulcet tone empty of malice.

"Anna the Gravedigger. Anna the Daughter, Anna the Wife. Anna the Sister, Anna the Friend, Anna with the spade in her hand."

"Merrick?" Annalise's voice grew louder, closer, and more desperate. There was fear and joy. "Merrick, where are you?"

Grau looked at Toader with grotesque pride.

"Anna the Gravedigger," the creature called. "Anna the Daughter, Anna the Wife. Anna the Sister, Anna the Friend, Anna with the spade in her hand."

"Merrick?" Yet louder, closer.

Toth's alarm surged. He had only a moment to decide an action.

Grau motioned for Toader and the soldier to follow him to the edge of bramble, preparing a trap of ensnarement. Toader yanked the soldier along, leaving the creature with a raven talon beside the antrum. The heat stirred his robes. Grau retreated toward the road. Once positioned to hide, Toader's heaving back rose from weeds like a boulder in grass. It was no matter. Their concealment was temporary, not meant to be tested.

The creature in the circle extended the sleeve of his burgundy robe, hiding the monstrous claw. His face shifted, breaking into amorphous fog. Then the body changed. The creature grew taller, the arms and legs lengthening. The thing crossed its arms and looked down, the picture of austerity in broken sunshine.

This is their way, Toth thought. *This is the culmination of the changeling.*

Toth steeled himself. He knew what was about to unfold, and he knew he couldn't stand by and watch it occur. He stood, collecting his thoughts, gathering his breath, steadying his heart. To say he was unafraid would be blasphemous in its scope of lying, but, behind fear, Toth worried for Annalise. His breath escaped in small gasps. He reached to his belt and removed the dagger from its scabbard. Toth gripped the handle for slashing.

Below, Annalise appeared from the wood. Mud soaked the hem of her dress. Her face was red from crying. Her mouth was parted. She hid behind crossed arms, locked tight as staves. She carried no tool, no weapon. Desperate hope was her only means of protection.

Toth pitied the woman deeply. Her grief was of a scope he couldn't fathom.

"Merrick," Annalise said to the changeling. Weakly, she spoke.

Thirty feet separated Annalise from the creature. The thing lifted his head and stared through Annalise, but he offered no reply.

The face was pleasing to her. Her voice softened.

"Why do you pray on bended knee?" she asked. The words trembled. "Why in this circle?"

When Annalise overcame doubt and stepped forward, Toth released his grip on Vinegar Tom's collar.

Fly swiftly, he thought.

The dog buzzed at the spine.

"Get him, Tom," Toth hissed.

The greyhound, with great power in his hindlegs, bounded through the grass toward the stairs. As the dog ran, and as Toth sprinted in his stead, wasps escaped their nest above, piling out into the sky.

May your confusion yet reign, Toth thought, peering above.

Tom glided down the steps, crossing four at a time. When he gained level ground, he dug his claws into loam and leaf, and he advanced like a projectile through undergrowth. Stretched to full length, Tom had the speed of a great cat. His beating presence, and the wasps that trailed him like a storm, drew the attention of Annalise, Grau, Toader, the soldier, and the creature that feigned prayer at an altar of mud. All turned an eye to the brindle greyhound of Kent.

Once seen, we cannot be unseen, Toth thought, struggling to keep his balance as he rushed down the steep stairwell. *Once the river is crossed, it cannot be uncrossed.* He damned caution.

"Back!" Toth shouted at Annalise. "Flee, Fräulein. Flee!"

Annalise split her gaze between the circle, Tom, and Toth. She stopped her advance. There was indignation in her doubt, anger at interruption and intrusion.

Toader moved from the undergrowth, rushing to intercept Toth.

The creature spun to meet the dog's attack, pulling back his robe, freeing his talon. Heat poured forth in a column at his back. Vinegar Tom was too quick, too determined. Without hesitation, the dog reached the edge of the mud and leapt. He struck the abomination at the shoulders, piling chest against chest, knocking him back with the swift blow. Down he went, his back crashing hard against the opening in the earth. The heat roared under his weight, scalding. Tom maneuvered, planting a mass equal to that of the creature, pinning him to the ground. The dog's jaw extended, showing yellowed, pointed incisors and fangs. As the changeling struggled to be free, working his talon, swinging and ripping at Tom's side, the dog went for the kill. The hound of blood grabbed the exposed throat and clamped with all the strength in his jaws. There was great power there. An audible grinding followed.

The creature shrieked like a mandrake as Tom rent his flesh, yanking, ripping, and tearing, stomping.

Toader broke into a sprint, mustering all the speed his great size allowed, and Grau came next, but both were slow and laborious. Both showed the weakness of their construction, of their lumbering, grinding bones, of an inferior god's design. The soldier came, too, far behind.

Toth moved between Annalise and the creature she believed to be Merrick.

"Flee, Fräulein!" Toth shouted.

Annalise watched, horrified and uncertain, angry and distraught.

Toth glanced at Toader, and his heart went cold with terror. His skin was pink like a hairless rodent, pocked by singular hairs that grew from mounds. Rather than engage the giant, Toth rushed to join Tom, crossing into the circle. The talon was free, striking Tom at the ribs, drawing blood, wetting his fur.

The hound crunched skin and bone, grinding sinew in his teeth, crushing the throat. Rather than blood, a muddied ichor that smelled like a putrefied intestine poured from the wound, coating Tom's muzzle, chin, and throat.

Toth grabbed the arm of the changeling, prying away the talon. The flesh was gelid to the touch, and it was hard. Toth stomped the forearm to the ground, cracking bone, drawing a wild look from the lead-eyed creature.

Heat seared the thing's back, running scarlet through his flesh.

No, Toth thought. *He's taking on my face. To look upon him is to look at polished glass. Even in agony, he imitates.*

Toth locked eyes with the abomination, and his mind went opaque with the noise of approaching wasps. The insects searched for a target, confused, hanging in the air.

Toader grunted with rage, nearing the circle, swinging briars aside.

Toth slid his boot to the creature's wrist, and he gripped the dagger. He stabbed at the talon. The blade passed through the palm, knocking against a bone that caved like chalk. Toth stabbed again and the blade passed through, entering mud. A rotten secretion jetted forth, spattering Toth's sleeve.

The creature shrieked through a broken throat.

While his boot locked the wrist, Toth pointed at the talon, exposing the repugnant form to Annalise. The long claws writhed and curled around the dagger.

"Does Merrick yet live?" Toth shouted. "Is this he? Flee, Fräulein!"

Behind Annalise, along the trail, came a white blur. Greedy Gut broke through the undergrowth with tremendous force. The dog rushed at Toth, beating her paws against the earth.

"No," Toth shouted. "No!"

It was too late. As Toader entered the circle, reaching a webbed hand for Toth's coat, the Pyrenees intercepted the giant, leaping without grace. Greedy Gut caught Toader by the hand, snapping her jaws tight.

Toth yanked Tom. The greyhound rose with a flag of skin and meat in his teeth, dangling white. Toth left the dagger pinned.

Toader swung at the Pyrenees, swiping, just missing her tail.

Tom, full of heat and rage, turned to Toader. A guttural bark escaped his heaving chest.

Toth forced the greyhound away, and both he and the dog ran to Annalise.

Greedy Gut dropped a chunk of finger to the mud. She dodged another blow from the giant, and then she raced after Tom.

The wasps, still uncertain, remained above.

Grau, Toth saw, moved in Annalise's direction, as well. She was so absorbed, in such a state of shock, that she failed to notice his proximity.

Toth ran harder, beating Grau. He grabbed Annalise's shoulder, and he pulled her toward the trail. Tom led the way, dripping blood, with Greedy Gut at his side. Shaken from her stupor, Annalise freed herself from Toth's grasp. Her renewed clarity was welcome. She nearly caught the dogs.

Toth, his lungs burning with exertion, looked back. His chest heaved. His hands trembled.

Toader gave up the chase. The giant knelt in the circle, taking the changeling into his arms, removing him from the antrum. The soldier stood by his side.

In his coat of black, Grau, too, relinquished the chase. With a contemplative stare, he stopped at the mouth of the trail, studying Toth. No expression of anger crossed his rat face. No word left his mouth. No threats. No promises.

When he stopped, the wasps finally descended, attacking Grau. Repeatedly and viciously, the wasps stung the driver's exposed flesh, burying barbs in his head and neck. Grau didn't acknowledge their presence, although the swarm was so great it obscured his face. He watched Toth until wasps draped his eyes. He was motionless as the insects ravaged. He experienced no pain.

Shrieking Hell, Toth thought, sprinting after Annalise and the dogs.

XXIII

CAPITULUM

Toth knelt by the greyhound and stroked his ear.

"That's a brave lad," he said.

Tom's breathing calmed. He lay on his side with the slashes at his ribs exposed, the crusted fur brushed back. The dog rested his eyes.

"Shhhh, now. That's a brave lad, Tom."

Toth uncorked a vial of gin to slather on the wound. He added drops to Vinegar Tom's cuts. The dog tensed, leaving his eyes closed against the pain. Nervous drool lined his mouth. He was loathe to show it, but Tom was hurting. Next, Toth retrieved a salve of ibex fat he'd purchased in Luxor. He removed his gloves, opened the concoction, and smeared the medicine on each cut. Although his breath quickened, Tom maintained his patience.

Annalise entered the house with the sun at her back. She carried a wash basin and towel over her shoulder.

"How is he?" she asked.

"His ribs aren't broken," Toth said, rubbing Tom's nape. "He'll be sore is all."

Annalise placed the basin on the floor. Water sloshed onto the planks where Bertram's mat had lain. The crusted fabric remained on the front stoop.

A shadow crossed the sunlight, and then a face showed in the doorway. Greedy Gut looked into the room with humble, downcast eyes. She reached a paw over the threshold, and when she wasn't shouted down for the act, she stepped inside.

Tom lifted his head.

"Good girl," Toth said. He snapped his fingers, calling her near.

Greedy Gut walked to Tom. She hovered over the greyhound.

"The mountain dog is a stray," Annalise observed.

"*Was* a stray," Toth corrected. "Although I can't allow her to carry such a name as Greedy Gut. She's too sagacious for it. She trailed me two days waiting for the moment when she was needed, Fräulein." Toth touched the dog's broad head. "An erudite animal, she is."

Greedy Gut sniffed Tom's wound. Then, with grace, she ran her tongue over the cuts.

"Don't eat the fat, Pyrenees," Toth said.

Tom sighed. He closed his eyes again and relaxed. When he did, Greedy Gut ate the food that remained at his nose. She looked up at Toth, chomping and crunching.

"*Ez jobb*," Toth said. *This is better.* "Good girl. What royalty you are."

"What language do you speak?" asked Annalise.

"My native tongue," Toth said. "Hungarian."

"It's the language in which you talk to animals?"

"Tom prefers English. He's from England, after all. Mayhap the Pyrenees favors French."

Annalise smiled.

"Did you locate Matthias?" Toth asked.

Annalise shook her head. She sat on the mattress. With her palm, she pressed wrinkles from the blanket. She was again in the throes of grief.

A remark from Grau went through Toth's mind. *The mad woman tucked the old fool in here,* he'd said, meaning the pit of fire. He wondered if the "old fool" was Matthias. Was the "mad woman" a changeling's conception of Cili?

Toth wetted the towel. As Tom winced, kicking his leg, Toth cleared the remaining blood. The cuts were superficial. The wounds would close and heal without the assistance of needle and thread. Toth scrubbed the rancid effluvium from Tom's snout and neck. Water softened the crystalized material. When he finished cleaning the greyhound, Toth took a handful of feed from his satchel to replace that which the Pyrenees stole. He placed the food on the floor.

Tom rolled onto his belly and sniffed the offering. He moved the feed with his nose. Then he pecked at it.

Greedy Gut watched with interest.

Toth stood, wiping his hands clean.

"Amazing animals, dogs," Toth said. "Ferocious each. Brave each. They sacrifice for us."

Annalise pressed her gown absentmindedly. Blood was gone from her face.

Toth sat on the opposite bed. He tamped tobacco into the bowl of his pipe. He lit it. His hands shook. Bludgeoning fear—a barrage of images—throbbed in his mind.

The Pyrenees flopped onto her side, shaking the floor. She landed with a sigh.

"You've said nothing of your father," Toth observed. "Where did Matthias go?"

"He's searching for Bertram," Annalise said. "I was also searching for my brother."

Toth exhaled smoke. He slipped on his gloves.

There was no need to express his trepidation about Matthias's whereabouts. Both he and Annalise knew the worry. If he lived, the old man was in the forest with Grau and his companions.

"Yet you called for Merrick," Toth said. He watched for a reaction.

Staring at the floor, Annalise nodded. "My father wants you to leave, Master Toth."

"He blames me for Bertram, does he not?"

She did not answer. Instead, she asked, "Master Toth, do you believe in divination?"

"Why do you ask that?"

"My father is a good Christian," she said cryptically.

"I don't doubt it," Toth said, although he did doubt, acutely.

"Last night, my father tried to divine Bertram's whereabouts."

Toth narrowed his gaze. When Annalise hesitated, he urged her to go on.

"He wasn't successful," she said. "This will sound strange to you, but he blamed his failure on Cili. Or better yet, Cili's spirit. He believed she was blocking him."

"I found the product of his anger," Toth said. "Matthias desecrated Cili's grave. He dug her up last night."

Annalise was silent for a moment. "He's a good Christian, as I said, Master Toth. I don't believe he went that far."

"He believes she is a witch, yes? That she's responsible for all this?"

"Yes."

"Why?"

"He saw Cili as I saw Merrick."

"He saw her in the flesh?"

"Yes."

"Is divination something that Matthias practices often?" Toth asked.

"Annalise shook her head defensively. "Only when desperate," she said.

"But he believes in the magic of it."

"He does."

"He's performed similar rituals before?"

"He's a good Christian."

"Has he or not?"

"He has."

"About Merrick?"

"Yes."

"Have you?" Toth asked.

"No," Annalise said adamantly.

"I'm quite serious when I ask this," Toth said. "I speak of rituals. Have you done more to call Merrick?"

"I've prayed for Merrick to return. I want to see him. I've prayed, but nothing more."

"I fear the changeling we saw knows this about you. He was preying on you today. He is the imitation you've seen and heard."

"Master Toth?"

"Yes?"

Annalise looked up. "What are those things? Because they are not men."

Toth glanced at Tom, who'd fallen asleep on his side. The rectangle of sunlight reached his form. The Pyrenees guarded him.

Toth drew on the pipe.

"They are the same creatures as the changeling I killed last night. They are in an advanced, I believe nurtured, stage of development. The others that you find by the pit are wild, as it were."

"Why does one look like Merrick?"

"They're creatures of mimicry, Fräulein. They imitate. I found one today that imitated a dead squirrel, preposterous as that is. It will starve because it imitates the motionlessness of death, but it was a near perfect imitation. That's why I believe these four are nurtured, shaped, and guided. The smallest—"

"—Shaped by what? What are they to begin?"

"There I can only conjecture."

"Do."

"They begin as the trapped souls of your dead. Once, they were people you knew. They begin as spirit and take on flesh. The great irony is that the dead lodged in the tithe barn are not subject to this transformation. It strikes me that your father ordered cemetery use to be discontinued. He ordered the corpses into the barn. Only the dead buried in the earth, buried in the body of Old Räum, suffer this transformation and torment."

"What is Old Räum?"

Toth laid out the case as he understood it. Around the pipe, he explained about the adversarial spirit called Räum, its pulsing call to ravens, wasps, and the dead, and burning antra that were, he posited, openings into the great body of Old Räum beneath the earth.

It did Toth well to put the ideas in the open for another to observe. A part of him desired Annalise to meet the theory with Groza's skepticism, but she seized on the aspect of mimicry. The clarity devastated her hopes.

"Merrick is dead," Annalise said.

"That much is certain. Your Merrick doesn't linger in the wood."

"Yet his voice…."

"Mimicked, I believe, as you *remember* it. Filched from your mind rather than Merrick's."

"How can you be certain of that?"

"I can't be certain," Toth admitted. "I can simply deduce."

Annalise hid her face in her hands.

"If I relinquish the illusion, I'll never see him again."

"God willing. What we saw today," Toth continued, "were the same creatures that snatched Bertram from your home. The helmet in this room belonged to the soldier among them. The effluvium on Tom's snout was the same as that on the helmet."

"What good does it do to know these things?"

"I must understand it in order to defeat it."

"Defeat it?" Annalise laughed, hollow and joyless.

Unamused, Toth said, "The Order of Saint Guinefort exists for no other purpose. I was not sent here to gather notes."

"Where did you learn to wield a dagger? Do they teach that to all brothers of your order?"

"A challenging upbringing," Toth said.

"Shall I apologize for assuming—"

"—You'll do nothing of the sort, Fräulein."

After a moment, Annalise said, "Thank you for what you did today."

"Anyone would have done the same."

"No, Master Toth, they wouldn't. Will they return tonight?"

"Of that I'm certain. Will Matthias? That's a better question."

"I have no secret knowledge of his whereabouts. I don't know. Did he really do such a horrible thing to Cili?"

"He did."

"Then I hope he does not return."

XXIV
CAPITULUM

top the Haflinger that plodded along the shore, weaving through sarsens, Groza shouted orders. His grating voice carried over the fields, invading homes.

Andreas walked in front of the horse, holding the reins. The unflattering scene resembled a child learning to ride a pony. The horse carried Groza up the shore and then down again, while masked men and women trailed in a procession. Their number had increased. As intended, the histrionics drew a crowd.

When Groza captured an audience, he shouted, "Is there no armory in this rotten asshole of humanity?"

A man informed Groza that Drunstall possessed no weapon house.

"How is it that you defend yourselves from marauders? Speak, man."

The man pointed at an outcropping on the mountain that loomed over the river. "When the beacon is lit, we leave for the safety of Karnstein. The chateau is armed."

Groza scoffed. "Does no one possess a musket to slaughter these infernal birds? Enough. Fetch my dueling pistols."

Toth followed Greedy Gut into the street.

The man brought dueling pistols, Toth thought, amazed at the physician's dedication to decorum.

Andreas handed the reins to one of the masked men, and then he left the shore to gather the weapons. He trudged toward The Cock's Foot.

The villager continued the procession, escorting Groza like a pasha on gilded litter.

"The ravens must go before I complete the bleeding," Groza said. "And there's another thing. I'm informed that a mass of corpses waits in the hillside tithe barn. Is this so?"

Annalise exited the house, joining Toth and Greedy Gut.

When Toth reached to pet the Pyrenees, the dog stepped closer, allowing his touch.

"It is so," answered a woman.

"Do you not understand the dangers of miasma?" Groza inquired.

"How does he not grow dizzy, moving to and fro?" Annalise asked.

"This is something he's practiced with a row of mirrors," Toth said. "I've little doubt of that. Groza isn't spontaneous."

"Do you know him well?"

"I know him as well as I wish to know him. More so."

"I say, do you not know the dangers of miasma?" Groza persisted. "Do you not understand the disease that you breathe? The gypsy Magyar will say you breathe demons by the throatful, but you breathe illness. You breathe miasma."

The ravens on the church shivered their feathers in unison, and the sound moved over the hushed crowd.

Andreas returned with a lacquered box of cherry wood. He carried the pistols with the care of a reliquary.

"Before the sun descends," Groza said, "two things will occur. I'll appoint men capable of using firearms to scatter the devil birds. They will not coat the House of God in their poisonous shit.

"Second, the tithe barn will be opened and cleared of corpses. I want men to sink a plague pit, and I want those remains hidden in the earth. I want to see a layer of dirt on the cadavers before dark. That barn is the chief reason you are suffering. Miasma carries every ailment known to man, including the ones up here." He tapped his wig. "Given time, I'll educate you on the matter, but let it suffice to say you breathe death. Aye, even with river air nigh, miasma cuts and penetrates. The rot of the charnel house is as ubiquitous in this village as smoke. It greets you on the road. It greets you a league distant. Either you bury the corpses or Andreas will torch them in a bonfire of the innocents."

"You'd damn them so easily?" someone asked.

"They're already damned," Groza said viciously. "You did that." He lifted his chin. "How can the soul assume the Heavenly shore if trapped in a cauldron of rot, sir?"

No one answered the jeremiad.

"Your pistols, Doctor," Andreas said.

"Why do your people readily obey Groza?" Toth asked.

"They'd follow you with the right tone. You're too kind to them."

"The barrier of their prejudice is so easily toppled?"

"That they allow you in this village says the barrier is fallen. You would've been halted at the gate two years ago. You would've been turned back, Master Toth, letter or not. No Jew or gypsy was allowed here then. Do you believe we're lost?"

"No," Toth said. "Only bludgeoned. You'll rise. If these people possess half your strength, then I've no doubt of it."

Annalise looked away, and a touch of color returned to her brow.

"Find men who can shoot," Groza ordered Andreas. "The rest of you gather spades and come with me. I'm cutting the seal of this tomb immediately."

Annalise started along the lane.

"Do you intend to stop him?" Toth asked.

"No, I'm going to dig. It'll give me time to think, Master Toth."

"Where's the gypsy?" Groza asked. Sitting straight in the saddle, he guided the Haflinger through the wheat. "Has the blasphemer and his mutt yet fled? Does the demon-haunted child yet cower under a pew? Does the caravan-bred Magyar tramp yet—"

"—I'm here," Toth shouted, "watching your skill unravel, Kaspar."

Groza approached Toth, touching his bangs as though doffing a hat.

"Careful, lest I have Andreas offer you one of the pistols, sir."

"How many died from your bleeding today, Kaspar?"

"If I had a gauntlet, and if the ground weren't mud, I'd toss it at your feet, gypsy."

"And I'd provide you with an agonizing death," Toth said in a moment of weakness.

"Is that right? What a violent, savage creature, you are."

"Fetch a spade, gypsy," the manservant said when he arrived. "We'll put you to work that even you can understand." Andreas took the reins from Groza.

The physician laughed. "What a sight that would make," he said. "Dorin Toth performing the labor of his forebears, exposed like an animal dressed in silk, a carnival bear who delights with tricks of the tongue."

"Fork-tongued gypsy, worthy of a woodcut," Andreas remarked, and he echoed Groza's laughter.

Toth neared the horse. Greedy Gut came with him.

"Although it's against my better judgment, I feel inclined to warn you, Kaspar."

Groza turned in the saddle. He adjusted his wig. "Warn me, gypsy? How dare you, sir."

"How dare you, indeed," Andreas echoed. He gestured at the gun box beneath his arm.

Toth leveled his tone. "There are four men in the wood who will enter this village tonight. They mean these people serious harm."

"Turks shudder before Leopold," Andreas said.

"They're not Turks delivering arson," Toth said. "Last night, these men captured a boy who lived in this house. Tonight, they'll pursue his sister. Annalise is her name." Toth motioned to the crowd traipsing to the barn.

"What are you suggesting, gypsy?"

"That you're prepared for a night without sleep," Toth said. "That you're prepared to defend those poor souls in your ward."

Groza scoffed.

"If these are highwaymen, we'll put these pistols to even better use," Andreas said.

"Oh, come off it, you bloviating fool. They're not highwaymen. They're not raiders."

"Then what are they, gypsy?"

"I'm hesitant to classify them."

Groza shook his head. "Demons, I suppose, with unintelligible names. Do Drunstall a favor and drown yourself in the river, gypsy. Andreas will provide you with a sack for the purpose."

"I was not alone in seeing them. What abducts a young man dying from pox?"

"Wolves," Andreas said.

"Yes," Groza agreed. "Wolves always ring a plague. And they mustn't be ghosts, you simpleton."

"Then call them wolves," Toth said, "but defend those poor souls all the same."

XXV
CAPITULUM

"Who placed this seal?" Groza asked.

From his position in the saddle, the physician scanned the crowd.

"Pray tell," Groza demanded.

A child's voice emerged in response. Sebastian, with Blancheflor holding his shoulder, separated from the throng. He was scarcely as tall as the horse's thigh.

Groza shaded his eyes from the afternoon sun. "Explain," he said.

"My mother made them. They're only linen, sir. They're not magic."

"Take it down, boy."

"It's nothing more than a charm," Blancheflor protested.

"It looks Jewish," Andreas said.

"It's French," Sebastian said.

"Enough," Groza interjected. "We'll all die here from the stench alone. Take it down, boy."

Sebastian stepped to a door covered in wasps. It was an odd sight: a child testing danger while men watched. The façade of the barn engulfed Sebastian, and he looked quite small as he unpinned the seal.

The ravens looked on.

Sebastian stretched the linen between his hands. He looked up at Groza for direction.

"Read it, child," Groza said. He spoke from behind his hand, clamping his mouth and nose with his palm. Death rot left him green to the ears, and his eyes watered.

"I can't," said Sebastian.

"Jesus Christ, be gone then. Move."

Sebastian folded the seal, and he returned to the crowd through a gauntlet of masked men. Toth found the child at the rear with Blancheflor. The woman wore a necklace of colorful petals that matched the flowers in her hair. She decorated herself like an herbalist. Given her reputation, Toth wondered if Cili had embraced the same air.

Floris and her bizarre infant were absent. Blancheflor comforted her brother.

"May I see that?" Toth asked. He knelt, making himself eye level with the boy.

Sebastian handed over the linen. The lettering was hand stitched. A lot of work had gone into its crafting.

"It's a harmless decoration," Blancheflor said.

Toth looked up at her. He stood.

"*La vie est un beau reve, mais ne vous reveillez pas,*" Toth read aloud. He watched the siblings. "It says, 'Life is a beautiful dream, but don't wake up.'"

He gave the seal to Sebastian.

"Your mother was a bright light," Toth said. He patted the boy's shoulder. "Don't let Groza convince you otherwise." *Or Matthias,* he thought.

"She made it for her brother, Loring," said Blancheflor.

Over the murmuring crowd, Toth asked, "Why is it not on his grave?"

"It was," said Blancheflor.

Toth furrowed his brow. "Here?"

"Yes," Blancheflor whispered.

"Why is Loring here if Cili lies in the cemetery?" Toth asked.

"Matthias had him dug up," said Sebastian.

"Two lads come forth," Andreas shouted.

Groza maneuvered his horse, admonishing the crowd for stealing his lane.

When the mass parted, two volunteers approached the door. Both men wore masks, and both were heavy in the shoulders.

Toth lifted his scarf, securing it over his nose and mouth.

"This will be scarring to see," he told the siblings. "If you insist on remaining, brace yourselves." He leaned closer to Sebastian. The child's hands were bloodless. "There's no cowardice in turning your back and closing your eyes," he said. "Your mother would've told you the same, would she not?"

Sebastian nodded. His eyes were deep and overwhelmed.

"Hide your eyes," Toth said.

Sebastian began to cry, but it was a sound lost in the growing din. To Toth's surprise, Sebastian buried his face in Toth's side. His back heaved with violence. Toth put his arm around the boy to calm him. He patted his back.

A nervous energy pulsed through the throng.

"Must you remain?" Toth asked Blancheflor.

Sadly, she nodded.

The men in hook-nosed plague masks, grotesque and birdlike, lifted the hickory stave that barred exit from the barn. The men grabbed the handle in unison. It was not labor for two, but there was courage in two. If nothing else, the guilt of desecration was divided. The door was thin, unfit for its purpose—planks wrapped with dual cords of metal. The sack of communion wafers hung from the handle. Above the door, suspended from the eave, was the witch ball with rosemary. Toth suspected Cili's children had a hand in hanging that charm, as well.

The door opened, grinding on rusted hinges, pressing grass that grew tall at its base. The next moment was one of great sin and shame. A wave of putrefaction eddied from the dark interior. The miasma was so heinous that it wounded everything it touched. The stench that escaped the fastened door was nothing compared to the odor that waited behind it.

A collective gagging ran through those present. Arms and hands covered noses and mouths. Even Groza, a man who knew death, lowered his eyes in horror.

Toth clamped Sebastian tighter so that the child was not tempted to see.

The masked men secured the door, leaving it wide. Sunlight lay over the barn's interior for the first time in weeks. This was no charnel house with bodies carefully stripped, cleaned, and arrayed. This was not a house of bones to honor memories. This was desecration and wanton disregard for the dead.

The corpses were thrown together, pitched through the door onto a mound of flesh. It was work performed in haste: the door opened, a body went inside, and the door closed. Fear of damnation kept the villagers from torching cadavers. One body after another for how long? There were, judging by the enormous size of the heap, at least twelve bodies within. Save for Loring, they were nameless, sexless creatures, decomposed to the consistency of mud, melting together. The flesh was black in stripes and white with foam. Blood, bile, and refuse pooled on the floor, so deep that it ran into the grass, soaking the earth.

Toth fixated on a bare leg and foot with skin discolored to the purple-black of a bruise. Moss sprouted at the heel where creases of light fostered growth. Maggots wriggled over the sole, breaking through an open sore, a borehole in the meat.

Groza collected himself when his horse shook head to tail. The physician fought the dizziness that everyone experienced. He gripped the saddle horn.

"What are you waiting for?" he shouted. "Either join the digging or get your hands dirty. Get these men hooks to pull out the cadavers."

It was then that a curious invasion left Groza speechless, arrested in awe.

The ravens lifted from the barn, leaving the thatch, ascending into the sky. Up went the birds at once. Then, when the ravens achieved a formation above the trees, they descended. All eyes turned up. Even Sebastian loosened his grip to see. The ravens flew hard at the open door like bats at dusk released to war on insects. *En masse,* ravens entered the barn, speeding with such ferocity that their bodies rippled in flight. Ravens from the church lifted, too, and ravens from sarsens by the river lifted, until the air was full, black as a storm. All descended on the tithe barn. Over his shoulder, Toth felt their approach. The air changed as the ravens beat their wings. All entered the barn's gaping hole, filling the interior, covering the pile of flesh.

Ravens fed with the intensity of starvation.

"Shall we shut the door, sir?" Andreas asked. The manservant had his hands on his wig, holding it in place. Like his master, he was on the verge of panic.

"I want the corpses out," Groza said, fighting to keep his horse from bolting. "Slaughter the birds if you must," he said, struggling. The horse turned, leaving Groza's back to the crowd. "Bury the ravens along with the rest. I don't care."

When the Haflinger turned again, Groza eyed Toth at the back of the crowd. He was unable to conceal the terror that crossed his face like shadow on the downs.

"Spades," Groza said weakly, gripping the reins, turning again. "Work the trench, men. Sink a hole."

"That's my child in there," a woman screamed. The masked men restrained her when she attempted to enter.

"And my Uncle Loring," Blancheflor shouted.

Toth gripped Sebastian.

A man split the crowd. He dashed through the front door, falling to his knees over the threshold. His hands sank into the muck. He flailed, scattering ravens.

"Get him out of there," Groza shouted. "Get them all out of there!"

Toth joined the child, shutting his eyes in horror.

XXVI
CAPITULUM

The sight of a man dragged from the charnel house left Toth sorrowful. He had no desire to see more of the gruesome excavation. As he crossed the lane, his thoughts were in disarray. He closed his fists to keep the tremble from them.

The hovel door was open, but nothing stirred inside. Toth passed through the gate, knocking it back with his knee, not wanting to sneak up on the dogs. Before entering, he glanced again at the barn. The crowd remained, as did the ravens, as did Groza, as did Sebastian and Blancheflor.

Toth kicked Bertram's fly-covered mat from the stoop as he passed.

Matthias's books and gadgets lay about the disordered room.

Tom was on the floor next to a pot. A layer of dust and dander covered the stale water. The greyhound slept soundly. His cuts were drying quickly, scabbing over. Greedy Gut, too, lay on the floor, but she was propped on her elbow and alert. Her watery eyes followed Toth. She panted in the shadow.

The sight brought needed warmth to Toth's heart.

He went to his knees between the dogs. He let Tom be, but he scratched the head of the Pyrenees. She leaned into his touch.

"*Vous êtes un protecteur naturel, n'est-ce pas?*" he whispered. *You are a natural protector, aren't you?*

Greedy Gut closed her eyes. When Toth scratched under the fold of her ear, she tilted her head with delight.

"They can't take the sentinel out of you. You'll always find your sheep to guard. I won't allow you to bear an ugly name, however," said Toth. "It's too vulgar. I've thought on it, and your name is now Basina. No more Greedy Gut nonsense. Do you like it?"

The Pyrenees closed her mouth, listening to a noise in the street.

"Basina is the name, *ma chérie*, of a Frankish princess. Does that not suit you?"

When Toth stopped scratching, Basina struck his leg, smacking down her paw. Toth rose and went for his satchel on the mattress. He was placing feed on the floor when a shape in the doorway blotted the sun. Toth turned.

"I must show you something," Blancheflor said, curt with urgency. Her loosening braids of red, disheveled, shone in the light. Her crown of flowers was askew.

"You left your brother behind?"

"Sebastian won't leave," she said. "I begged him."

Toth looked at the Pyrenees.

"Please guard Tom," he said.

Basina lapped at the feed. The hard morsels scraped the floor. She drew them into a pile with her paw.

Outside, Blancheflor said, "That is my uncle's dog, Master Toth."

"Yes, so I was told. And Loring named her wrathfully."

"How so?"

"My God, Greedy Gut. How dare he? You don't mock a Pyrenees. They're proud animals. They work, and they're loyal, and they're ancient. Romans used them in the field. King Louis made them the Royal Dog of France. You do understand that honor, don't you? The Royal Dog. They return respect when given, ridicule when given, and anger when given." Toth set his jaw. "She is called Basina. I will not tolerate her being slurred as Greedy Gut."

"Your relationship with dogs is troubling, Master Toth."

"So be it, Fräulein. A dog has yet to slur me as *gypsy*."

"We thought her dead. We'd given her up," Blancheflor said.

She knows she's been abandoned, Toth thought, but he let the anger pass.

He looked Blancheflor in the eyes. "What is it that you wish to show me?"

"*Le meneur de loups,*" she said. "I'm sick of suspicion falling on my mother."

"The leader of wolves," Toth intoned. Zeal chased his fatigue. "Very well," he said. "Is this something you've concealed from me?"

"Yes," Blancheflor said. "Come."

With haste, Toth trailed the woman through the fields.

"I imagined Dr. Groza would've spotted it from his perch on the horse," she said, "but it escaped him."

"Much escapes you when the world's a mirror," Toth said.

A thousand footfalls cratered the shoreline between sarsens. Blancheflor walked past the derelict mill where the settlement ended and the forest began. An enormous boulder jutted from the mud at the tree line, a chunk of mountain rolled down in ancient times. Brown water lapped against the bottom of the rock, trapping sticks, pine needles, and rubbish like the pylon of a bridge.

"Everything catches here," Blancheflor said. "My mother used to hunt for treasures on the bank."

She ascended the stone, clasping the hollows. Climbing was the only way around the boulder. High weeds choked the side not touching water.

Toth proceeded upward. He pulled himself to the top.

Blancheflor gestured at a pool on the opposite side.

Pressed into the mud, submerged to the chest, and covered in wasps, was the broken-necked corpse of Matthias. His skull was open at the right side. The flesh beneath was washed clean and grey. The tide shifted his beard, but there was nothing uncanny about the movement. His skin was charred black, burned in the manner that Cili was burned. His face was a death mask, and his creased eyes were still as marble. A piece of his jaw was pinched away, and this was the only opening that was raw and red.

Toth was numb, but his mind went to Annalise. The death of Matthias left the woman alone in the world. A breeze moved over the current, rippling the muddy water. The corpse, and the truth it revealed, gave Toth a touch of vertigo. He turned from Matthias, watching the wood on the far side of the river.

Blancheflor stared at Matthias. Wind tussled her hair, leaving strands of red across her nose. Her features were hard.

"Was it murder?" Toth asked.

The mad woman tucked the old fool in here.

"Matthias did what he accused my mother of doing. The act washed him to this shore, as it washed my mother to this shore."

"I've seen Cili's remains," Toth said. "She was burned thus."

"Yes. You exhumed her?"

"I did not." Toth watched her keenly.

"She was said to have torched herself on a pyre in the wood. Perhaps, Master Toth, Matthias torched himself on a pyre in the wood."

"And he ended here?"

"As my mother miraculously ended here."

God, cure this land, Toth thought. *Cure these people.*

"Did you see Matthias die?" he asked. "Did he step into one of the burning pits?"

Blancheflor said nothing.

"Did you push him?"

Toth touched the amulet beneath his scarf.

"How do you know Matthias is *le meneur de loups,* Fräulein?"

Blancheflor looked so deeply into Toth's eyes that she peered inside him. The effect was unsettling. Lack of emotion rendered her something less than human, but old anger has that consequence.

"My mother, Cili, she knew. She saw him in the act."

Blancheflor reached out, touching the damp lace at Toth's wrist. He recoiled.

"Matthias was a conjuror," she said. She swallowed.

"And Annalise?"

"I don't know what Annalise knows. Either she aided Matthias or she is ignorant."

"Aided him in what?" Toth asked.

"*Conjuration*, Master Toth. Don't say you haven't suspected he is to blame."

"Is this murder, Fräulein?"

"Matthias torched himself like my mother torched herself," Blancheflor said. "It's an old and honorable way to pass."

Toth gazed at the corpse in the mud. A centipede split the old man's teeth, wriggling into the wire of his beard. The lips were burned off.

Ars goetia, he thought. *The art of conjuration.*

So it ends.

XXVII
CAPITULUM

rau turned from the barrel, disgusted, distracted, and furious. He leered at the forest. His face was swollen.

"Fish it out," he said finally.

The Lieutenant stepped into the cart. Metal creaked and the horses shifted. The soldier removed the lid of the outermost barrel. Then, as Grau monitored, he reached into the brine, submerging his arm to the elbow. The liquid was cold and thick, and a skin coated the top. The creature within made no effort to avoid capture. It floated, nearly lifeless. The Lieutenant wrapped his hand around the oily trunk—so miniscule that his fingers and thumb overlapped. He pulled the creature from the solution. The slick skin dripped. A small mouth puckered in a face with no eyes.

The thing's veins and inner workings were visible. As Grau asserted, the creature wasn't developing properly. In its stillborn shape, the thing resembled a cave fish. Arms and legs would never grow from the trunk.

"Will it not live...and change?" The Lieutenant asked. "How...do you know?"

"It's a failure," Grau replied.

Grau didn't hide his frustration. He walked from the road, entering the wood. His head was bent, and he was troubled. Beyond the trees, he met Toader, who sat on the ground next to The Stripling like a guardian, vigilant for dogs. A chunk of Toader's finger was missing. A bead of uncoiling fungus grew in the sore.

The Lieutenant hopped from the cart.

"The animal ruined you," Grau said to The Stripling.

Toader made the sound of a whimpering hound.

Indeed, The Stripling was mangled. His throat was torn, layers of flesh opened like a grotesque flower, and his talon was crippled, unmoving. The creature lay by the pit in agony, unable to sleep and unable to cope with the pain. Periodically, he moaned with the force of delirium, withering inside his robes.

"He needs to feed," Grau said.

The Lieutenant approached with the limp fetus. He shook the thing clean. The creature's mouth moved. The head was a slick knob above the single orifice.

"Tonight," said the soldier, "we should…go after the man… and his dog beasts."

"How deep is your anger?" Grau asked. His features shifted gracelessly, slowly.

"This…is my brother," said The Lieutenant.

Grau's breath rattled.

"All of us need to feed," he said. "And not on children of pox. The man in the scarf, yes, but I say we find one for each of us. And you, too." He looked at The Stripling. "You shall have your own. Perhaps the animal who did this to you will suffice."

Toader whimpered.

The Lieutenant held out the fetus.

"It yet…lives," he said. "What do you…wish to do?"

"Give it to Toader," said Grau.

The Lieutenant did so.

Toader held the creature in his palm. The puckering mouth was the only sign of life. Like a bothersome stitch, Toader ripped the fetus in two. Bile oozed over his hands and splattered the ground. The fetus made no noise as it expired. The mouth became fixed. Its heart and stomach dripped into the mud.

"For every success like you," Grau told The Stripling, "there are ten failures and one cretin." He knelt.

Toader handed over half of the fetus.

"Open up," Grau said. He pried apart The Stripling's jaw.

The Stripling screamed in agony when the motion bunched his neck.

The Lieutenant began to sob. "How can he…feed…if he's… in so much pain?" He wiped his face.

"Why do you cry?" Grau asked. He bit a piece of fetus, chewed it, and spat it into The Stripling's mouth.

Toader stuffed it down the throat with his finger.

"I'm going to kill…that dog beast," said the soldier.

Grau mumbled behind his chewing. When Toader pried The Stripling's mouth wide, he spat again, and Toader pushed the morsel into the throbbing membrane. Bile pooled in The Stripling's mouth.

"Tonight," Grau said with finality. He reached up and peeled skin from the soldier's arm. He put the ribbon in his mouth and chewed it.

Toader whimpered to The Stripling.

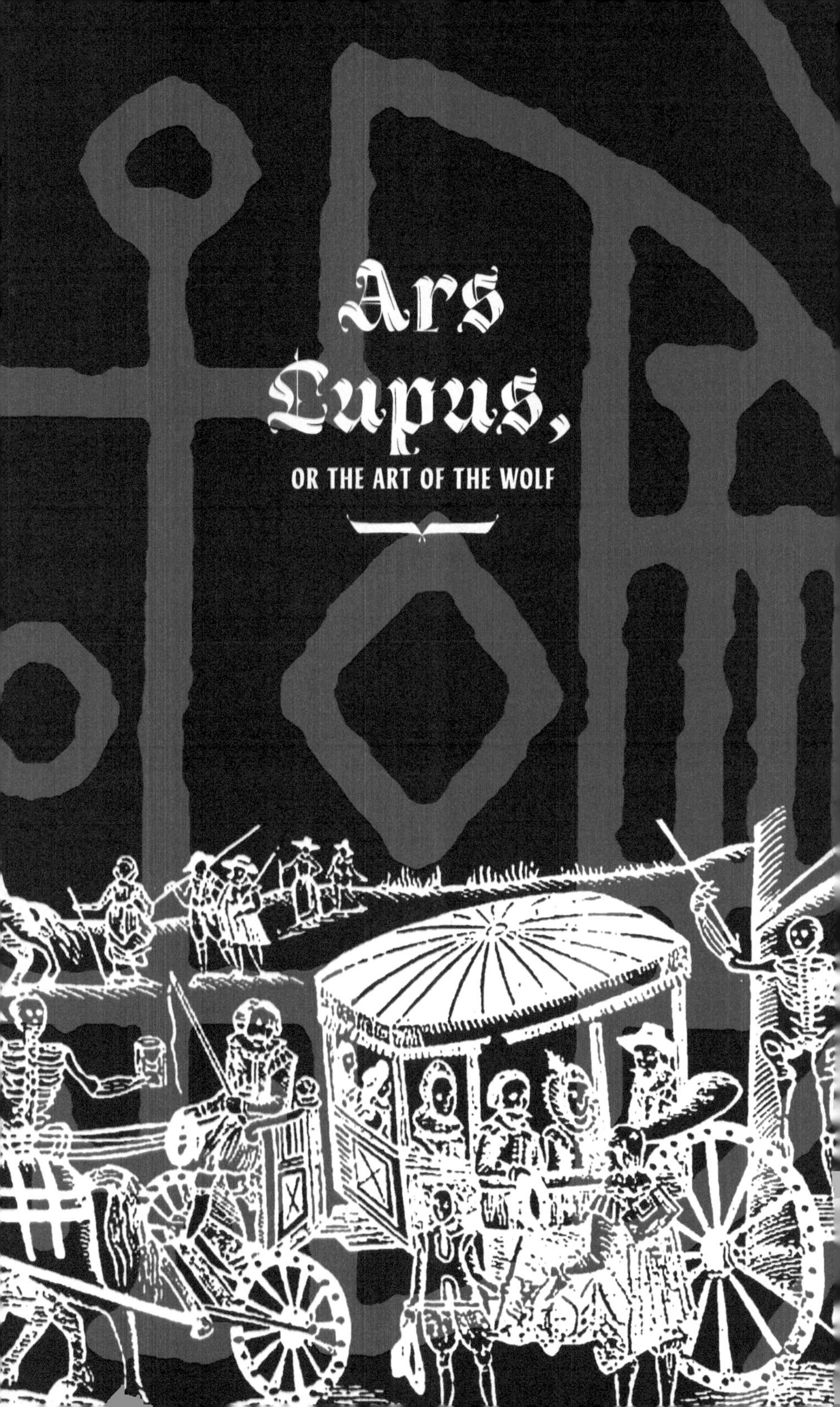
Ars
Lupus,
OR THE ART OF THE WOLF

XXVIII

CAPITULUM

In from the river they came, speaking in the low tones of the guilty. The burden of knowing was upon Toth. As he and Blancheflor crossed a field of buckwheat, flowering white in the evening sun, he asked, "When did your sister have Loring, her child?"

Blancheflor walked at his side. She frowned.

"Is that an attempt at humor, Master Toth?"

"I find nothing humorous about today."

"You speak of the doll. It isn't a child. And it isn't Loring."

Toth stopped. A raven shadow crossed his path.

"How do you mean?"

"It isn't real. Look closer. It's carved from wood."

"I did look closely," Toth said. "It had flesh. I watched it draw a breath. Floris said it shared your uncle's name."

Blancheflor's frown straightened.

"Why would she carry a doll?" Toth asked.

"Because Floris is fragile. She believes...." She hesitated. "She believes our mother's soul is inside the doll."

"Why does she believe something like that?"

Fighting embarrassment, Blancheflor said, "Floris believes she caught her spirit like the devil in a bottle."

"Do you not find that bizarre? All of it?"

"I find it horrifying," said Blancheflor. She looked at the ground. "Sometimes, Master Toth, I hear the doll breathing. Therefore, I don't like hearing you call it an infant, much less calling it Loring."

Toth stood quietly, drawn inward, pondering.

"Regardless of her fragility," she said, "we must speak with her. She'll tell you what I cannot. Come along."

The Cock's Foot waited in the shade of elms. The hogs next door fought the heat by rolling in mud. One of the Haflingers and two stout workhorses paced restlessly. The stench of pig and horseflesh mixed with the moldy heat. Despite ongoing labor at the plague pit, the crooked tavern was not without life. An elderly man with a grey beard waited at the gate with his leg on an empty trough. A faded sign on the pole at his side held the tri-toed symbol. The man had the air of watchmen and gossips. His grey cat rested on the fence. The feline was missing one of its ears, and its fur was matted.

To Toth's relief, Basina and Vinegar Tom greeted he and Blancheflor at the rain doll tree. The dogs came wandering from an empty hovel. They'd been exploring. It did Toth well to see the greyhound on his feet again. He walked balanced and hardy. Tom sauntered through the street behind the Pyrenees.

Toth knelt and stroked Tom's neck. The dog's wounds were clean. The shimmer of the salve was gone, however. Basina had licked the fat away.

"The medicine isn't food," he said to the Pyrenees.

Toth scratched her snout. Basina closed her eyes to enjoy it.

"She hasn't allowed a soul to touch her since Uncle Loring passed," Blancheflor said.

"It's more important that Tom accepts her, which he seems to have done." Toth stood. "I daresay they're infatuated. Come, Tom," he said. He pointed at the greyhound reproachfully. "Gingerly now. Don't exert yourself."

The grey man at the gate watched as Toth, Blancheflor, and the dogs came near. His demeanor made it clear that one must speak to him before passing. His face ticked with palsy. His sinewy frame trembled.

Toth had not spoken to the man previously, but he'd seen him at the gathering in the church.

"What's your name, gypsy?" the old man asked, although a person of his inclination made it certain he already knew. He had learned, possibly, everything there was to know about Toth.

Toth suffered the irreverence. "Dorin Toth."

"What's your accent?"

"Hungarian."

"Magyar, eh? Dark as a Turk, too," the man said. "Tsk tsk."

"And your name?" Toth asked.

"I'm Dragoslav, and this is Snip Jens." He gestured at the cat.

The feline flicked its tail with agitation, staring daggers. The crusted fur at his nape raised.

Basina and Tom tilted their heads. A quick motion by the cat would've sent them reeling, but Jens wasn't so ignoble as to hop and flee. Snip Jens straightened his spine, maintaining his look of superiority and displeasure.

Blancheflor leveled a withering gaze at the old man. Her anger was palpable.

Dragoslav failed to meet her eye. "What is it, gypsy, that you want here?"

"A word with your barmaid," said Toth.

Ponderously, Dragoslav processed the request. He was an artless man of vice, a troublemaker. The descending sun spread over the lane.

"Pay for it," he said.

"Is this your establishment?" Toth asked.

Dragoslav nodded. He patted the cat. "Mine and Snip Jens'," he corrected. "Ol' boy's a rat catcher extraordinaire. Why, once he—"

"—Is Floris inside?" Toth asked.

"Pay for it." Dragoslav held out his hand.

"I have the same privileges here as Groza," he said. "You'll cooperate."

The old man quivered at the chin, lip, and eye. His pox scars were ancient. He'd live until he was slime under a rock.

"You'll find the wench at the bar, gypsy," he muttered. He leered at Blancheflor then. *"Je t'ai dans la peau,"* he whispered. *I have you under my skin.* He licked his lips.

"Enough," Toth warned. He pointed a finger at the old man.

Dragoslav laughed. "Or you'll sic your mutts on me and the kitty, eh?"

"Don't tempt me," Toth said.

"Don't you stay in there long with them fleabags, gypsy."

"Sir, there's no chance of that."

When Toth, Blancheflor, and the dogs walked past, Dragoslav offered no further protest. He and Snip Jens stayed at the trough. The old man laughed again, and he turned his attention to the barn. The cat watched the dogs with rage.

Once inside the alehouse, Toth understood why Dragoslav waited outside. The heat within was strangling. The building was windowless and stank of yeast. What little air there was moved through the front door. Not only was the tavern windowless, it was austere. An array of roughly hewn tables crossed a plank floor. Timber columns braced the ceiling. There were seven empty tables scattered between the columns. Woodsmoke clung to the building's fibers, although the soot-coated hearth was cold, dark, and dead. A metal cauldron hung above ash.

Tom and Basina sniffed the air. The dogs split around a table and met again on the other side, which pleased the Pyrenees.

"Dragoslav's a nasty old bastard," Blancheflor said. "He's never been different."

Toth deemed the assessment fair. He didn't argue.

As promised, Floris was behind the bar. With her red hair knotted at the top of her head, she looked forlorn and puzzled. Sweat beaded on her brow and glistened at her nose. Her blanket-wrapped doll lay on the bar between a decanter of wine and jug of ale.

As Toth neared, and as he reached into his pocket for a gulden, a familiar voice called his name from the corner of the room. He turned, searching for the source. He'd assumed the tavern empty of customers, but Andreas waved from a table in the far corner. He sat vainly in the dark, drinking alone. A stein and empty trencher rested on his table, and he was flush with sun and drink.

Toth found it curious that the manservant was absent from Groza's side.

"Dorin Toth," Andreas said, grinning wide. He pushed through chairs, leaving them askew, crossing the floor.

Tom emitted a low growl. Basina stilled, casting her alert eyes on Andreas.

Floris watched with detachment. Asleep on her feet, she'd yet to greet her sister.

"You look startled, gypsy," said Andreas. "Call off your mutts, sir."

"I can't control them," Toth warned.

Andreas waved away the danger, but his discomfort showed. In only a few words and gestures, he established his drunkenness.

"Whatever brings you here?" he asked. "I understand your kind should refrain from the delights of Bacchus, but, then again, *Bache, bene venies.* Is that how it is, gypsy? Do the mutts get ale?" He laughed.

Andreas shoved between Toth and Blancheflor, which perturbed Tom. The greyhound attempted to wedge between, but Toth grabbed his collar gently, restraining him. Basina made no pretense by offering threat. She possessed the confidence of an animal that broke bones in her jaws. Toth admired her stillness.

With a demand rather than gulden, Andreas procured a drought of wine. He used the Bishop's name, and then his fist came down against the bar, rocking the doll.

Toth offered his coin, regardless. He glanced at Floris's Loring. What had been flesh was grained wood.

Floris cupped the money, then she handed over an inelegant earthenware stein. The wine inside was warm and topped with a ring of bubbles. The heat of the day and Andreas's obnoxious proximity built a craving, so Toth drank the alcohol to the finish. It was acidic and full of water. He breathed deeply to compose himself.

"That ought to rejuvenate you for more digging, gypsy. Dr. Groza's been asking for you."

Toth looked at Floris over Andreas's wig.

"I need to speak with you, Fräulein," he said.

Floris touched the face of her doll. She said nothing.

Andreas scoffed. He grabbed Toth's arm, but Toth pulled away violently.

"Sir," Toth warned. He straightened the sleeve and lace wrist of his coat.

Tom growled. Basina rose on all fours.

Andreas looked down at the Pyrenees. Her head was higher than his waist.

"Do you not understand you're unwelcome?" Andreas asked. "I bear you no ill will, gypsy, but your place isn't here. You can't be in this establishment when a German's present. Or maidens, for that matter. You know it as well as I. Why not treat the village the same?" He looked at Blancheflor. "Why are you with this man?" he asked. "I demand to know."

"I trust him," she said.

Toth looked into the eyes of Andreas. The fire of hatred was in his chest.

"Has Groza ever told you why he loathes me so?"

"Of course. He's never met a gypsy he loved."

"It was a matter of murder, of gloves bathed in arsenic," Toth said. "He was convinced it was a case of witchcraft. I humiliated him. He's been trying to return the favor since."

"In Prague?" Andreas acted incredulous. "Ludicrous." He peered at Blancheflor. "They're slanderous people, these gypsies. I imagine you'd have to be impure to trust such a man." He licked his lips. "Are you impure?" He faced Floris. "And you, my dear? Do you trust a man raised in a caravan of dogs?" He laughed. "A man who commands fleas and ticks."

"Move aside," Toth said.

Andreas pretended to feel a sting. His mouth shriveled into a wound. "I speak for Dr. Groza now," he said, feigning sobriety. "You're expected to leave for Graz in the morning and admit your errors to von Thun. If you do, the good doctor will treat you kindly when he publishes his findings. He'll omit you, but only if you're gone come morning."

"Careful that *you're* not gone by morning," Toth said.

Andreas shook his head. "Violent creatures, these gypsies. Clanging with knives as they walk, ready for slashing. Thieving." He split his gaze between the sisters. "Whoring."

"Andreas, the only reason I do not give you violence is that you're an ignorant pig. Go to your lord," Toth said, "and succor him. Leave us be."

"Gypsy—"

"—I said leave." Toth stared. "I will no longer speak to a man who is not my equal."

"Not your equal? Sir, I will arm myself—"

"—If you want to convey a message, have Groza speak to me. I'm through tolerating an underling."

Andreas's face reddened, and his decorum slipped. "See to it that you're gone by morning, gypsy. See to it."

Toth turned his back.

From behind the bar, Floris stared without emotion.

Andreas stomped through The Cock's Foot, shaking dust from the rafters. The door parted, light entered, and then the door slammed shut.

Basina and Vinegar Tom trailed the manservant.

Andreas barked an order at Dragoslav, but its exact nature was lost in the muffling. His shouting continued up the street.

"He's a disgusting worm of a man," Floris said. "I won't repeat what he offered me in private."

"He's offered it to every woman in the village," Blancheflor said to Toth. "Some of us twice, and he hasn't yet been here a day. He's as disgusting as Dragoslav."

"He has a letter from the Bishop," Floris said, "that forces us to comply with his lust. So he claims."

"That isn't a real letter," Toth said. "He simply knows you can't read."

Alone with Cili's children, Toth rested against the bar.

"What do you know of Matthias?" he asked.

Blancheflor gave her sister a nod of approval.

Floris unwrapped Loring's face. The carving was not a fine one. The features were crude, the work of a hobbyist. A small hole for the mouth, uneven almond indentations for eyes. Ants crawled around the ear where three hairs sprouted.

"He was a man even more disgusting," said Floris. "At least Andreas presents what he feels. Matthias hid behind godliness. He was not the saint or the scholar he proposed."

"So I've gathered. Have you told her what happened to him?" Toth asked Blancheflor.

"Yes, she knows better than anyone what happened to him. Tell Master Toth what you saw before our mother's death," she said to Floris.

"I was with my mother," Floris said. She grabbed the vessel of wine, and then she poured a drought. She drank it down.

Loring's dead eyes trailed the stein to her mouth.

Toth steadied himself. "Go on," he urged.

"Perhaps, Master Toth, it is better to show you. If Matthias is dead, then his den is unguarded. I don't know who knows. I don't know if anyone knows."

Toth took the pipe from his coat. He packed the bowl with tobacco. He lit it with a candle behind the bar.

"Did Matthias kill your mother?" he asked.

"Yes," said Blancheflor.

"Does Sebastian know this?"

"No," Floris said. "We shielded him from the truth."

"Does Annalise know?"

"We have no love for Annalise," said Floris.

Toth exhaled a cloud of smoke. "But you're uncertain if she knows?"

"We suspect it," said Blancheflor.

"I want to request something from you," Toth said. "After you show me, I want you to take your brother and anyone who is willing to follow, and I want you to leave Drunstall. I want you to be on the road before nightfall."

"Why leave now?" Blancheflor asked. "With Matthias dead, is it not over?"

"It's far from over. He no longer controls what he conjured."

"Being on the road in the dark is a danger in itself," Floris said. She rubbed a smudge from Loring's face.

The rash, Toth thought. Soot spread where the pox rash had been.

"As true as that is," Toth said, "any highwayman will be less dangerous than what will befall your settlement tonight. You must leave."

"Dr. Groza?" Blancheflor asked.

"He'll be in as much danger as anyone. I'd order him to leave, too, if he wasn't obstinate. The brood that took Bertram last night will return. Tom wounded one of them grievously today."

"What are they?" Blancheflor asked.

"If what you say of Matthias is true, then they're a product of his meddling. Annalise called them 'goblins'. There is no proper word for them in your tongue, but I prefer 'changeling'."

"Changelings," Blancheflor said.

"Call them what you will. My belief is that it's a distorted soul of the dead. A trapped soul and a creature of mimicry," he said, glancing yet again at the doll. "Not unlike capturing the devil in a bottle, Floris."

The sisters were quiet. The tobacco burned to the finish. Tom watched Basina sniff under the tables, eating crumbs of stale bread.

"Will you leave for Karnstein?" Toth asked. "I'll bribe you if I must."

"What if we aren't received there?" Floris asked. "Travelers aren't welcome."

"Then huddle at the gate. Not being in this village is the only important matter tonight."

"We'll go," Blancheflor said, "but only if you say nothing of Matthias."

Toth sighed. "I can't stay silent about Matthias forever, but I'll say nothing of your involvement."

Floris wrapped Loring.

"Shall we show you then?" she asked.

XXIX
CAPITULUM

lancheflor and Floris guided Toth and the dogs from the back of the tavern toward a stone wall behind the church. Either by force or inclination, the gluttonous ravens had departed the barn, and the full-bellied beasts lofted again on the belltower, watching. The mill stood across the fields, and behind the mill Matthias's corpse awaited discovery. Toth felt the burden of its presence. Vinegar Tom sniffed the air, but Toth called him back when the dog started in that direction. Basina remained in the shade.

Covered with a square plank door, a cavity opened at the base of the wall. Blancheflor crouched with a candle from the tavern burning in her grip. When she lifted the door, a wave of cool, musty air emerged, cave-like. The room below was hacked from stone.

"Come," Floris said.

She handed Toth her doll and placed a foot on the rung of a ladder.

Toth accepted Loring gingerly. As Floris descended, he studied the face. The eyes were more lifelike than they had been in the alehouse. These were not the roughly sunk almonds. The pupils had gained definition and texture. The scrape of lashes ringed the eyes like starbursts. The mouth held complex lines like crow's feet. Twin ants moved across the lips. Another ant circled the ear. Loring seemed to squirm within the tight blanket. His leg shifted.

Tom lifted his nose.

A peculiar stench issued from the doll. Toth brought it closer to his face in an effort to determine the odor. He put his nose to the grained cheek. *Sulfur.*

A breath escaped Loring's carved lips, brushing Toth's flesh.

Toth recoiled. The mouth had not moved.

Now or never, he thought.

He unwrapped the wool, exposing the head, chest, and shoulders. Indeed, the features were of wood grain. He peeled the blanket until the wrist was exposed. The wood grain ended here. The color changed. What began, he could not say, but he had an idea. He didn't have a chance to reveal the hand.

"Give him to me!" Floris said. "Don't ogle Loring like a Peeping Tom."

Blancheflor ripped away the doll, and then she handed it to Floris at the bottom of the ladder.

"Why did you do that?" he asked, jarred. "I thought you were concerned. Why keep it hidden from me?"

"So, she found it," Blancheflor said.

"Where, you mercurial woman? Where did she find it?"

Blancheflor descended without answering the question, her flower diadem dipping from sight. The candle flickered with the draft.

You don't want to be certain, Fräulein, Toth thought. *Damn you both.* He attempted to collect himself.

To the dogs, he said, "Cause a ruckus if anyone approaches." He scratched Tom's ear and then Basina's.

With a mix of reticence, anxiety, anger, and curiosity, Toth descended the ladder.

"Mind your ribs, Tom," he said as he submerged into darkness, but his thoughts were on Loring.

The cellar, carved from limestone, was oblong in shape and quite deep. Twilight sun covered the ladder and floor below the entrance. Blancheflor's candle lit the other end feebly. The beaten planks of the church floor stood six feet from the hard pack, barely enough space for Toth to stand erect. The footfalls above shook termite dust from the crossbars. Someone paced in the nave, passing through the array of pox victims with vigor.

"She's dead," the voice said. "No, the bleeding did her no good. She's dead. Drag her out to the pit."

The din permeated the cellar.

Tom lowered his head into the opening, peering from side to side.

"Don't even consider it," Toth warned.

Tom blinked with innocence.

The cellar was a neglected hole. An assortment of barrels draped with cobwebs lined the walls. The wood was generations old and rotten, the staves warped, the innards exposed. The imperial insignia was burned into each. The center of the floor held a battered table, around which Blancheflor and Floris waited.

A mound of splinters, dead insects, and rat feces was below the slab. A machine stood on top.

Candlelight exposed Blancheflor's expression of worry. Floris was stoic and shadowed with Loring in her arms.

"Do you know what this is?" Blancheflor asked.

Toth stepped nearer. The device was familiar, but he had never seen one outside of Vienna, and he had never seen one in the possession of someone without wealth. This was an expensive rarity, a plaything for noble halls. The machine stood upright with a chamber of unlit candles at its rear and a glass lens at the fore. A platform connected lens and light. Beside the mechanism were squares of glass, transparent save for images painted at their center.

"It's called a magic lantern," Toth said. "It's not something you see often."

"What does it do?" asked Blancheflor.

"It's difficult to put into words," Toth said. "It magnifies and throws images with light. It's better to show you."

He took the candle from Blancheflor's grasp. With its flame, he lit ten candles at the back of the machine, and then he latched the chamber. A circle of light emanated from the lantern with the force of a torch. Light covered the bare wall.

"Fantastic," Blancheflor said.

With delicacy, Toth lifted a glass square. He slid it upright behind the lens of the device. He knew a magician in England, Roya Jasper, who used a magic lantern in his work with automata. Toth learned the mechanics of operation from the man. Despite its appearance of complexity, the machine was simple.

"It's marvelous," Floris admitted.

The image was a full moon with sleepy eyes and a grin. The moon was stationary against the cellar wall. Toth inserted another square of glass. Now the moon watched over a tranquil sea. A lone boat with a fisherman inside floated on the surface.

Blancheflor stepped into the light. Her shadow erased the images, casting the wall dark. She moved to the stone and touched where the moon and sea had been. When she moved from the light, the images returned. She touched the moon, and her fingers met limestone.

"It's a mechanical trick," Toth said. He looked at Floris. "Is this what you and Cili saw Matthias using?"

Gadgets like a magic lantern appear diabolic to the rural mind, he thought.

Floris shook her head in dissent, however. She walked to the table, and she rifled through the glass slides. Delicate clinking filled the cellar, an undercurrent to the footfalls above.

"This," she said.

She handed the glass to Toth.

He examined the slide in the light, and his heart thudded at the mute testimony. The painted image was a sigil, carefully drawn by hand. The lines were like those in the *Hieroglyphs of Ba'al* and stabbed into hazels. The nave, transept, apse, and diamond were the same. A magic circle surrounded the sigil, and carefully traced runes of Honorius, the medieval alphabet of magicians, edged the glass.

"Old Räum, indeed," Toth said. The name pulsed with the beat of his heart. "And worshipped thus."

Toth withdrew the moon, sea, and boat. He inserted the sigil. The cartouche-like shape spread over the wall. Black lines. Simple. The runes were etched with care. Toth was no stranger to the language of Honorius.

Adjuro was the word, spelled without the second and third vowels like ancient Hebrew.

Adjuro. I adjure.

Matthias used the magic lantern in rituals of conjuration, Toth surmised. It amounted to a marriage of technology and necromancy. *What better way to attract Old Räum, a lover of baubles?*

Toth worked to calm his mind.

"Do you understand what this symbol means?" he asked.

Neither sister answered.

"By form, it's called a sigil. It functions like a signature. The symbols are used in summoning adversarial spirits."

"The thing that stole Matthias's son?" Blancheflor asked.

"A higher power than that, I'm afraid." Toth bit his mustache. "Those creatures are but symptoms of the disease on this land." He pointed above. "The ravens, too. They're symptoms. And many other things besides. They all emanate from the same fount." He walked to the wall, avoiding the throw of light. He cast shadow only when he traced the lines of the sigil. "This is the signature of a malevolent spirit called Old Räum. A name received and accepted by a being quite powerful. I hesitate to call it demonic, because I do not think of it thus, but there are men who use the term. There are men who think Old Räum a Prince of Hell. I imagine Matthias understood Räum thus. He framed his conjuration Biblically. See here."

He lifted a slide inscribed with *Dominus et Miles.*

"Lord and Knight," Toth interpreted.

"There's more than that," Floris said.

Toth returned to the lantern and removed the sigil. Light through the wicked seal made him uncomfortable.

Floris stepped to the barrels. She worked a lid loose with her free hand. She moved to the next cask and then the next. It took four attempts to find that for which she searched.

"What was Matthias doing when you and Cili found him?" Toth asked.

"He had the symbol on the wall and many candles lit." Floris reached into the barrel, lifting a wooden box from the bottom. It was plain enough, unpainted, splintered, fastened with pegs. It covered the woman's palm and outstretched fingers. "He held this," Floris said, "and he spoke in the tongue of the Church."

Toth accepted the box. Despite its size, there was weight to it. One side had a simple hinge.

"Do you know what's inside?" Toth asked. He didn't deny his nerves. His body tensed. Hair rose on his neck.

"We've looked many times," Blancheflor admitted.

Toth opened the box. His heart was in his throat.

An earthy stench coiled from the chamber, the smell of ash and flesh. Toth extended the box into the light of the lantern. Inside, spread over the base, was a human heart ruined with fire, flaking into charred petals. Particles moved like dust from the box. The shape was coming undone, but enough of the heart remained to identify. Seared blood with the consistency of tar coated the wood.

The gravity of murder pressed Toth's thoughts, condensing his mind to the tunnel-visioned question of whom.

Why not the heart of one already dead? he countered, but intuition said otherwise. He grew faint with the implications. *Cili murdered. Matthias murdered. And this soul murdered. How many more?*

Blancheflor and Floris watched expectantly.

Toth formed the question. "To whom does the heart belong?"

Floris hugged Loring.

"There's more in the box," urged Blancheflor.

Toth placed the container on the table. With less delicacy than a surgeon, he moved pieces aside, blackening his gloves.

At the bottom, flat at the edge of the heart, was a disk with a borehole. Fire had scorched and discolored the lead. Toth pulled the medallion free, crumbling a piece of the heart. The disk was slightly larger than a coin. In his palm, he held the piece in the light.

"What does it say?" asked Blancheflor.

"It's an identification tag," Toth said. "For imperial troops going to battle."

One side of the disk was engraved with the oath of allegiance to Emperor Leopold Habsburg. A crucifix was carved into the soft metal. Toth read the perfunctory note. On the opposite side was a name and station of base.

"Merrick Weltz," Toth read, his graveled tone filling the room. "Schloss Greinberg."

He stared between Cili's children.

Dust fell from the rafters as someone above dragged a mat and body.

"Annalise's Merrick," echoed Blancheflor, but she was neither shocked nor saddened.

"Did Matthias have reason to harm Merrick? Was it the same reason he harmed your mother?"

"He believed our mother a witch," Floris said quietly. "He believed our mother afflicted him. I doubt he believed that of Merrick."

"What is Castle Greinberg?" Toth asked. "And where is it?"

"It's a fortress," Blancheflor said.

"It's the rendezvous point for soldiers when the beacon is lit," Floris added.

A fortress to protect the road to Graz, Toth thought. *Like many others.*

"The Turks destroyed it," said Blancheflor. "It's in ruins, I hear."

Toth's mind went to work. He paced to the ladder, leaving the box on the table, wringing the amulet under his scarf. The air was lighter, his breathing easier. Tom and Basina lay at the mouth of the hole, paws draped, gazing down.

"The worship was here in the village, but the summoning was not. The thing called Old Räum," Toth said, "hides where? Where was he summoned?"

Schloss Greinberg, he reasoned.

He looked across the cellar with determination. Light lay across his broad shoulders.

"You'll leave for Karnstein tonight. I have an additional request," Toth said to Floris. "You do not have to tell me when and where you found that creature you hold, or why you keep it, but I want you to destroy it. Throw it in the river if you must. Or burn it."

"Why would I do such a thing to Loring?"

"It's a changeling. Given time, it will grow. The days of its flesh will be more than its days of wood."

Floris said nothing, but she glared, and she gripped the doll tighter.

"And you know this as well as I," Toth said to Blancheflor.

XXX
CAPITULUM

The physician left his horse, and he marched from the barn to the church, his cape trailing in the wind. Andreas walked in his stead. Two masked men followed down the trail.

"What is this call to evacuate?" Groza shouted.

Annalise was the last to leave the plague pit. The task was incomplete, the mound of flesh hooked, dragged, and moved to the ditch but left uncovered. Angrily, she placed her spade against the scarlet crucifix on the wall of the barn. She slipped off her mask of spiced fragrance.

Below, fronting the corral, Blancheflor prepared a wooden-wheeled ox cart for departure. Rather than sheaves of wheat, four children filled its bed like refugees. A few men and women moved busily around the wheels. Blancheflor was gesturing and directing. Two plow horses were harnessed to the cart. Despite Groza's hostility, a mass evacuation it was not. More men stood on the porch of the alehouse, holding steins.

Dusk spread over the river, closing in on the village. Insects clouded the fields. The ravens sat stationary, patient for the night.

A breeze stroked the sweat in Annalise's hair, and a chill went through her body.

"Where is the gypsy?" Groza demanded, his voice distant, his shouts so ubiquitous now that they were part of the environment.

Groza was a blustering toad of a man, the opposite of Dorin Toth. Annalise scanned the crowd, but she saw no sign of Toth or his hounds. She had no trust for the physician, but she had to wonder at the level of trust she put in the occultist. Toth was confident, even arrogant, and his quiet certainty inspired belief. He was a man of books and ink, and he was a man, he'd shown, of blood. She would've doubted the latter, doubted it to the point of ridicule, if she hadn't seen him wield a dagger and pierce flesh. Ferocity hid behind his velvet mask.

Master Toth put himself in danger to protect you, Annalise thought. *Would Groza? Of course, he wouldn't. He'd hide behind a tombstone. The blustering is empty. Andreas, doubtlessly, would unite with the attacker. Would your father help? No, he wouldn't. Would anyone down there do the same as Toth?*

Heavy with exhaustion, Annalise wiped sweat from her forehead. Dirt caked her hands. Her fingers and forearms buzzed from hours of digging. Long exposure to rot and spice numbed her senses.

Evacuation, she thought. *A handful of souls. To where? How far could they go?*

Annalise moved to the pit, mask in hand. With the work of ten, the trench was dug in a day. The pit stretched fifteen feet in the length and dropped five feet. Groza could not be faulted for his generalship in that regard. He forced people to action. Still, the burial was incomplete. The gas-bloated corpses, split and peeled by ravens, were at the bottom of the pit, arranged face-down in layers, stacked, waiting to be hidden with earth. Maggots wriggled in their folds. Scraps of clothing, tufts of hair, broken-jawed expressions, open eyes on turned faces—all these things inspired memories. If she stared long enough at the mound, she saw friends and relatives rather than piles of decay: she saw life in death.

A fresh corpse, that of a young girl who died from Groza's bleeding, was the most pitiful and heart-wrenching sight of all. Apolonia had died that very day. Her older brother, Nikolaus, helped cover her with small shovelfuls of earth.

Stay the night and hide them, Annalise had urged, but the men fell away, retreating to ale at the tavern. *Wolves will drag them into the forest*, she'd pleaded. With the barn cleared, Groza lost interest. *There are few wolves in these mountains*, the physician said. A simple layer of dirt on flesh satisfied he and Andreas. The rest would wait for morning.

When a voice moved through the wood, scattering Annalise's thoughts, despair wrapped her heart.

It was not the voice of Merrick, but the voice of her father.

"Crawl to me," Matthias said. "Anna the Gravedigger. Anna with a spade in her hand."

A changeling, she thought, recalling Toth's words. *Mimicry. What if Master Toth is wrong?*

Annalise pretended to be unbothered by her father's absence, but it was only to soothe her mind. The thought of losing her brother and her father in a matter of hours was unbearable. It wasn't real. This voice, though, was very real. It wormed into her mind, igniting hope.

She walked closer to the tree line, despite fear. The foreboding shadow of the forest exerted its pull.

"Crawl to me, Anna. Come to your father."

Annalise dropped the mask and walked into the wood. She descended the trail to the burning hole in the earth.

"Crawl to me, Anna," the voice beckoned.

A column of heat shot upward, shaking the limbs of an overhanging tree. The air at the lip was distorted into waves. In the mud she spied a rope. A broken end, charred black, lay in the muck. The other end snaked into the weeds. Movement in the undergrowth made her skin crawl.

She tensed, turning, half-believing Matthias would be there, half-believing Toth's changelings would emerge.

Annalise paused.

It was an animal. A crouched black figure moved through ropes of dead briar. It was a dog.

Vinegar Tom, she thought.

She whistled. The thing acknowledged the call, but it proceeded so slowly, shifting with great pain. The animal inched, dragging itself. It was tall for a dog. The crouched shape was unnatural.

Annalise whistled again. Her first thought was that the flame of the pit had scorched Toth's hound. When the animal was only yards away, however, her heart lurched. The black exterior was not fur. It was burned flesh.

A horrible face turned to her, and Annalise recognized the eyes, naked of char. The eyes belonged to Father Haas. With skin hanging in ribbons from his bones, dangling like strips of worm, the priest crawled toward the road. The man was a husk. His thigh was as thin as a branch. His legs, eaten away, were gnawed stumps, ending jaggedly at the knees.

The voice of Matthias came from the wood again.

"Crawl to me, Anna."

Father Haas came nearer, struggling through the thorns. The rope was knotted around his waist. He rasped.

"Help me, Annalise," said the priest.

In revulsion, Annalise stepped back, moving from the pit toward the barn.

Haas collapsed in a pile, crying out in agony, his face wrenched, crumbling into the dirt.

Matthias's voice continued on the wind.

"Crawl to me, Anna. Crawl to me."

Haas clawed the earth, propelling himself forward with his arms, his brittle skin flaking away.

"Help Father Haas, Anna," said Matthias. "Help him. Lift him. Comfort him."

When Annalise could take no more, she ran.

XXXI
CAPITULUM

The man in the mask fell, crumpling as though his legs were reduced to cartilage. He struck the ground with the force of unconsciousness. The mask's protuberance of a nose snapped under his weight, and rosemary spilled against the dirt. The box he carried tumbled free, rolling over once and opening. Vials crashed. Precious blood soaked the lane. Those moving in concert around the man stopped, but none of his fellows tried to help. Disbelief held sway.

An alert raven was the first to react, gliding down from the belfry. The bird navigated shattered glass, dipping its beak in clumps of bloody earth.

Drunken Andreas screamed vitriol at the lad for his clumsiness. He preceded Groza from the church, waving his arms with rage. The masked few turned to watch the manservant. Andreas lifted a burning torch pinned by the entrance. He brandished the flame as he yelled, throwing droplets of fire.

The young man did not respond. Unmoving, he lay injured.

Or ill, Toth thought.

He returned his attention to Blancheflor and Sebastian in the front of the cart. He handed a lantern to the boy. Fire burned behind the glass. A halo of light spread to the horses.

"Where is Floris?" Toth asked.

"Floris isn't leaving," Blancheflor said. There was pain behind the words. She gripped the reins.

Not many are, Toth thought, frustrated. In the past hour, the number of evacuees decreased from eight to six, from pathetic to woeful. It was a miniscule segment of Drunstall. Four children orphaned by the plague joined Blancheflor and Sebastian. That was all.

Toth doubted that Groza influenced Floris to stay. She possessed, he feared, reasons beyond. *The changeling doll,* he thought, and he regretted the sensation of a layer of wood, thin as hide, writhing against his arm, of breath escaping fixed lips.

"Unfortunately, there's no time to convince Floris otherwise," Toth said. "So be it. Leave, and Godspeed to you."

Blancheflor hesitated. The children in the back of the cart murmured fear.

The road ahead darkened with the approach of another storm.

"Think of your brother," Toth said. "Floris will fend for herself more capably than he."

Sebastian didn't protest. He shifted the lantern, uncomfortable.

Blancheflor nodded. "Master Toth?"

"Yes?"

"Godspeed to you, too."

"I'll need it," Toth said. "Thank you."

Sebastian handed Toth the linen seal crafted by Cili.

"Will we see you again?" asked Blancheflor.

"I hope so," said Toth.

Dusk deepened. The mountains disappeared from the skyline.

With a flick of Blancheflor's wrist, the horses started forward. Hoofs slopped through the muck. The wooden wheels groaned. When the cart rolled past the last of the homes, gaining the road to the Karnstein fork, Toth returned his attention to the church.

Basina and Tom were at the scene of the fallen man. A few strays hung at their heels, forming a ragtag pack. Tom moved well, without pain.

Groza followed Andreas from the church. Uncharacteristically, the physician was exhausted into silence. He pushed through two women, and he knelt beside the young man. He lifted the head and removed the mask. He felt for a breath and pulse.

Andreas waited at Groza's side, red-faced, kicking after a raven, lamenting the loss of precious blood. The torch burned in his grip, crackling, casting harsh light over the nearby faces. Smoke coiled into the air. Andreas did not see the man in the dirt, nor care. He saw the loss of a day's labor, a day's bleeding.

Toth approached the throng.

"The pox rash is on this young man," Groza said. He gestured at a streak of vermillion near the temple. The case was already advanced. That the man had worked through the day, regardless, did not bode well for his chance of defeating the illness. Pox would consume him tonight, erupting over his skin.

"Ambrus," a woman said, offering the man's name.

Groza had no care for names. Here was another victim. Here was one for the ledger. Here was another to replace the girl he lost in the makeshift hospital.

Male, 20, deceased. Toth envisioned the note scratched into a journal.

"Ready a pallet," Groza ordered. "And find someone with the strength to carry him inside. He'll need close attention." The physician stood. "How many of you are hiding pox?" he asked. "How many of you are infected and say nothing?"

"Come away," Toth said to the dogs.

Tom acknowledged the call, but Basina ignored it.

Groza locked on Toth. He gestured at the gate and road.

"And you'd have them carry the disease to the four corners of the globe," he said. "How many people departed this village tonight?"

"Six children," Toth said. "I wish it were more."

Groza shook his head. "To deliver pox to Karnstein," he chided. "And beyond when they're turned from the gate. Why not grind scabs into their food?"

"I must speak with you in private, Kaspar," Toth said.

"I don't grant you the privilege," said Groza. He peered at the motionless onlookers. "I said I need men with strength to move this fellow inside."

Two masked men came forward. They strained to lift Ambrus from the dirt. They, too, were ill.

"You worked them too hard," Toth said.

Groza sneered.

Andreas shook his torch, and beads of flame became embers, drifting to the ground.

"I'll speak to you, gypsy," said the manservant. "I'll tell you what you need to hear if you'd be so humble as to lower yourself to my standard." He laughed.

Toth ignored him.

Tom, however, raised his hackles. Basina shifted her eyes.

With the assistance of a third man, Ambrus was escorted into the church. Groza departed, absorbed and unreachable.

Andreas extended the torch, barring Toth from trailing the physician. The flame leapt, and shadows moved over the dogs.

"Gypsy, I—"

Whatever insult he had loaded went unspoken. Toth smacked the manservant in the mouth, mashing his lips against teeth.

Andreas's eyes went wide, but he did not move to fight back.

Toth stood over him.

The crowd susurrated.

"I'll see that you burn for that, gypsy," said Andreas. "You *dare* lay your hand on a German."

"I have had enough of you. I warned you not to speak to me," Toth said. "Consider that a second warning. And consider it the last."

Andreas spat blood. A line of red crossed his teeth.

"You're fortunate that I—"

Toth clenched his fist and Andreas flinched, but it was not the threat that cut off the manservant. Rather, a scream from the tithe barn sliced through the village, leaving anyone within earshot cold. A hush fell between sound and spasm.

The dogs reacted first.

"This isn't over," Andreas said, but Toth had his back to the man.

Annalise sprinted out of the forest, emerging like bas-relief from the darkness.

"I saw the priest," she screamed. "I saw Father Haas."

"Haas is dead," said a man.

When two lads tried to restrain Annalise, she split between them, running the distance to Toth. She stopped with force, gripping him like a raft on the open sea.

Toth embraced her.

"Father Haas," Annalise said. "I saw him, Master Toth. I saw him."

"You're certain of that?" Toth asked.

"He was burned," Annalise said. "He was barely living." She looked in Toth's eyes. "He crawled from one of the holes in the ground."

The revelation gave Toth pause. *Burned like Cili, Matthias, and Merrick,* he thought. *Did Matthias murder Haas, as well?*

"You're saying Father Haas has returned to us?" someone asked.

"The priest is dead," Andreas countered. He walked forward, nursing the blood on his lip. "Bishop von Thun knows it thus. This girl stokes fear for the gypsy. She's in his employ. Look how they confer with comfort. No doubt she comforts the Magyar in other ways."

"She's crazy like her old man," another said. It was Dragoslav. He wheezed.

"Everyone, you must shelter in place tonight," Toth said. "Go to your homes or go to the church."

"Pay him no mind," said Andreas. "He'll be leaving you soon enough."

"Come with me," Toth said to Annalise.

Men parted as Toth led Annalise to her home. Tom and Basina followed, while the other dogs ventured into the wood to explore. The villagers, steered by Andreas, retreated to the church, talking loudly, obnoxiously, of Annalise's madness and Toth's primitive anger.

"There was a rope tied to his waist," Annalise said. "The other end was burned at the pit."

The house was dark, the shutters open, the door closed.

"The rope was burned black," Annalise said. "As was the priest. He asked me to help him. He was in agony."

"If it's Father Haas," Toth said, "and not a changeling, his fate is sealed. He's beyond help. We must shelter tonight."

The dogs hung back while Toth opened the door. The slab creaked. Tom wanted to be with the strays, hunting the wood, exploring. Basina was content to remain and guard.

The interior of the house was stygian and hot. The timber columns had the shape of men waiting in the dark.

Annalise turned her saturnine face to Toth's. Inches separated them. Toth felt her warmth, and he smelled the dried sweat of her labor.

"I heard my father's voice," she said. "I was following it when I found Haas."

Toth's mind went to the old man's corpse in the river. When was it right to tell the daughter of Matthias? When was it wrong to withhold? He formed the confession of Matthias's death but left it unsaid. He moved from the woman, and he groped for candlesticks in the dark. The dogs rushed inside.

Annalise waited at the threshold, watching the river. When the room was lit, Toth led her to the bed.

Toth gathered feed and placed it on the floor for the hounds, and then he fastened the door and the shutters, closing out the night. A semblance of safety overcame him, and he relaxed his demeanor. The candles cast orbs at the corners of the room. The columns lost their mystique.

"Describe Haas to me," Toth said. "The way he was in life."

Annalise stared at the wall. "My father said he was simple and dimwitted. He said only dunce priests ended up in mountain villages."

"Was he as your father said?"

"No, it wasn't true. Father Haas was a charming man. He had a kind heart. Master Toth, it was horrible to see him that way. What happened to him?"

Toth stifled the accusation of murder. Instead, he asked, "Was the priest curious like your father? You said he brought home one of the changelings."

"He often walked in the wood," she said. "He was the first to bring back one of those things."

"Do you mean others did the same?"

"Not intentionally," Annalise said.

Such as Floris, Toth thought, *who brought one home after it had begun the process of change. How many others suffered these unique agonies?*

"Is Haas foolish enough to crawl inside one of the pits?"

"I think not." Annalise gripped her head, distracted. "Who would?"

"Would your father push him? Why did Matthias do the terrible things that he did, Anna? I know he is responsible for all of this."

Annalise looked up. Her mouth tightened. Red ringed her eyes.

"What would I find if I ripped up these floorboards and dug in the walls?" Toth persisted.

"You've been listening to Cili's children."

"Yes, I have. I have, indeed, Fräulein."

Annalise wiped tears from her cheek. She rose from the bed and walked to a corner of the room. She moved aside a stone in the wall, and then she reached inside the cavity. Candlelight pulsed at her back.

"You would find a great deal in these walls. Cili's family called my father *le meneur de loups,*" she said.

"Yes. The Leader of Wolves. A conjuror."

"Cili called him that first. She often hissed it at him in the street. Do you know what Cili and her children call me?"

"No."

"*Salope des loups.* Slut of the wolves."

Annalise pulled two items from the hole: a manuscript and a small box. The book's pages were waterlogged and curled. The box was a twin of that hidden with the magic lantern beneath the church. When she returned to the bed, she handed both to Toth.

"*Sworn Book of Honorius.* This is a grimoire," he said. "One must open it with a desire in mind. Whatever the answer, you'll find it in the so-called runes of Honorius. This is a strange text, a dangerous book, for a Christian to possess. You admitted he was a diviner. But he was more, wasn't he? What was it that Matthias coveted so that he would turn to this?"

"His wife," Annalise said. "My mother. He wanted his family returned because she was taken from him."

"Matthias conjured something. Did he do it to bring your mother back from the dead? Did he transform the earth so that he could bury her in it and watch her rise?"

"You don't know the depths of it. He worked for months, Master Toth. Open the box. See the depths of that which he was capable."

Toth unlatched the wooden container.

"Your mother died before pox struck?" he asked.

"An entire year before. I first heard him in the wood. He dragged my mother out there while she yet lived, and he shouted into the dark. He said, 'Take back this woman, who is sick and belongs to you, and return my wife, whom you have stolen.'"

"To whom did he speak?"

"Cili the Witch."

The box held a cache of medallions, each of which belonged to an imperial soldier stationed at Schloss Greinberg. The names ran together, and all were unfamiliar to Toth. He passed them through his hands like coins.

"What is the meaning of these?" Toth asked.

"He overturned an entire crypt to acquire those tags. He never did wash the grave dirt from his hands."

Chips of bargain, Toth wondered. *Or memento mori. Or baubles for Old Räum.*

"I assume you've searched for Merrick's name in the pile."

"I have." She shook her head.

"How distant is Schloss Greinberg?" Toth asked.

"Four leagues toward the mountains," said Annalise.

"Did Matthias travel there often?"

"He took my mother there, when she was ill."

The conclusion arrived in whole, entrenching like Toth had always known it as fact.

Drunstall is the site of worship, he intuited, *but Greinberg is the site of summoning. Old Räum hides in the fortress.*

"What was it, may I ask, that killed your mother?"

"Cili and Loring killed her. The incestuous garbage. They poisoned her with a shrove cake. Haas had no interest in witchery. He refused to investigate. My father took his concerns to the magistrate in Voitsberg, but nothing was done."

Toth set the manuscript and box aside.

"My father didn't intend any of this," said Annalise.

"Did Matthias kill Haas?"

"I've long suspected it, although this is the first time I've uttered it."

"Did he kill Merrick?"

"No. Merrick died a soldier. He died fighting the Turks."

I can't bring myself to tell you, Toth thought. He left the matter of Merrick's charred heart unspoken.

"I want—"

"—Hold," Annalise said. Trepidly, she walked to the center of the room.

The dogs lifted their heads.

"Listen," she said. She wiped a tear from her cheek.

Toth listened. To his astonishment, he heard a voice outside the walls of the house. The voice was his own, as though he stood in the street, calling in, calling for Annalise.

XXXII

CAPITULUM

At first, the words were indistinct. The voice. The accent. The learned inflection. They were the same.

"An echo," Toth said, tempering fear that spread in his heart.

Annalise shook her head. She was correct to deny him. The voice spoke when Toth was silent. The words were not his words, but the voice was his.

Tom heard it, and the paradox unsettled the hound. He uncurled and stood. He tilted his head at the shutters.

The planks on the window rattled with a touch. It was a prodding of exploration rather than demand, and the force emanated from outside.

The voice was so close now, the words were clear.

"Anna, come nearer. Crawl to me, Anna." Thus spoke Dorin Toth.

Astonishing, he thought, and it was the mortal terror of a ghost outside the flesh that bound his heart. It was a fear of existence.

Toth gathered himself. He whispered to Anna.

"Is this what your father said to you? Is this what Merrick said?"

She wiped at her eyes. Tears streaked her hands. Behind the struggle, she nodded.

Basina joined Tom at the wall.

A hand outside the window worked the shutter, pulling harder, shaking the latch. The odor through the walls was the fragrance of the river, and decay was at its core.

"Anna, come nearer," said the voice of Toth. "Crawl to me, Anna."

Basina shocked the room to action when she released a single bark, deep, guttural, and sharp. She raised on her hind legs and smashed rock-hardened paws against the shutters, snapping the latch and splitting them wide. Outward the boards swung, and night entered the room with a rush that extinguished a candle.

In wonder, Toth looked upon the shape of Matthias standing at the window. His hands dripped and his clothes were soddened. His neck was bent, and the side of his skull had a hole the size of a fist. Maggots writhed in his beard. His skin was burned black. The mouth curled.

It was from Matthias that Toth's voice issued. The man opened his mouth to reveal wasps packed in his throat.

Old Räum's ink and Old Räum's voice. Legions indeed.

"Anna, come nearer. Crawl to me, Anna," the changeling mimicked through the vibration of insect wings.

The voice was Toth's. Then the voice was that of Matthias. Then it was the voice of Merrick. The taunting words were the same.

"Anna, come nearer. Crawl to me, Anna."

Matthias stared through dead eyes coated black. Something long and thin like a snake slithered from the wound over his ear.

"It's but mimicry," Toth cautioned.

Annalise looked at her father in awe, and her horror pulsed in silence.

"Your father is dead," Toth said.

"I am here," said Matthias.

The soldier with a face of glass appeared in the darkness then, shuffling from the window to the door. He emerged like a touch of fog at Matthias's shoulder, materializing out of the night. Light glinted on his skin. Fungus grew under his eyes.

Toth leapt and threw his weight against the door. His mind rushed with panic.

The soldier tested the slab with a push. And then came a stronger, more desperate thrust. The door heaved inward, unbalancing Toth.

Tom and Basina were unsatisfied with waiting. The Pyrenees, erect with her paws on the sill, standing tall as a man, leapt through the hole with one terrific plunge. Her hind legs landed on the sill, and then she darted out, her massive back a blur of white.

Stirred to bloodlust, Tom mirrored her boldness. He, too, gained the sill and leapt, damning the scabbed wound at his ribs.

Matthias was the target of their anger. Basina unhinged her jaws, showing a wide mouth full of teeth. She clamped the old man's wrist, grinding as she bit down. Matthias's dead-eyed stare turned wild, animated, and his mouth parted with a shriek that flooded Drunstall. It was the same mandrake scream as the changeling by the cemetery.

With pain, Matthias began to morph, losing shape. The protuberance in Basina's mouth turned from the burned flesh of a man to the claw with a crucifixion wound in its palm.

The door heaved, harder still. Toth's boots slipped back on the floor. Annalise, jarred to the reality of the moment, rushed to join him, throwing her weight against the slab. The timber columns rattled.

The changeling fought to free its arm from the Pyrenees. It shrieked again. With its neck unprotected, Tom darted upward with precision, biting flesh. Tom sank his teeth into a wound already raw.

The figure diminished in size, and its clothes changed into a robe of burgundy and grey. The thing swung its free hand at the Pyrenees, but the effect was that of smacking a fist against a boulder. The meat on its arm opened as Basina reached bone. Once locked, the dog could not be budged. The changeling swung again to no avail, screeching.

Tom caught the free hand, and he bit down. He shook it with violence to snap bones.

With surprising strength, the soldier cracked the door-frame, opening a fissure. In shot his arm, lodging between. Toth pushed harder to smash the limb, but the arm was inside to the elbow, and the door was too thin for severing.

The hand was webbed, creating twin protuberances like a malformed claw. A bed of mushroom-like fungus grew from the palm. The soldier grasped at Toth's coat.

"Through the window, Fräulein!" Toth said.

At that moment, the soldier withdrew his arm. The door slammed shut. The creature lumbered toward his fallen companion.

He was, Toth realized, after Vinegar Tom. The realization brought a surge of rage. Toth's mind went red.

"My father keeps a hatchet," Annalise said.

"Get it," Toth ordered. "Now."

Annalise moved through the room. She rummaged, pushing over a chamber pot, and she pulled free the stout hatchet of a woodsman. The blade was dark and oiled. The handle was hickory. Toth took the weapon. It had a fine weight for cleaving.

"I want you to run to Karnstein. Go to the chateau there," he said. "Don't stop running until you're at the gate."

Before Annalise protested, Toth pulled open the door. He peered into the night. Basina had the creature on the ground, stomping at its chest and ripping its face and neck. Tom was gone toward the darkness of the fields, and the soldier followed. The hound was leading the creature away from his master.

Wrath blotted Toth's fear. As he passed through the gate into the lane, Basina looked up from the changeling. The creature was unconscious, its face and throat in ruin. The skin was translucent, all mimicry bled from its form. The Pyrenees was full of blood, bristling and huge. Along with Toth, she started after Tom.

"Make haste," Toth told Basina.

Tom emerged from the wheat crop and rushed to the shore, slopping through mud and darting around sarsens.

The soldier chased the greyhound, driven with tunnel vision. The metal of his plates clamored through the shadows.

Toth was twice the speed of the lumbering changeling. He cut through stalks of wheat, emerging on the shore. When he neared the soldier, fear pushed back on his anger. His chest tightened. It was not only the soldier's proximity that frightened him. Toth witnessed another attack emerging from the river.

Toader, the giant hidden beneath a monk's habit, was at the waterline, pulling something large and glistening from the current. The cowl had fallen from his skull. The skin was slick, the head bald, the face pinched. Toader crushed the thing that he dragged with a hammer strike of his fist. In a cacophony, insects swarmed into the night. A dark orb formed over the water, growing to the size of the mill. It was an orb of wasps. Their buzzing cut through the village.

The ravens mirrored the insects, lifting into the air. Hundreds of birds filled the sky, black against the black storm clouds churning at the rim of the mountains.

Villagers poured from their homes.

Fire erupted at The Cock's Foot. Flames engulfed thatch, reaching into the trees. The heat made the animals wild, and pigs and horses escaped their corrals.

Tom sprinted until he touched the water, and then the greyhound of Kent turned with deep courage to face the advancing soldier.

Despite his effort at heroics, Vinegar Tom did not face the soldier alone.

Basina and Toth came running from behind.

When the soldier neared Tom, Toth damned himself, ducked his shoulder, and rammed into the back of the moldering creature. The soldier fell with a crash, splashing into the river. Tom leapt out of the way. Toth was on top of the thing, keeping the hatchet up so as not to cleave himself. Basina stomped through water, putting herself between Tom and the melee.

The soldier attempted to throw Toth by turning onto his shoulder, but the Hungarian managed to stabilize himself. He pressed his knee into the thing's back, smashing its chest against the mud beneath the river. Water splashed in a torrent as the soldier and Toth struggled.

Toth swung the hatchet. The first blow cleaved into the back of the skull, opening bone at the base. The creature screeched with the same timbre as its companion. Toth swung again, this time with balance. The blade struck the neck clean, and it dropped an inch into meat and cartilage. Muddy effluvium seeped from the wound, mixing with the water. The stench was atrocious, that of fungus in dead meat.

Possessed, Toth swung again, splashing the current. The neck cleaved further, splitting like a stalk of rhubarb beneath the weight of the ferocious blow. Toth swung again and again as the soldier's fight weakened, his resistance lessened, his force waned. With a final strike, nothing but sinew connected the head. Toth grabbed hair and ripped until the head was severed from the body. He released his grasp and the skull drifted into the current, floating wild-eyed, as the trunk contaminated the river with its filth. Tapeworms squirmed from the open throat into the water.

Toth rose, heaving, struggling for air. As water rushed around his boots, he checked Tom's safety. The greyhound and Pyrenees stood side by side on the shore, dark ichor coloring Basina's fur. She guarded Tom.

Toth's breath escaped in short gasps. With no time to think, he stared back into the night. He did not find Annalise, but Groza and Andreas were in the lane on the opposite side of the fields, shouting orders to men who ran for escape. The ravens crashed into walls, bashing themselves against stone. The wasps swarmed open doors.

Grau, garbed in black, exited the church. He and Toader advanced, converging on Groza and Andreas.

If you're too ignorant to flee, thought Toth, *so be it. Make peace with God, Kaspar.*

Annalise waited by the gate, watching the wasps and ravens that invaded her home. Toth hurried from the water, ducking past a sarsen that glistened black from the current's spray. Swiftly, the dogs followed.

I doubt anything can harm you, Toth thought, admiring the hulking Pyrenees.

Basina rolled her shoulders with pride as she ran.

The first wasp barb, a hot pinch that throbbed in his neck, found Toth. And then another strike landed behind his ear. He brushed off the buzzing, writhing insects, stuck in his hairline.

"Anna, we must leave," Toth shouted.

A crowd rushed around Annalise, sprinting toward the gate of broken wood. The road from Drunstall was thick with refugees. No one escorted the pox victims to safety. Those suffering were left behind in the church.

"Anna, take the dogs and go with those men."

Shaken from her stupor, she asked, "Dorin, what about you?"

Toth searched his person, making certain he'd lost nothing in the water. The amulet hung below his scarf. He gripped the hatchet in his fist.

When he looked down the lane, he saw that another fire had erupted in one of the homes against the hillside.

"I must help them first." Chest heaving, he asked, "Whose home is it that burns?"

Annalise counted down the row.

"Cili's," she said.

"Dear Christ. Floris." Toth turned to run. "Take the dogs and go," he said.

Without hesitation, Annalise, Tom, and Basina sprinted after him rather than away.

"Senki sem hallgat rám?" Toth shouted. *Is no one listening to me?*

Ahead, flames on the consumed thatch ignited the hillside, spreading through a patch of nettle. The blaze neared the neighboring roof.

In front of the church, Groza shouted, "Show them von Thun's letter, Andreas! And fetch my pistols."

The manservant was frozen in place. A hundred wasps draped his arm, coating it red. His eyes were lost in agony, and his mouth was agape. A tremor through his jaws was his only motion.

"God damn you," Groza said. "Sirs, depart this village. You have no right to be here."

The giant descended upon the physician.

Groza arched his back in defiance.

As Toth watched in horror, Toader struck the doctor with his open hand, knocking the man's wig to the mud. When Groza doubled over in pain, Toader grabbed him at the armpits and lifted him from the earth. He bit at his chest, ripping silk. The glow of flame was between the toe of Groza's boot and the ground.

Ravens flew close, ringing the physician and his manservant.

Rather than assist his master, Andreas went to his knees to beg life. The wasps reached his neck and chest, growing by the second. No one remained to help. The masked men were gone. Andreas and the physician were alone.

Toader bit Groza on the mouth, aborting his protest, aborting his scream.

Grau, cadaverous with shadow, swollen at the back of his skull with the poison of wasps, pushed through the circle of ravens. He stepped to Andreas and stood above him. Grau was more methodical than his companion. There was delight in the cruelty of his slowness.

Toth ran to the immense heat of the fire. Ravens swirled in smoke above Cili's home, adding to the terrible din of the night.

The roof burned, and the columns within were streaked with flame, but the stone façade had yet to catch. The doorway was free of fire. The shutters burned like torches.

Toth stepped to the door, looking over the threshold. Through rolling smoke, he spied Floris on a lone chair in the middle of the room. Black smoke engulfed her form. Fire ran the length of the rafters, dripping like wax to the floorboards.

Floris rocked in the chair, back and forth, speaking in the rhythm of hymns to her child.

Loring squealed, cried, and squirmed.

"Flee while you have a path, Fräulein!" Toth shouted through the doorway.

Indeed, the route from chair to door was clear of flame, but it was a path that would only last moments. Soon the floor would erupt with fire, and the flames below would embrace the flames above.

Floris refused to move. She rocked in the chair, back and forth, back and forth, obscured by smoke.

Shrieking Hell, Toth thought.

"Keep those dogs back!" he shouted at Annalise.

The matter of living with himself, of duty and pride, pushed Toth into the danger of the burning hovel. He crashed through smoke, lunging at Floris in the chair. He grabbed her arm, which was so hot that it burned through his glove.

The swaddled changeling, the bottom of its blanket ignited, lay cradled in her arms, crying. The wooden face was contorted, the mouth parted. Hundreds of ants streamed from the orifices in black swaths, frantic.

Toth pulled Floris to her feet. Smoke invaded his lungs and burned his eyes.

"We must leave," he urged, coughing, choking. He shook Floris.

A flap on the blanket opened, revealing the chest of the doll. Ghastly pale flesh covered the ribs.

Floris shifted her eyes to Toth. When she stole a glance at the open door, Toth acted. He ripped Loring from her grasp, stripping its blanket. The body was a mix of wood and flesh, marbled from the neck to jointed knees. It possessed claws that were sharp and transparent to the bone. A trapped wasp writhed inside one of its fingers, granting motion. The feet were black with ants.

Toth threw the changeling into the flames.

"No!" Floris said.

A piercing cry escaped the fire.

A change came over Floris then, as if she woke from a dream. Toth pulled her free of the door, into the open night. The air was a salve to his beaten lungs.

Grau and Toader took notice of Loring's scream. In unison, the ghouls turned their rat-eyes to the fire, and they rose from the bodies of Groza and Andreas, spasming in the mud. One by one, ravens landed on the corpses.

Blood covered Grau's mouth, neck, and hands. The blood glistened in firelight.

"We *must* go," Toth said to Annalise. "We can lose them in the wood."

When screaming died inside the fire, Floris looked from the flames to Toth. Rather than concede and depart, she did the opposite.

"Loring!" Floris cried.

She dashed through the door into a wall of fire. She dropped to her knees and buried her hands in burning ash, screaming in agony but persisting. Her red hair caught, and then her back. She dug for Loring until she collapsed, and then flames ate through the woman.

Toth stood in awe.

"Another child of pluck," said Grau from behind.

The moment, the connection, left Toth altered. He felt Grau dig in his heart, scrape his mind. The sensation was physical.

Toader whimpered like a smashed dog. His eyes were incapable of expressing depth of hate. He stared with nothingness.

Tom and Basina shrank against Annalise.

Grau stopped. He locked on Toth. Fire reflected in his dark eyes.

Flee, damn you, Toth thought, stealing a glance at the dogs and Annalise. The flames were hot at his back.

"Yes," Grau rasped. "Flee, damn you. You have no place here, Dorin Toth. Why do you guard the Child of Matthias?"

Toth gathered the courage to speak. *This is an abomination,* he thought. *Stand and face it.*

"Yes, an abomination, child of pluck. Stand your ground. Why do you not allow a scourge to run its course?"

"I have no other purpose," said Toth, "but to collect devils."

"Come nearer," said Grau. "Crawl to me."

"You're weak, Grau. Your companion opened like a rotten gourd." Toth touched the hatchet at his waist. Gore covered the blade.

Grau looked at the weapon.

"Kill his animal," he told Toader.

"Who were you in life, Grau?" Toth asked, backing closer to the fire. The heat reddened his neck and scalp. "Or are you simply a thought from Old Räum?"

Grau's black lips curled into a smile.

Toader lunged for Vinegar Tom then, and the greyhound jumped back, spurring Annalise and Basina to run. Toth ran, too, fleeing a budding storm of raven, wasp, and fire.

Grau and Toader followed as far as their fallen companion. Toader dropped to his knees beside the gutted corpse, hammering at the exposed ribs, shattering what remained. He bellowed with rage—a sound that pressed the dogs closer to the ground.

XXXIII
CAPITULUM

Storm clouds blotted out the moon, leaving the footpath treacherous. Wind gusted through the forest, overturning leaves, casting pale shoals on the trees. Rain began with a drop that spotted Toth's glove. Thunder moved over the hills.

"Hold," he whispered. His lungs burned from running.

When Toth left the trail, Annalise and the dogs halted.

After crossing through wind-bent grass, Toth climbed the limbs of an elm, lifting himself from the ground. He gazed down the path into darkness. The trees shuddered, but nothing followed. Grau gave chase as far as the forest, but Toth didn't know if the changeling had ventured within. Whether he and Toader were lying in wait or in retreat, Toth couldn't say.

Returning to Schloss Greinberg, possibly, with their fallen brethren.

"How do you feel, Tom?" Toth asked from the perch.

Vinegar Tom's ears perked. The wounds at his ribs hadn't reopened in the melee, and for that Toth was relieved. Basina had gone far to protect the greyhound from harm.

Toth hopped to the ground, splitting nettle. He waded through weeds to rejoin Annalise. Teeth and barbs filled the bramble. Steadily, the rain intensified until it drummed the treetops, drowning every other noise.

"They're no longer in sight, Fräulein," Toth shouted. "Either they've given up the chase or they're waiting."

"This path forks toward the barn," Annalise said. She was not breathless like Toth. Rain washed in rivulets down her neck. Her eyes were red with starburst veins. "We can circle and return if you deem it wise." She brushed aside soddened locks.

"Unless you know a cave to shelter in, that is best."

"And if the changelings remain?"

Lightning flashed, illuminating the night. The wood shimmered like oil. Thunder rolled over the mountain. The wind strengthened, snapping dead branches.

"They lost two of their fellows," Toth said. "Even if gone, they'll return."

The feeling of the hatchet cutting gristle stayed in his mind. The smell that poured from the soldier's neck quickened his heart. Although he was not eager to use it, the hatchet waited in his belt. Rain washed the blade clean.

Basina shook her coat. Toth reached down and loosened a tangle behind her ear.

"Lead on," he said.

The trail wrapped around a brackish pond ringed by pines. On the opposite side, the path weaved into a grove, beginning its return to Drunstall. Lightning flashed with rapidity, and the pine trunks were like black, swaying columns. The flashes were so constant, beat after beat, second after second, a flash of day, a flash of night, that the kaleidoscopic turns kept Toth's eyes blind to the deeper dark. Fronted by the dogs, he and Annalise walked close together.

"Why did Floris do it?" asked Annalise, opening a subject that neither wanted to examine.

The trauma of seeing the woman burned alive surfaced for both she and Toth. Toth's mind throbbed with the image, the sound. The smell. It wouldn't be forgotten.

"The doll she so adored was a changeling. She believed it to be her child. She called it Loring."

"Her first child, his name was Loring. He drowned in the river," Annalise said.

Toth felt despair for the woman. A jarring suspicion of Matthias occurred to him.

"That was shortly after my mother died," said Annalise. "It was an accident." Wind blew hair around her chin, wrapping it like a scarf. Foul clarity pulsed in her eyes.

Was it an accident? Toth thought.

When the roof of the barn came into view, dark against the flashes of white, the air along the trail thickened into steam. Mist passed through the foliage, breaking into tentacles, stretching from the antrum where heat belched. Toth asked Annalise to wait with the dogs, and then he plodded forward. Rot permeated the mist. Rain beat against the mud circle, pricking until the ground moved like boiling water.

A chill raised the hair on Toth's neck.

"Is this where you found Father Haas?" he asked. "He had crawled from here?"

Like crawling out of Hell, Toth thought.

Before Annalise responded, Basina dashed any hope of entering the village in secret. The Pyrenees released a tremendous bark that shook the wood. Toth grew ill at the idea of Toader lumbering from the church in response. He leapt out of his skin to clamp Basina's snout.

"Stop it!" Toth said. "What is it?"

Basina and Tom crowded a shape that lay coiled in the bushes.

"It's Father Haas," said Annalise, turning away.

"Back," Toth told the dogs, cutting through the brush.

If truly alive and not a changeling when he crawled from the hole, Haas was dead now. Whatever friction moved him had abandoned him or failed. Rain beat his weak flesh apart, exposing meat. Toth counted five changelings arrayed over the priest's body, languid as leeches, working their jaws to eat skin and drink rain. The largest of the creatures shifted, dragging its belly, pulling itself along with well-developed claws. Its eye sockets were brackish pools—the same as Grau's eyes. There was something distinctly intelligent about the way the changeling lifted its head and opened an oddly slanted, oddly wide mouth, catching rain in its maw.

Oblivious to everything but feeding, the creatures didn't acknowledge Toth. He ripped away the largest of the brood. The creature's mouth moved against the air even though no morsel waited between its teeth.

God forgive me, Toth thought, but his rage was too strong.

With a quick whip, he slid his gloved hand to the diminutive legs of the changeling, and he swung the head against a tree trunk. The first blow connected with a thud, breaking the skull.

The other changelings continued to feed.

The creature hissed weakly, so Toth swung again, opening the brittle head fully. Cracked to the brain, the thing ceased squirming. The mouth stilled into a frozen slash, and no hissing escaped its throat. The head oozed.

Tom jittered with excitement.

"This is the true nature of Floris's doll," Toth said, holding the limp body in his grip. "And of Merrick, Matthias, Grau, and Toader. They all began thus."

Annalise looked away in disgust.

Toth threw the changeling deeper into the wood.

Beneath the feeding, Father Haas stirred. The first movement was subtle. The second was not. His arm flinched to life and swung out.

Toth reacted too late.

A charred hand connected with his boot, gripping, sliding upward to the flesh of his calf. The grip was weak, but the heat of fire remained in the digits, passing through leather, singeing the garment, burning skin.

When Toth screamed out in pain, the dogs rushed in.

"No," Toth shouted, struggling to keep them away.

With his burning grasp, Haas pulled himself. The changelings on his hide fell away, sliding into the muck.

With his free leg, Toth kicked at the skull. Brittle bone caved with the blow. He kicked again, but the action was unnecessary.

Annalise split the hounds, dashing from the path. She gripped a muddy stone, wielding the rock like a primitive axe. With great courage, she struck Haas, opening a hole in his skull. She struck him thrice, and when her violence was complete, the priest's head was shattered. The brain was as loose as vomit, streaming into the mud.

The changeling expired.

"No more of this," Annalise said, determined. She discarded the dripping stone. "I'll accept no more of this mimicry."

Tom and Basina sniffed the corpse.

"Come, Fräulein," Toth said, his voice sturdier than his heart. "If Toader and Grau remain, they know we've arrived."

Toth, Annalise, and the dogs moved past the plague pit to the barn. Although the trench squirmed, Toth did not investigate. Changelings slithered over the corpses, thick as maggots, feeding. Rain brought forth the creatures like worms.

Annalise refused to look.

An air of ruin hung over the village. Rain had quelled the flames on Cili's home and the alehouse. The smoldering remains stood as blackened husks with fallen roofs, burned floors, and consumed entryways, all in piles of orange and black between the walls. Smoke trailed into the sky and tinged the air.

Drunstall was a hole of mud, feces, and gore. Loose animals walked between the houses and through the crops. Over the fields, the tumid current reached high, breaking a lock on the mill's water wheel, turning the grinder with rhythmic groans.

The ravens huddled on corpses in the lane, pinching flesh. The wasps had fled for shelter. Dragoslav lay face down beneath the rain doll tree, the back of his skull open. Two masked men draped in carrion birds lay at side.

There was no sign of Toader and Grau. Only their carnage remained.

Groza and Andreas lay crumpled, surrounded by puddles and voracious hogs. While Annalise sprinted to the church, Toth and the dogs approached the physician and his manservant. Blood infused the air. The hogs fled when Basina barked.

Toth stood over Groza. A chewed face and marble eyes stared into nothing. Toth had no respect for the man, but he pitied Kaspar Groza for his deep ignorance.

Even Groza was somebody's father, he thought.

The physician had suffered, which brought Toth no satisfaction. His wig was gone. His lips were torn, his nose opened, and his cheeks bitten wide, leaving a hole at the center of his face. Eyes over the cavity made for a grotesque caricature of the yelling German. The maw gathered water, pooling in the bruised, constricted throat. Toader had eaten deeply, as deep as Groza's tongue. The root, a jagged piece of meat, lay at the back of his mouth, peeking through rainwater.

Pathetically, Groza clutched Bishop von Thun's letter. The ink had run into the earth.

Andreas was in worse condition. Beside the extinguished torch he lay, ravaged by hogs and wasps in ways that Groza was not. There was no flesh where his face had been, leaving a raw mask. Rain rearranged the meat. A silver crucifix lay clean against the gore of his chest. His hands were gnawed to bone.

"Come, Master Toth!" Annalise called.

Toth was ill as he approached the church. Red visions of the carnage within assailed him, leaving him weak. With Tom and Basina at his heels, he entered. Under shelter, the dogs shook water from their coats.

Annalise waited in the center aisle of the nave. Waning torchlight fell over the pews. She was shaking her head.

Groza's bleeding apparatus was smashed, the vials shattered.

Toth counted the sick. Nine of the twelve pox victims lay on their mats on the floor. Of the three absent, he saw no sign.

"Toader dragged them into the river," said Annalise.

Men, women, and children stood around the contour of the room, locked in prayer. Periodically, a choked sob interrupted the litany. One by one, they found Toth.

"All is lost," said Annalise. She collapsed into the pew and buried her face. "They'll return for the others. I know it."

"It isn't lost, Fräulein," Toth said. He touched her shoulder. "Not yet. Can I request your help? The matter will push you to your limit, but I know you have the strength inside to do it. I trust that."

Annalise nodded. Blood was in her eyes. Hair was matted to her scalp, her gown was sopping, and her face was ashen, but the turbulence and vigor below the surface endured.

"When the sun rises, evacuate everyone to Karnstein Chateau. Including these poor souls. They'll listen to you now."

"Will you not come with us?" asked Annalise.

"No," said Toth. "I'm leaving immediately for Schloss Greinberg. I must undo what Matthias started, and I must do so at the source."

"I'm sorry for my father, Master Toth."

"I'm sorry for him, too, Fräulein."

Toth walked up the aisle, stepping over bodies, crunching glass. He eyed the sobbing form of Nikolaus by the side door.

With a gust of speech, Toth ordered the evacuation to Karnstein Chateau. In the spirit of Kaspar Groza, he invoked the name of Bishop von Thun, he invoked the military, he invoked God. He demanded rather than pleaded.

"You will leave at dawn," he finished.

The prayer started again, but it was disorganized and distracted in the heat of the nave. Woodsmoke drifted through the door.

XXXIV
CAPITULUM

A sign in three scripts—High German, Bavarian, and Slovene—stood in the fork's joint. The sign bade warning to any man unarmed and not in uniform. The post was cracked and leaning, reduced to target practice, loose in the soil.

To the left of the fork, the road began a winding incline to the fortress. The trail was thin, steep, and choked with rutted mud. Through the mist, a mountain fortress came into view. Blackened stone towered on the cliff. Dawn pierced the rain and fog, breaking red over the battlements.

The road to the right snaked through the ruins of a feeder settlement and farm. Tall stakes, tools of impalement driven by Turks, crossed the land. A human skull and spine hung from the remains of a gallows. There were ghosts in the stillness of the village.

Toth guided the Haflinger left, beginning the ascent to Greinberg. He felt anything but courageous for the choice. Vinegar Tom and Basina walked near the ledge, watching the broken rooftops grow distant.

Nests spotted trees lining the road. Wasps darted between the patches.

Upward Toth and the dogs climbed, the weight of anticipation keeping Toth silent. When the horse broke through the uppermost layer of fog, the fortress waited at Toth's left. Ominous and defeated, the dark husk of stone overlooked the mist. No pride remained in the fortress. Soot and vine provided the bunting and flags, while weeds offered fringe. The heraldry was mockingly tattered, and enormous nests smothered poles from which the flags hung limp.

It was four years prior that Turks overran Schloss Greinberg on their way to Vienna, slaughtering men like cattle and burning the fortress and the village it harbored. Greinberg once represented Habsburg strength in the highlands, but now the fortress demonstrated frailty.

If Tom and Basina shared Toth's wariness, the dogs refused to show it. Each animal moved eagerly. Toth was glad for the display. Their resilience pushed him forward.

Toth guided the horse to a gate in the rock. Three dead torches and three leatherbound skulls, wrapped with vine, hung at the keystone. The portcullis was in jigsaw pieces on the ground, jagged as broken teeth where a portion remained lodged in the upper edge of the arch. The curtain wall that stretched from the gate was sickly, pitted with cannon and mortar blasts. Large chunks of stone had fallen to the earth, leaving portions of the wall ineffective, marred with open wounds. The keep, impressive in girth and height, rose behind the wall. From the valley floor where peasants once toiled, Greinberg must have been godlike and seemingly impenetrable when in full vigor, but now the fortress was a *memento mori.*

Even the great, Even in Arcadia…and so forth, Toth thought.

The fortress was intact enough to use as a rendezvous point for surrounding villages, for soldiers marching to the Balkans, but no sentinel was on duty to stop trespassers from penetrating the rotten shell when not in use. Greinberg was quiet as a tomb.

The Haflinger carried Toth through the open gate, passing beneath the mangled maw. Three portly ravens looked down, opening their mouths without cawing. The dogs navigated a path through metal debris and sharp stones.

Within the walls, a complex of buildings spread out, with bunkhouses, barns, and storehouses ringing the central keep. To varying degrees, the buildings were torched. Most of the roofs were gone, leaving skeletal rafters. Nothing stood pristine. The keep was dark with soot, rising four stories. A staircase, pitted like the walls, fronted twin doors of iron. The doors hung askew.

Matthias, Toth thought, *killed Merrick here. Matthias conjured here, far from his home. Did the old man purloin the magic lantern from Greinberg, too?*

Toth dismounted. He left the horse to graze in a patch of weeds beneath a black poplar, one of several circles of foliage in what had been a courtyard. Now the grounds formed a sea of mud. A breeze pushed fingers of fog through the trees. For reasons he didn't wish to dwell on, Toth did not tie the horse. He patted the Haflinger, whose name he did not know, and he lifted his satchel from her flank.

While Tom marked the tree, Toth studied the foreboding tower. The keep was the obvious place to begin his search for Old Räum. Toth was armed with a hatchet at his waist and two manuscripts in his satchel. He carried the *Hieroglyphs of Ba'al* and Matthias's *Sworn Book of Honorius.*

If Old Räum were an adversarial spirit, as Toth deduced, then the hatchet would do little. Fighting a flood with a knife was more efficacious. The adjuration magic in the grimoires would, he hoped, prove more effective. A Christian face on the incantations made the ordeal an exorcism, but Toth denied the reduction. He thought more broadly. Adjuration magic was a ritual of commands to remove the entrenched.

Toth's heart, as it had been for two leagues, was busy against his chest. Everything inside urged him to leave. How simple it would be to return to the horse. To pass through the gate. To retreat through the fog. To leave Styria behind.

The carrot before him was the transformation of knowing. *With success,* he thought, *you'll rewrite the chapter on the spir-*

it called Old Räum. You won't speculate or approximate; you'll know. That was enough to drive Toth into the dragon's den.

Toth freed the *Sworn Book of Honorius.* According to legend, the grimoire was compiled when the great magicians of the world met in a Dark Age cemetery, and the men agreed to commit secrets to a single text. The mysterious Honorius played the role of scribe. Of truth, there was little in the story, but the *Sworn Book* was a masterful compendium, regardless.

Toth stepped beneath the poplar's canopy to protect the pages from rain. He opened to a section on adjuration magic. Although he'd committed the incantations to memory as a student, he read the pages again to calm his nerves. The incantation was one of binding. Adversarial spirits could not be killed, but rendering a spirit dormant was another matter.

Returned to sleep, as the Order of Saint Guinefort phrased it. Slumbering dragons filled the world.

The ritual forced a spirit to assume the shape a man could control. *Ba'al* claimed Old Räum took the form of a raven when bound, but that was conjecture.

Toth ran through the lines of the ritual thrice.

Basina lay in the grass as she waited. The clemency of heaven was in the dog. Tom, the agitated sort, paced.

"Come," Toth said to the dogs. "It's time."

Toth crossed the courtyard to the stairs. On the opposite side of the tower, abandoned in a garden of weeds, was the cart he knew from the cemetery. Tom and Basina smelled the wheels. The planks were ancient, rotten as coffin wood, and the metal was rusted through. The ebony horses were skeletal, all knobs and ribs, but they did not feed on the grass. Long strips of pale gossamer marbled the flesh on their thighs. Ants crawled over their necks in bands as thick as bridles. The horses, too, were changelings.

The front seat was empty, but the cart was not. The decapitated soldier lay stiff between the drums. Dead worms hanging from his neck, pasting the boards in their attempt to escape, gave the appearance of cut flowers. So close, Toth saw the curious writing scratched into the breastplate—the gibberish scrawling of a child or lunatic rather than language. The soldier's head, too, was collected from the river, and it rested by the diamond-shaped springs of the seat, scraped by teeth, half consumed. The skin and hair were gone, but meat remained fastened to bone.

Stuffed into one of the casks was another corpse, that of the smaller changeling. Any resemblance to Matthias had vanished. The body, robed in burgundy and grey, was draped over the barrel lip. The neck and soiled ruff were tattered. The raven claw hand reached down, a nail scraping the bed. Basina had opened the changeling well. A ball of wasps dangled from the throat, tethered with sinew.

Grau and Toader collect and mourn their dead, Toth thought.

The cart's presence erased doubt about what awaited him in the keep, and the thought of Toader in the throes of grief brought mortal terror. Vinegar Tom watched Toth, alert to the swell of emotion. Toth petted the greyhound's neck.

"I need your courage, Tom," he said. "And I need your strength, Basina."

Toth clutched the amulet beneath his scarf, and he recited a prayer of protection. When complete, he ascended the steps. Ravens occupied the keep's arrow slits.

Warm carrion air pulsed through the iron doors. Toth and his hounds entered. The hall was high, long, and cavernous. Morning sunlight pierced fissures in the eastern wall, casting gold a bevy of raven nests in the rafters. Toth met their beady stares and then looked away. He walked on. A layer of dried mud, feces, and sprouting weeds covered the floor. Inaccessible doors, barred by hundreds of casks piled two deep, lined the way. Like the drums in the cart and church cellar, the imperial insignia branded the staves.

The ravens were idle, but the wasps were not. Insects filled the air twenty feet above, flying in formation, tracing ephemeral sigils. Periodically, a wasp dropped to the floor, having died in the air.

Toth watched, fascinated.

Not unlike a battery of magic, he thought, *an engine.*

At the far end of the hall, a light pulsed orange in an alcove of shadow. A familiar sound emanated from that direction, as well as beneath Toth's boots. The floor hummed with intensity. The vibration reached his knees. It was the din of burning antra.

Basina jumped then, kicking out her back leg, and she bit at her rear. At the same time, a sharp pain jabbed Toth's neck. He looked up. The sigil failed, erasing in layers, as wasps flew downward.

Toth and the dogs ran, sprinting the length of the hall, fracturing mud. He heard the wasps, many hundreds of them, swarming over his shoulder, closing in. The barbs entered his neck three at a time, spreading poisonous agony. Tom outpaced the insects, but Basina was slow and cumbersome. She cried out when a wasp caught the flesh of her ear.

A doorway waited in the alcove. Toth swung open the twin doors without thought, allowing the dogs to enter, and then he ran inside, snapping the doors shut behind him. A few wasps darted around the room, but most of the swarm remained in the hall, committing suicide against the panels. The sound was akin to sleet.

Toth rubbed his throbbing neck and caught his breath. Numbness spread to his ear, and the flesh swelled. Tom was unscathed, but Basina was hurt and angry. The dog flopped onto her side, panting and drooling. The wasps that entered slinked over the ceiling, losing direction once separated from the whole.

Collecting himself, shaking off the pain, Toth surveyed the room. Copious light streamed through a lead window that stretched floor to ceiling. The ruin of the hall was not evident here. This was a special place to someone. Matthias's abode of late, Toth reasoned, but to whom it belonged prior was a mystery. A commanding officer, no doubt.

The outer hall suffered for the richness of this inner chamber. All the finery that Turks left behind in Greinberg had been filtered into the room. It was opulent with partially scorched tapestries and portraiture of armored men. The doors were ornate with a scene of Melusina, the mermaid of old, carved into the panels. Chairs, desks, a wardrobe, a table—all medieval in age, German in skill, and Italian in beauty—cluttered the floor.

The dragon's hoard of gold, Toth thought. *A treasure room for Old Räum.*

Atop the desks were machines and playthings: a mechanical clock, an automaton bird, and a companion for the automaton beetle that Matthias had proudly demonstrated to Toth. Glass slides for a magic lantern were stacked near a mound of parchment. The runes of Honorius marked the foremost slide, but the other slides were toys, layers of a pastoral windmill scene.

The windmill disturbed Toth, not for insidiousness but for its innocence. Things had escalated for Matthias. The man had lost control. Or his mind.

Basina licked her stings, while the greyhound hosed a wardrobe. Toth comforted the Pyrenees, burying his hands in her ruff, scratching. Her ear was hot and scarlet. Fury brimmed in her eyes.

In addition to furniture, Matthias had collected an array of arms. Tom nudged a pike that leaned against a wall of blades, knocking the long shaft to the floor. Toth navigated through the couches and lifted the weapon. The pike was as ornate as the room, with silver inlay and ostrich feathers. Decorative or not, the weapon had a good weight. Toth kept it, carrying the pike to the door. If needed, he liked the distance it afforded as opposed to the hatchet.

The dimwitted wasps hadn't the patience to keep after quarry long. Within minutes, the swarm in the hall faded, the buzzing growing distant. When another minute passed, Toth cracked the doors and peered out. A few wasps crawled on the wall, but most of the attackers had returned to sigil making. A handful of wasps lay dead on the ground.

"Quietly," Toth said to the hounds.

He led the way, leaving the doors parted, carrying the pike with two hands. Directly opposite the chamber was a stairwell that descended into the bowels of the fortress. The roar of an-tra, steady like a great machine, emanated from the cavern.

Toth prayed, girding himself, pushing back against fear.

No lantern flame illuminated the stairs. Rather, stuffed into an arched recess was the cross-legged corpse of a man, his limbs thinned to bone. Pox scabs and fire blackened his skin. His stomach was opened wide, and hot coals burned in the bed of his pelvis. Lines of orange veined his flesh. Wasps shifted in his eye sockets.

The image brought Bertram to mind, but then another thought struck Toth. Where Bertram's hair was dark like that of Annalise, the hair on the corpse was blond. There was an unskillful cavity in the chest where the heart was butchered and removed.

Merrick, Toth thought then, and he felt sorrow.

Poor Annalise. The only consolation is that she is not here to see him thus. This is not the man who lives in her memory.

Toth steadied his breathing. He positioned the pike to stab, and then he pushed into the foul wind, leading the dogs down the stairwell. Sulfur and decay belched from the chamber. The animals moved willingly but cautiously. The air grew hotter with each step, and it was not a leap of apocalyptic fancy to imagine the descent as sinking into Hell. Despite his effort, Toth breathed rapidly, keeping pace with the thud of his heart. The air blistered his lungs.

What he had fathomed was not what greeted him at the bot-tom of the stairs. A crypt-like room with a dirt floor stretched below the main hall. Great columns of stone, fifteen feet high, girded the ceiling. At intervals, rectangular boxes like sarcoph-agi decorated the ground. One wall was that of a mausoleum, a comb of burial niches. The holes held the busted coffins and ripped shrouds of disinterred soldiers. Toth thought of Mat-thias's collection of identification tags, and the foul realization was upon him. In his rituals of conjuration, Matthias had pil-laged the graves, collecting.

Taking in the vast darkness, Basina and Tom lost their ea-gerness to explore. The dogs flanked Toth, keeping close. Vinegar Tom shivered at the ribs. Toth's hands sweated inside his gloves. He listened, but reverberation through the crypt consumed any nuance of sound. The rumbling emanated from a far corner where a chasm of light opened in the earth.

Toth crept through the sarcophagi, stopping to look and listen with each advance.

A hulking shadow at the pit caught Tom's attention. The greyhound and Pyrenees stepped from Toth's side, splitting around a pillar.

Toader knelt at the edge of the chasm, bathed with orange light. His monk's habit was gone, and the pink flesh of his boil-covered back and arms showed in the darkness. His spine heaved and his bare shoulders worked. He resembled a skinned rat, gnawing, whimpering.

An act of worship and retribution absorbed the giant.

If he turns, we're dead, Toth thought. It was not a warning but a matter of fact. There was nowhere to run here, no forest in which to hide.

Smothered in the gaseous heat, Toader cradled Grau in his arms, pinning him with webbed hands. Grau moaned. Toader's unhinged jaw worked on his skull, scraping meat with two incisors. The skin was gone, eaten from Grau's face. He was a slash of raw red above the dark collar.

Crouched nude, Toader gnawed, and he whimpered like a broken wolf.

They mourn their dead, and they avenge their dead.

Dorin Toth looked at the greyhound and Pyrenees for courage.

If he turns, we're dead. He saw himself in Grau's position. More distressingly, he envisioned the hounds with the giant's whimper in their throats. The fear and dread were almost paralyzing.

There was no time to plan or think. Toth's attack was not careful or precise. He gripped the pike, steadied it, and he ran past a sarcophagus toward the roaring pit.

As Toader loosened the vise of his jaws, swiveling his head to see, Toth connected with the spearpoint, driving steel into the side of Toader's neck. The hide was hard and ungiving. The blade did not sink far.

The giant shrieked, dropping Grau. The blow did not have the force to unbalance Toader. With the long pike protruding from his neck, he began to stand.

Toth stood in terror, watching Toader work his way to his knees, shrieking like a banshee. Pawing at the blade, cutting his hands, he ripped the pike free and threw it to the ground.

Toth was petrified, but Basina and Tom were not. The hounds raced past their master, moving with incredible swiftness.

"No," Toth shouted. "No!"

Tom leapt first. Basina, with greater force, followed. Both dogs struck Toader before he was upright and balanced, knocking him over Grau. The giant toppled backward, falling into the pit. There was no sound of Toader striking the bottom of the chasm, but the depths consumed his shrieking.

Tom fell hard against Grau, breaking his momentum, but Basina was less fortunate. The Pyrenees fell with Toader, dropping hard on her hip at the precipice. She slid through dirt, carving trenches with her paws, her hindlegs and tail falling into the shaft. Mad and alert, she clawed and gripped the earth, digging in with her stone-like nails.

Toth was after Basina in an instant. He dove onto his stomach and reached, grabbing the Pyrenees before the weight of her rump carried her into the hole. She cried as the heat singed her fur. Toth reached into the fire, his hands burning through leather, and he grasped her rear. The greyhound came then, taking Basina's ruff into his mouth. Together, Toth and Tom hoisted the heavy Pyrenees, yanking her back from death. She crawled on her stomach when she was free of the hole, and then she collapsed on her side, panting with her mouth wide.

With labored breath, Toth shifted his attention to Grau. Despite a broken skull, the changeling watched Toth with curiosity, his dark eyes folded in raw meat. He had no strength to fight, but he worked open his lipless mouth.

Tom stood guard over Basina.

Toth lifted the pike from the ground. He put the spear-point against Grau's chest. The rat eyes never left him. Grau watched until the last.

"Child of pluck," he rasped. "Collector of devils."

Toth said nothing. With a great thrust, he shoved Grau over the edge, dropping his broken body into the pit. The changeling made no attempt to grab the ledge. Unlike Toader, Grau did not shriek as he fell.

Silence did not reign long. As Toth checked Basina, brushing back the seared fur on her tail, the ground quaked with fury. Toth put his hand against the dirt. The tremor ran to his shoulder.

Old Räum moved in the earth.

It is time, Toth thought, bracing himself.

XXXV
CAPITULUM

When the great columns trembled, gravel rained from the ceiling, spattering the ground. Toth shielded his head from falling stone. He was as distant from the stairwell as he could be in the crypt, but he mapped a route. Before he attempted escape, the floor convulsed, and a hole opened in the earth. Like a hungry mouth, a growing chasm pulled rock and barrels downward. Toth's route to the stairs grew less certain, more treacherous. Then another fracture ruptured wide, creating an island, sending a sarcophagus tumbling into the dark. The tumult rattled the wall of tombs, spilling the mummified remains of soldiers, spreading cadavers over the ground. The din was astonishing. Greinberg was coming undone.

Toth spied a trace of the being that moved like an underground river through stone. As Old Räum passed beneath the stretching cavities, his form was that of a flood. Dark water breached the rim of one of the holes, and a boiling, bubbling stream of scum spread over the ground, taking shape around a pillar. The water, brackish and reeking, held an outline, a shape Toth could only describe as a face. It was like no face he had ever seen, but symmetry was present. Eyes emerged, scarring the Hungarian with the image of horror.

"Protect Basina, Tom," Toth ordered.

He dropped his satchel, positioned himself in front of the dogs, and he began the incantation from *Honorius*, reciting the lines in a dialect of corrupted, vulgar Latin.

The water reacted, halting its advance, undulating at the fringe.

Toth ran through the incantation again, his voice strengthening with each intonation.

Slowly, the boiling scum receded into a shaft like a withdrawn hand. Abruptly, the walls, ceiling, and ground ceased shaking. The antra calmed. Heat no longer roared. In the face of destruction, a hush passed through the crypt. Toth filled the air with another recitation. He gathered his breath, deepened his voice, and intoned the words with authority. Then once more.

From the far end of the cavern, on the stairwell to the keep, came footfalls, echoing heavily.

The conclusion in *Ba'al* was incorrect. Old Räum did not assume the shape of a raven when bound. Merrick appeared at the base of the steps, but this was the man that Matthias knew, not the youth that Annalise had locked in her mind, arrested in time.

The corpse had risen from the shelf above the stairs. The coals in his open stomach burned hot. The charred flesh seeped light like a Baroque angel of God. Merrick stepped with blunt motions, shedding scales of flesh as he crossed the crypt. His eyes were the white of fire, as was the membrane of his wasp-infested mouth.

A deep horror moved through Toth, weighting his limbs, occluding his mind. Again, the desire to flee seized him. Vinegar Tom and Basina stared, mystified and motionless.

"You are the spirit called Old Räum," Toth managed to say, breaking the spell of obfuscation. He cast the declaration in four languages, repeating the name. The pidgin of Latin in *Honorius* brought a response.

Merrick creaked at the neck, breaking flesh, judging Toth, considering the dogs, and contemplating the pit of fire that consumed Grau and Toader. There was a touch of wonder in the turn of his head, the flow of fire in his eyes. It was fascination with the achievement of an inferior being, and it passed from Merrick's face like shadow.

"You are bound in this form, Old Räum," Toth bellowed. "You are bound to remain in this form and obey." His voice echoed through the cavern.

Merrick stared. He reached into his stomach and grabbed a coal, wrapping it in his hand. He started forward again.

"I commanded you to appear in a likeness familiar to me. I commanded you to obey, Old Räum. You *will* obey."

A wasp-wing voice emanated from Merrick, vibrating in his throat, splitting char.

"Dorin Toth," he said.

Toth grew ill at the sound of his name. Thoughts and memories were physical to spirits like Räum—they saw these things as clearly as if they were features of the face. Nothing was secret to him. Nothing was hidden. He knew his entire being. He knew his deepest fears.

"What do you call yourself? Is it Old Räum?"

Merrick closed his mouth over the wasps.

"I command you to *speak*," Toth said. "You are bound in this form. You are bound to obey."

"Dorin Toth." The tone was one of arrogance—brimming with the finality of knowing, understanding.

"Old Räum, you are banished from this place. You are *banished* from Greinberg. You are *banished* from the wood. You are *banished* from Drunstall. You will no longer trouble these people. Matthias, the conjuror who brought you forth, is dead. You are no longer bound to him. You are bound to me."

"Anima," he said. *The soul.*

"Find Matthias's soul and keep it. That's your prerogative. That is your treasure to hold, but you must depart."

"Dorin Toth," he said. "Lugos. Son of Almos."

The words chilled Toth's heart, giving him pause. He was born in Lugos. Almos Toth was the name of his father, and it was also the name of his elder brother. The words amounted to a threat of retaliation, a web of retribution.

With Toth's pause, he wore his terror.

Merrick's face broke into a thin smile. He shuffled, brandishing the coal in his crumbling fist as if it were a weapon.

"Depart, Old Räum!" Toth commanded. "You are bound."

"Dorin Toth," he said. "Collector of devils. Collector of hounds." Old Räum raised his arm at the greyhound.

Basina and Tom did not move. Räum was inside their minds, cowing them.

Merrick's smoldering corpse shambled, closing the distance, shedding skin. He reached the dogs. Mesmerized, the animals closed their eyes, dropping their tails. Their fur smoothed.

"What are you called?" Toth asked, his voice losing force. *One touch and the dogs will be engulfed*, he thought.

Old Räum did not answer. When the corpse lowered his hand toward Tom's skull, prepared to ignite the hound, Toth freed the hatchet from his belt. He had no other choice. He gripped the handle and swung the blade with little thought, striking the outstretched limb. The weapon caught the back of the hand, bashing rather than cleaving.

Old Räum's fingers crumbled with the touch, deteriorating to ash. The coal dropped to the floor in front of Tom. The dog was blinded, oblivious, unmoving.

Toth breathed heavily. *He's saved you many times*, he thought. *Now is the time to save Vinegar Tom.*

Old Räum did not react to the loss of his digits.

"What are you called?" Toth demanded.

He struck at the corpse again, but Merrick reached out with his other hand, grabbing Toth's forearm, blocking the blow. The crushing grip seared through, melting cloth against flesh, burning into meat.

Toth vented his agony, screaming until his voice choked. The hand passed through his skin like a breath of Hell.

"Dorin Toth," said Räum.

Toth fell to the ground, acrid heat roiling from his flesh. His mind pulled inward to find balance. He maintained his hold on the hatchet.

"What are you called?" he gasped.

"Dorin Toth," said the spirit.

Toth shoved away the dogs and kicked at Merrick. His boot connected, stripping a chunk of meat from the calf. Then, with a jolt of strength, Toth ripped his hand and hatchet free. He swung steel at the weakened leg, splintering a calcined bone.

Old Räum went to his knees, joining Toth. Coals tumbled from his stomach, spreading hot ash over the floor. The veins on Merrick's hide dimmed. His back pulsed, flickering out.

"Dorin Toth," he said to the ground.

Toth got to his feet. He was delirious with pain, but he pointed the hatchet. He wielded the blade like an executioner above his quarry. It was in his mind to open the skull to the wasp nest brain inside, but he had to know more.

"What are you called?" he demanded. "What is the seven-fold name that you hide, spirit? You are bound, Old Räum. You are bound to obey. You are bound to depart."

"Isis knows," came the reply. "Dorin Toth."

The goddess who knows everyone's name, Toth thought. It was a mocking reply, and it was a play on Toth's own name, another god of Egypt.

Toth struck the skull, cleaving brittle bone.

Old Räum dipped his head still lower. He chewed wasps tunneling from his throat, and the mashing rhythm was that of laughter. His jaws flaked away in large chunks. His shoulders fell away.

"Depart this place," Toth ordered. He gripped his arm in an effort to stem the pain. Then he struck again, shattering the unfused sutures at the base of the head. Indeed, a tightly packed orb of wasps pulsed between splinters of bone.

Old Räum placed his broken palms on the earth. Then, beginning with a seam at the spine, his form fell into ruin. The spirit burst into seven ravens, full of winged vigor, that flew hard past Toth, upward to the ceiling. Before smashing against stone, the ravens broke into a thousand wasps, a sea of insects that diffused like a great splash. A streak of black and red, the wasps raced to the stairwell, then flew through the keep above, finding fissures in the walls, and dispersing into the fog of the valley. The wasps spread leagues apart, carrying away Old Räum's essence to safety.

Although the stink of sulfur and smoke remained, the pits did not reignite.

Toth kicked aside the coals at his feet, and he cursed. He gripped his arm tighter. His head swam with the pain.

Although Old Räum had fled, the spirit was not defeated. Räum was simply exorcised, stripped of his abode.

With a swell of emotion, Toth dropped to his knees. The dogs, freed of their binding, closed in on him eagerly. The animals understood the change in the air. What residue the spirit left behind in the hounds, Toth could not say. What residue remained in his own mind, he could not say. Time alone would reveal the cancers of such probing.

Toth wrapped his arms around Vinegar Tom and Basina, and he hugged each of his companions close. Their fur, cool to the touch, was a great relief.

"Bold hounds, your courage is unmatched," he said, choking back a sob.

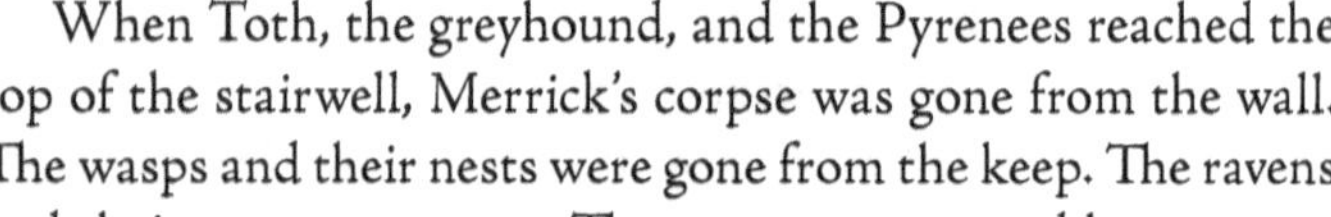

When Toth, the greyhound, and the Pyrenees reached the top of the stairwell, Merrick's corpse was gone from the wall. The wasps and their nests were gone from the keep. The ravens and their nests were gone. The wagon, cargo, and horses were gone.

Old Räum was gone, lying dormant, waiting, scattered in the wood.

Toth moved into the officer's chamber to rummage the drawers and nurse his wounds. Through the window over his shoulder, bright morning invaded the shell of Greinberg, stretching across the floor, streaking the wall of blades. Toth pulled the salve of ibex fat from his satchel to tend the deep burns. The flesh was ghastly, spotted with pieces of melted cloth, and the sight left him ill. The danger of infection was acute. He steadied himself on one of the couches.

Basina flopped down in the doorway, sighing.

"When you joined us, you got more than you bargained for, *Chien de Montagne des Pyrénées*," breathed Toth. Despite the pain, he smiled at his new companion.

Vinegar Tom hopped over the exhausted Pyrenees, entering the room to continue the business of exploration.

XXXVI
CAPITULUM

I t was the height of noon when Toth and the dogs reached the fire beacon that overlooked the Lavant. Drunstall, with its wooded trails and fields, spread out below, unhidden. Even the hilltop cemetery, a garden of stone between the trees, was visible from on high. Toth had encountered no ravens upon his return, and the carrion birds no longer painted the valley dark. The church belfry, the tithe barn, and the sarsens were clear.

Basina found shade near the stone building behind the pyre. The Pyrenees stretched out in the grass, reaching with her paws, exhausted. Vinegar Tom rolled onto his back, kicking his feet in the air. The dogs deserved a rest, so Toth dismounted. The Haflinger joined the animals in the lengthening shade.

When manned, the fire beacon existed to warn of raiders. When flames rose high enough to see from the valley, the people of Drunstall gathered what they could carry and fled to safety. It was an ancient method of survival. Unmanned, however, the beacon was dead, robbed of its purpose, emptied of fuel. The guard house was in disrepair. No watchman protected the village.

While the animals lounged, Toth walked to the edge where grass ended against a flat rock. The stone was broad and long like a stage. From its perch, he took in the vista. With everything in bloom, Styria was a beautiful sight—an idyllic, pleasant canvas. Even the river had subsided, running brown but contained within its shores. A great calm lay over the forest. Swallows chirped in the trees. Save for thin smoke rising from Cili's hovel and The Cock's Foot, the day appeared normal.

Carefully, so as not to jostle his wrapped arm, Toth retrieved a spyglass from his satchel. He'd filched the gadget from the officer's chamber at Greinberg. Being useful to curious men, the device was one of Matthias's playthings, he presumed. Bound in leather, with a lens at each end, Toth raised the military tool to his eye. He trained the glass on the village. To his chagrin, there was movement in the lane that stretched from the church.

The pack of strays, thought Toth, but the longer he observed, the less he believed this to be true. The animals were too large for dogs. His heart went cold when he isolated one in his sight. The banded fur of grey, white, and brown told the tale.

Wolves, he thought miserably. *A pack of wolves from the mountain. How long had they been lying in wait?*

Five grey wolves dragged corpses from the plague pit to join the bodies of Groza, Andreas, Dragoslav, and others whose names Toth never learned. Two wolves fought over the rotund physician, digging in his open gut. The predators feasted greedily.

Ars lupus, Toth thought with revulsion. *The art of the wolf.*

He recalled a phrase that Annalise uttered in a moment of despair.

The promise of plague wolves, she said. *Wolves encircle tragedy. Wolves descend at moments of great weakness.*

Wind gusted over the river, scattering debris around the rocks like blown chaff. Toth lowered the spyglass. Gripping his throbbing forearm, he turned to the dogs and horse.

"We must make Karnstein Chateau before nightfall," he said apologetically. "Come. Make haste. The wood is full of wolves."

Grumbling, Vinegar Tom got to his feet.

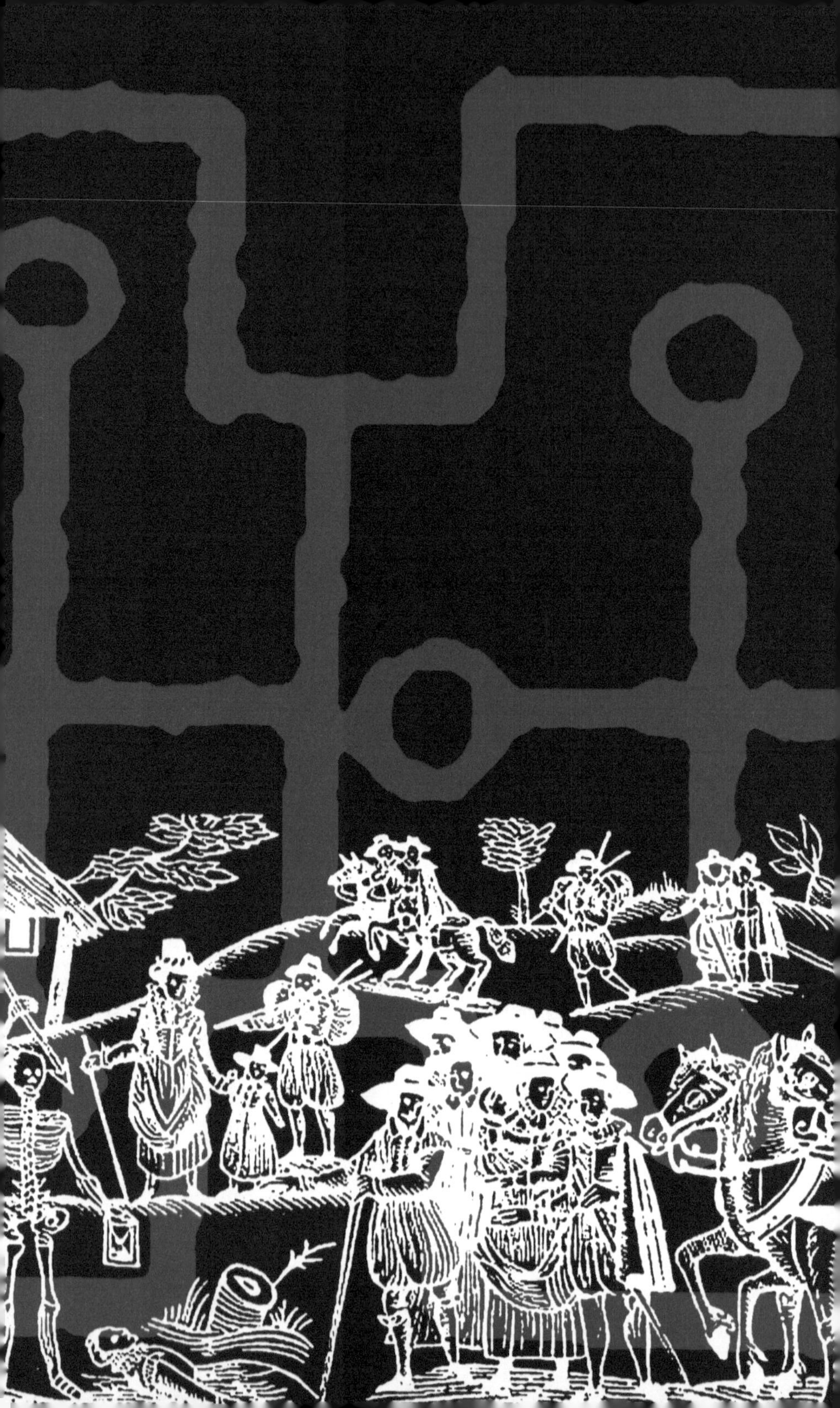

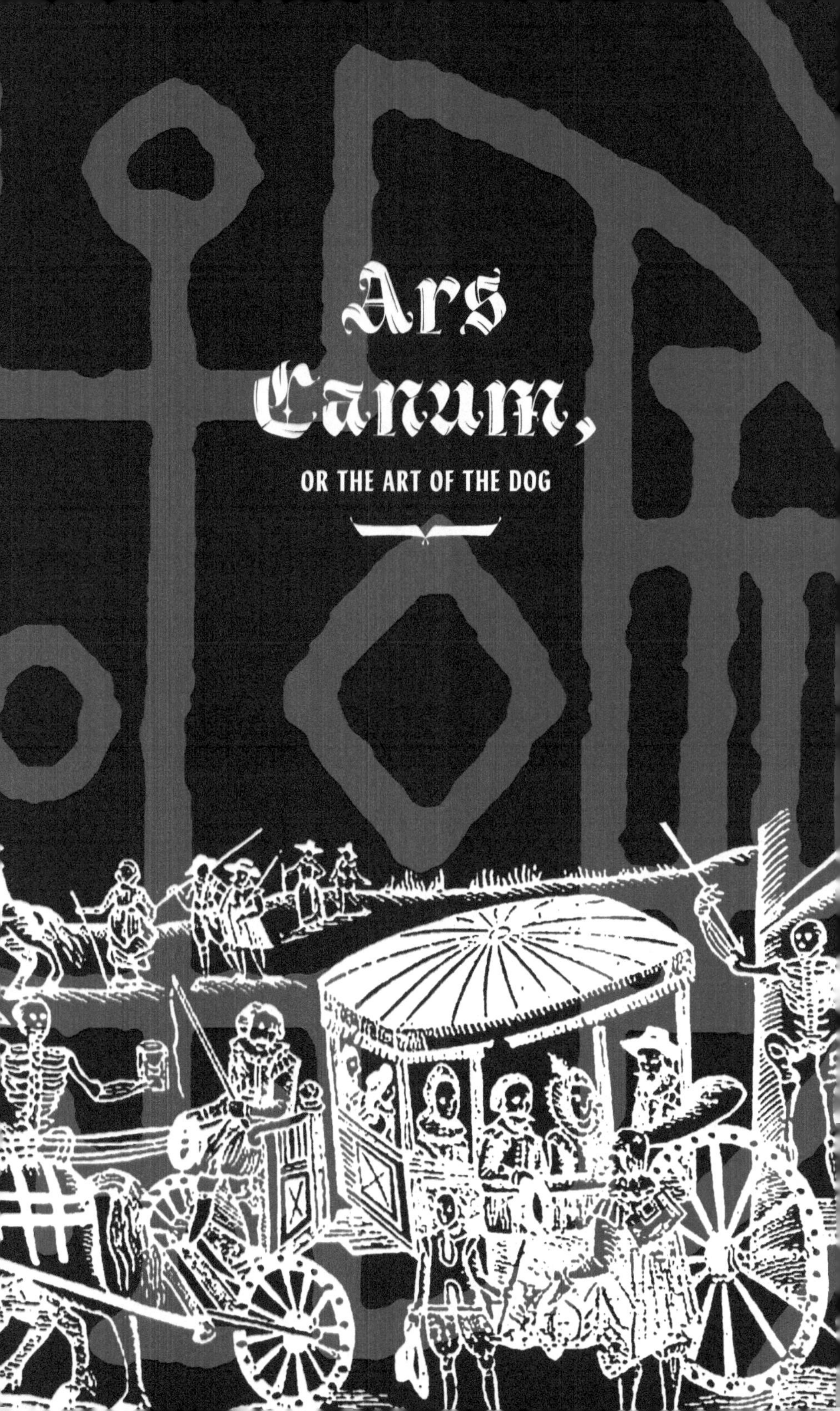

Ars
Canum,
OR THE ART OF THE DOG

XXXVII
CAPITULUM

Beneath great frescoes of angels in the library at Admont Abbey, Dorin Toth and Brother Abelard walked through rows of gold inlayed bookshelves two stories high. Windows stood recessed between each set of shelves, so that sunlight striped the marble floor. The gold shone divinely, as did the simple tables at which Benedictine monks studied and prayed.

Freshly returned from a case in Nubia, Brother Abelard of the Order of Saint Guinefort was in good spirits. Although Toth's efficiency and thoroughness pleased him, the elder explored Toth's conclusions with a wry frown.

"This fellow, Matthias," Abelard whispered, "why did he do such things? He was a learned man."

The pair passed under a great arch of white gold filigree that led to another dome of angels, a window into the rim of Heaven.

"A dangerous concoction of arrogance and grief," said Toth. He admired the leatherbound books so neatly arrayed at his left. "Matthias lost his faith in the correct things, so he filled the void with faith in himself. Grief has done worse to men."

Abelard nodded. "Were his intentions noble?"

"They were quite selfish, in fact. He had no intention of helping his people, even his child."

"You believe Merrick was Matthias's initial offering to the spirit called Old Räum?"

"I do. Matthias killed the man his daughter loved to save his wife. He had his own ideas of magic and witchcraft, and not all of them founded."

"Apparently effective enough."

Toth smiled. "In a pragmatic sense, that's true."

"His own ideas of filial obligations, too, it seems."

Toth nodded. "He blamed a woman named Cili, an outcast, an herbalist from what I gather, for his wife's death. If there were other offerings to Old Räum, I didn't uncover them, but I know he killed more than Merrick." Toth counted the victims: Merrick, Loring, Cili, and Haas.

Abelard shook his head. "A rueful matter."

"How did Bishop von Thun react to news of Groza?" Toth asked.

"There will be an inquiry. Groza was too well-connected for there not to be."

"Anywhere there's an inquiry, there's want of blame."

"You'll be shielded, Dorin. Blame or not, it will be of no consequence. Tell me this: why did Old Räum acquiesce to your binding?"

Toth stopped beside a gilded bust.

"Like many of his line, Old Räum is bound by his myths," he said. "He's come to believe them over millennia. He exists solely within the framework of mythical logic. Its importance is Biblical to him. He knows what we write about him. He knows what I'll write about him. Those things, too, he considers."

With a smirk, Abelard said, "God forbid he become enlightened." He laughed at his joke and asked, "Was it truly Räum?"

Toth shook his head.

A monk's footfalls echoed through the library.

"I was unable to coax his true name, although I tried. Old Räum is as good a name as any, for *räumen* means 'to empty.'

What better name for a spirit thriving on pestilence, preying on weakness?"

"He isn't vanquished," observed Abelard.

"He certainly isn't," Toth said, "but now he's dormant again."

"Until another dabbler rouses him from slumber."

"Yes. May millennia pass before that wise fool is born. Old Räum has his eye on me, I'm afraid. He has my name and my father's name. I don't think he'll soon forget my line."

"Nor will you." Abelard gestured at Toth's forearm.

Toth looked at the bandage, damp with red. "Even if this wound heals properly, Old Räum left his mark. No, I won't forget."

"I value your conjecture, sir, so tell me one more thing: what did the spirit intend?"

Toth thought for a moment. "It's my belief that Old Räum, once loosened from the grip of Matthias, intended to send a changeling, the diminutive creature that mimicked with such skill, among the people as a savior, a Christ figure. The Christ would clear the problem and build a cult around the worship of his father. I've no doubt Old Räum once enjoyed the prominence of deification. Naturally, the spirit desires a return to godhood."

"I imagine it's a unique agony."

The Brothers of the Order of Saint Guinefort exited the abbey and walked into a garden courtyard. The sun was bright and hot, shining over rows of flowers, footpaths, and cropped hedges.

Annalise sat on a bench in the shade with Matthias's beetle in her hands. Vinegar Tom was attentive at her side. Basina lay stretched in the cool grass, unburdened. The Pyrenees was brushed clean of mats, tangles, and burrs, and her coat dazzled white in the sun. She wore a collar of royal blue, studded with silver. A *fleur-de-lis* stamped the face of each stud.

Abelard whistled for his greyhound. A moment later, the dog named Godfrey, whom Tom did not love, separated the hedges. The animal was elderly like his master. He eyed Tom with disdain as he passed. Abelard patted Godfrey's side.

"Greetings, Fräulein," Abelard said to Annalise. "I understand you're traveling to Vienna with Brother Toth."

Annalise set the beetle aside and rose. Her dark hair and eyes were striking in the garden, beauty layered with beauty. Weariness was not absent from her face, but she was mending. Her cheeks flushed red.

"Yes, father," said Annalise.

"Have you ever seen such a city?" Abelard asked.

Annalise laughed. "Truth be told, I've never left the mountainside. It'll be a brand new experience."

Abelard smiled.

Looking at Godfrey, she asked, "Do all of you travel with dogs?"

"They're as much a part of the order as we are," said Abelard. "We certainly do." He looked at Basina, panting at his feet. "Is this your savior?" he asked Toth. "What a magnificent animal, eh, Godfrey?"

The old greyhound stared, unimpressed.

"This is Basina," said Toth. "Of course, you know Vinegar Tom."

"How could I forget? That reminds me," said Abelard. "I have a gift for you, Dorin."

Toth looked at Annalise with embarrassment.

Abelard released Godfrey and sat on the bench. From his satchel, he pulled a manuscript.

"At the university," Abelard said to Annalise, "Dorin has a colossal library of canine literature. Here's one more for your shelf, sir."

Abelard handed Toth a book titled *Of Englishe Dogges*, a 1570 zoology of hounds by John Caius.

"Oh, marvelous," said Toth. "How marvelous." He opened the text.

"Never ask him questions about a dog," Abelard warned. "About any dog at any time. He knows them all."

Annalise smiled. She sat on the bench.

"I told you Basina is a *Chien de Montagne des Pyrénées*, did I not?" Toth asked.

"You did, Dorin. Twice, in fact."

"Did I tell you King Louis marked her the Royal Dog of France recently?"

"Yes, twice," Abelard and Annalise said simultaneously.

"Listen here, Tom," Toth said, turning pages. He read aloud, "'Of the dog called the greyhound, in Latin *Leporarius*. Incredible swiftness,' it says, Tom. Is that you?" He flipped through sections. "Ah, and here you are, Basina, under the shepherd's dog. English arrogance at work. 'The coarser sort,' he writes. Unkind of him. Tsk tsk. I'll tell you what it doesn't say about Vinegar Tom," Toth said to Basina, stepping onto a manicured trail in the hedges.

Basina, Tom, and a jealous Godfrey moved around his heels. Basina's collar shone beautiful in the light.

"I imagine you've never heard the story of Saint Guinefort, the greyhound," Toth said. "Like yourself, he was from the land of Charlemagne."

Abelard shook his head at Annalise. He patted her hand.

"How many times have you heard it?" he asked.

"Twice." Annalise laughed.

"Dorin is an enigma, you'll find," said the monk. "Serious to a fault, perhaps, but hounds are his great weakness. He's human around them. A brilliant man."

Annalise lifted the beetle, parting its wings of bronze.

The monk eyed the automaton. "It's over now, my dear. In time, you'll find peace."

Toth's voice, reciting the well-worn tale of Guinefort, faded behind the hedgerow.

A NOTE ON THE TYPE

The text of this book is set in Adobe Jenson Pro and captures the essence of Nicolas Jenson's roman and Ludovico degli Arrighi's italic typeface designs. The combined strength and beauty of these two icons of Renaissance type result in an elegant typeface suited to a broad spectrum of applications. Designed by Robert Slimbach of the Adobe type design team, Adobe Jenson Pro is part of the family of Adobe Originals historical revivals.

Nicholas (or Nicolas) Jenson (c. 1420–1480) was a French engraver, pioneer, printer and type designer who carried out most of his work in Venice, Italy. Jenson acted as Master of the French Royal Mint at Tours and is credited with being the creator of one of the finest early Roman typefaces.

Working separately but concurrently with Johann and Wendelin of Speyer (de Spira), Nicholas Jenson is popularly thought to have made the final definitive break from blackletter style towards a fully evolved roman letterform.

During the 1470s Nicholas Jenson's technical skill and business acumen helped establish Venice as Italy's publishing capital and in centuries since he has been celebrated for perfecting roman type, the rebirth of Latin inscription.

Ludovico Vicentino degli Arrighi (Cornedo Vicentino, 1475?–1527?) was a papal scribe and type designer in Renaissance Italy. Very little is known of the circumstances of his life. Around 1510 he was a bookseller in Rome. He was employed as a scribe at the Apostolic Chancery in 1513. His experience in calligraphy led him to create an influential pamphlet on handwriting in 1522 called *La Operina*, which was the first book devoted to writing the italic script known as chancery cursive.

He turned to printing in 1524 and designed his own italic typefaces for his work, which were widely emulated. His last printing was dated shortly before the sack of Rome (1527), during which he was probably killed.

Composed by Clever Crow Consulting and Design,
Pittsburgh, Pennsylvania

ACKNOWLEDGMENTS

My gratitude and thanks to the following authors, artists, and colleagues for their guidance, support, and friendship:

Michael August
Brian Berry
C.W. Blackwell
Brian Bowyer
Damien Casey
Wendy Dalrymple
Kathy Edwards
Nicole Eigener
Stephanie Ellis
Adam Hulse
Sarah J. Huntington
Derek Hutchins
Jon Joy
Pam Klinepeter
Rob Langford
Beverley Lee

Paul John Lyon
Regan MacArthur
Remo Macartney
Catherine McCarthy
Ronald McGillvray
Chris McGinley
Dave Neal
Jennifer Ostopovich
Greg Parker
Anthony Perconti
Christine Scott
Austrian Spencer
Patrick Stanley
Kyra Torres
Jonathan Tripp
Sebastian Vice

ABOUT THE AUTHOR

Coy Hall lives in West Virginia, where he splits time as an author and professor of history. As a historian, he studies Medieval and Early Modern Europe. History influences his fiction, with many of his stories set in the distant past—sometimes the real past, sometimes an imagined one, but most often a mix of the two.

GRIMOIRE OF THE FOUR IMPOSTORS

THE HANGMAN FEEDS THE JACKAL

Nosetouch Press is an independent book publisher
tandemly-based in Chicago and Pittsburgh.
We are dedicated to bringing some of today's most
energizing fiction to readers around the world.

Our commitment to classic book design in a digital
environment brings an innovative and authentic approach
to the traditions of literary excellence.

NOSETOUCHPRESS.COM
*We're Out There

Science Fiction | Fantasy | Horror | Gothic | Supernatural | Weird

YOU MAY ALSO ENJOY

THE FIENDS IN THE FURROWS I
An Anthology of Folk Horror

THE FIENDS IN THE FURROWS II
More Tales of Folk Horror

THE FIENDS IN THE FURROWS III
Final Harvest

SONG OF THE RED SQUIRE
C.W. Blackwell

THE CURSED EARTH
D.T. Neal

THE THING IN YELLOW
D.T. Neal

WAX & WANE
A Gathering of Witch Tales